"ARREST THIS MAN!

"Book him for fraud."

Three massive bors wearing the yellow sambrowne belts of Thember policemen entered and marched with heavy, thudding treads to where Slith sat. The troops lifted Slith by his arms—skinny arms next to their borrish ones—and marched him toward the door, his toes dancing on the floor, his heels never nearing it.

"Wait! What is this?" he squalled. "They are mine!"

"That remains to be seen . . ."

ARBITER TALES
L. WARREN DOUGLAS

THE WELLS OF PHYRE

An Arbiter Tale

L. WARREN DOUGLAS

A ROC BOOK

ROC
Published by the Penguin Group
Penguin Books USA Inc., 375 Hudson Street,
New York, New York 10014, U.S.A.
Penguin Books Ltd, 27 Wrights Lane,
London W8 5TZ, England
Penguin Books Australia Ltd, Ringwood,
Victoria, Australia
Penguin Books Canada Ltd, 10 Alcorn Avenue,
Toronto, Ontario, Canada M4V 3B2
Penguin Books (N.Z.) Ltd, 182-190 Wairau Road,
Auckland 10, New Zealand

Penguin Books Ltd, Registered Offices:
Harmondsworth, Middlesex, England

First published by Roc, an imprint of Dutton Signet,
a division of Penguin Books USA Inc.

First Printing, July, 1996
10 9 8 7 6 5 4 3 2 1

To Cornell William "Luke" Lugthart, Sr.
June 15, 1990–February 1, 1995

Acknowledgments

Allan Cole, Leo Frankowski, Chris Bunch, Shawna McCarthy, and Amy Stout for suggestions, much appreciated enthusiasm, and sharp criticism, among other things.

Sue, for enduring all too many miserable facets of this writer's life without getting much benefit from the good parts.

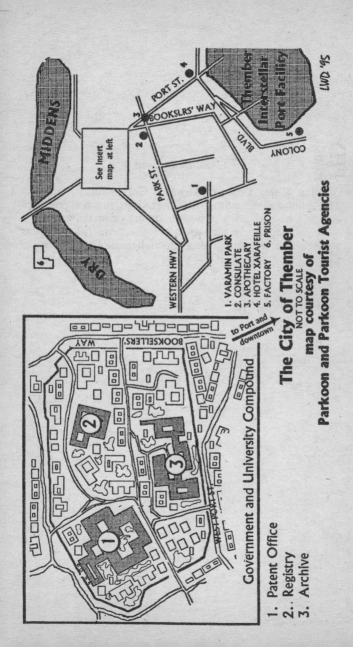

Government and University Compound

1. Patent Office
2. Registry
3. Archive

The City of Thember
NOT TO SCALE
map courtesy of
Parkoon and Parkoon Tourist Agencies

1. VARAMIN PARK
2. CONSULATE
3. APOTHECARY
4. HOTEL XARAFEILLE
5. FACTORY
6. PRISON

PHYRE
The Environs of Valbissag

1. Where Slith & Bleth met
2. Bilous Seep
3. Mt. Curble
4. the pissberry valley
5. the High Pan
6. the rootmat valley
7. Karibekl Cave
8. Thplet's and Bleth's cave
9. Jandissl palace
10. Krat
11. CIM pit mine
12. Blanderstan quarry
13. Fednap Formation subsurface mine
14. Ballanbuff Reservoir
15. Mt. Afkak
16. Valbissag Town and spring

PROLOGUE

Phyre was the harsh, only planet circling the star also named Phyre, the two hundred and seventy-first inhabited solar system of the Xarafeille Stream.

The Xarafeille Stream, in turn, was a bright, sweeping banner of stars, ten thousand gold, five thousand red, and a scattering of blue, white, and intermediate shades. Those stars that had inhabited planets—and there were thousands of them—were all numbered: the Xarafeille Stream, where the seven races of man commingled in a peace that was often uneasy, and where only the mysterious Arbiter with his great fleet and his poletzai legions kept the peace at all.

The origin of man, or humans, was lost in the mists of antiquity, though perhaps the Arbiter, perusing the recorded wisdom of his predecessors, knew how they came to be. He was, after all, John XXIII, and his late father was Rober VIII, and there had been a dozen named Shems (or sometimes James) as well; thus there had been forty-three Arbiters, and each had reigned for most of a long lifetime, each had contributed his wisdom and his discoveries to the great Archive on Newhome, orbiting Xarafeille Prime. Any man who read a tithe of those recorded memories would know more of human origins than any man before or since. But ordinary men cared little for truth, preferring comfortable legends and dignified lies.

Bors and ikuts were bulky, furry men, dark- and white-furred respectively, though some ikuts' fur was almost golden. Trogloditic bors believed they originated in mountain caves on some cool, forested, long-forgotten world. Ikuts told of Sea, a lost world where the words for all sixty-three kinds of ice originated. (Though only seventeen words were in current use, or had been identified on inhabited worlds of the Xarafeille Stream, all were memorized in ikut schools.) There were no ikuts on Phyre, because even at the poles there was no ice, no cold.

Wends were slender and brown-furred, and sometimes had lighter tufts atop their mobile ears. They originated, so their myths claimed, on Forest, where their remote ancestors had chattered in treetops and subsisted on nuts and fruit pits. There were also mantees, graceful watermen, on some worlds. Mantees claimed origin on a world variously named River, Everglade, Mooskeg, or simply Home. No living mantee claimed to have been there, though all believed themselves *from* there, at some remove. There were no mantees on hot, dry Phyre, because except in the encapsulated spaceport towns there was no pure, flowing water, there were only wells, seeps, and solute-rich springs.

On Phyre were a few tarbek tribes, but mostly fards: golden-furred, white-bellied, swift, and clever fards, desert-wise, hard, enduring fards who wrested livelihoods from the driest deserts, who sipped strong, dense, mineral-laden water from seeps and springs. Every seep, every spring, every damp spot in Phyre's habitable zones had a name, and was owned. The fards who owned them were harsh men, and they bred sons as hardy and as unrelenting as were they themselves.

To every rule there is an exception, of course. Among the sons of Fladth Wrasselty, lord of the spring named Valbissag and the stone town that surrounded it, the exception was the child of Fladth's old age, who was called Slith. Slith Wrasselty was tan-pelted like most fards, with soft, white belly down and short creamy fur from digits to knees and elbows. His whiskers were long, black, and fardlike, projecting from the corners of his mouth and from his brows. He was quick of movement, and his pink, mobile nose was never still. His long-tufted ears, like hyperactive radar antennae, never ceased their scanning. Fards did not seem quick to other fards, of course.

Among them, Slith seemed ordinary, or perhaps even a bit sluggish at times, but members of the other races of man would have deemed him jittery and abrupt—like all fards.

Mentally, Slith Wrasselty was quite unfardlike, mainly because, unlike his brothers, he actually *liked* his aging father Fladth (which was quite strange) and he had no desire whatsoever to slay him (which was unnatural and almost unheard of, if not quite perverted).

Slith's strange, unfardlike attitudes had shaped his behavior in other ways, too. Because he had no wish to be a parricide—and because he made no secret of it—his two older brothers and two younger ones had no use for him at all. They did not even bother to plot his death, though all of them nursed glorious schemes by which they hoped to slay or emasculate their other siblings as soon as one of them succeeded in assassinating old Fladth. Though men of other races deemed such fardish preoccupations cruel and inhuman, the contest over succession and inheritance unquestionably bred quicker, smarter, and more ruthless fards, and the Wrasselty clan, longtime owners of Valbissag, stood high among those. Slith, should his brothers not change their minds and slay him as a matter of principle, a mere trimming of a loose end, would be an unusual Wrasselty indeed—a living brother of Valbissag's owner.

Of course it might not be much of a life. If he pledged fealty to whoever won the struggle, he might be so lucky as to be granted a seat by the spring, where he could breathe its life-giving vapors and ladle its flavorful water to his lips. He might even be allowed a patch of sand to sleep on in an outer courtyard within the palace walls. If his elder brother Gleph inherited, he would surely make Slith work all day, likely at some noisome task, for every privilege. If Thradz, the next oldest, won, Slith would be lucky to catch a single breath of Valbissag's steam, let alone a sip, unless he paid for it in solid coin. If either Thplet or Splath, his younger siblings, took claim of Valbissag, palace, and town, he might have an easier life of it, because both seemed to look on him with distant affection, but there was no guarantee of it. People changed when they became successful, and the nature and direction of such change were always unpredictable. It was not wise to count on anyone whose self-interest was unclear.

On other worlds, among other kinds of human folk, different adaptations prevailed. Mantees did not practice murder as an ordinary means of determining inheritance. Though mantees were otterlike (when born in certain environments) or more similar to dugongs or seals (when born in warmer or colder places), their breeding practices most resembled those of certain social insects, as only one female of an entire tribe, called a throng, became fertile and thus mother to an entire generation.

Bors females gave birth in pairs, one male and one female at a time, and inheritance was a kind of matrilineal primogeniture. Fathers were not slain, but they were of no importance to anyone except their own sisters' get, for which they were responsible. Male bors might share a sister's inheritance, even her rule, if she were of a dominant line, but it was most on sufferance, not graven in law.

Wends ... but there were few wends on Phyre, and those only in the large spaceport town of Thember, and there were no ikuts at all. There were tarbeks aplenty, but those strangest of all the human kinds inhabited only the lowest valleys where nasty volcanic fumes accumulated, and where springs trickled water so acid it would burn the fur off any other men's hands and the skin from their throats. Tarbeks, unless they wore filter veils, were unwelcome among other folk because their breath reeked of sulfides, carrion, and even more noxious things. No one knew, and few cared, what odd reproductive or successional strategies tarbeks employed.

Then there were old-humans, but only in the cities on Phyre, who practiced odd and ancient customs—though no one except perhaps the Arbiter himself, on the planet Newhome, orbiting the star known as Prime, or Xarafeille I, had access to the databases and the histories that described them.

"Daddy?" demanded Parissa, breaking into her father's reverie. "Daddy!"

"Yes, dear?" John Minder acknowledged his youngest child.

"I won't let Robby sassipate you! Not ever! I'll sassipate him first, if he tries it. I'll put stuff in his food, or . . ."

"What? I'm sorry dear, I don't understand."

"Sarabet says some rotty boys sassipate their daddies, and I won't ever let Robby sassipate you." The child was obviously distraught; tears ran down her cheeks.

Her father swept her up onto his lap, smiling to allay her fears. "That's *assassinate,* Parissa—and only the fards on Fellenbrath and a few other very conservative and old-fashioned places do that. We are old-humans, not fards. Your brother will not have to slay me in order to inherit. In fact if he did so, he would inherit nothing at all."

Parissa was impressionable, imaginative, and intelligent—a dangerous combination in a child only just out of toddlerhood. Her fund of knowledge was limited, but her ability to extrapolate from the bits and fragments of truth she did acquire were considerable. The conclusions she drew, though—however logical they were—were often disastrously wrong. He would have to caution her older sister Sarabet—and her brother Rob, too—to be careful about introducing Parissa to isolated facts without adequate context to understand them.

"Old-humans like your mother and me do not merely mate, dear. We *marry,* and as a rule we remain together all our lives, and just as we love and care for our children, they in turn care for us when we are old." Minder explained how old-human inheritance worked, in general terms, idealized ones, until he was sure Parissa was able to distinguish between her brother and the brothers of men like Slith Wrasselty. When her fidgeting indicated to him that she could absorb no more, he suggested that her neglected dolls were surely becoming lonely. . . .

"When I began telling Slith Wrasselty's story," John Minder said sternly to his eldest children, "I purposefully excluded Parissa because of her youth. I'm sorry you didn't see fit to keep my confidences."

"I'm sorry, Dad," began Sarabet.

"It's my fault," said Rober Minder, who might some-day be Rober IX. "I started it. I was just teasing her. I didn't think she'd take me seriously."

"And when she came to me, I guess I made it worse," Sarabet concluded. "I tried to explain about fards so she wouldn't be so upset, but she just doesn't know enough to make sense of it all."

"I suppose now that she's exposed to the hard facts of the fardish codes, we should include her in future lessons," Minder said. "At least I'll be there to straighten out any misunderstandings, in future."

"Aw, Dad. Do you have to? She's always asking questions, and every story takes twice as long for you to tell."

Minder shrugged. He did not remind Rob that he had brought it on himself. He did not have to. Rob was not stupid, though his father was sure he would consider himself so, for a while. He was not malicious, either, but he was overly fond of teasing, and because Parissa was intelligent, Rob often overestimated her degree of comprehension, and her ability to reason correctly. He would have to learn better, if . . . John Minder shut that thought off. He was himself a young man, still, and had no need to think about picking a successor—but it was difficult, watching his children, not to wonder which one of them might someday be Arbiter of the Xarafeille Stream stars.

PART ONE

OROGENY

Granites, Lavas, and Basalt

CHAPTER 1

Where is the Arbiter? Here on Glaice, mantees
are drowning baby ikuts, and ikuts have revived
the ancient practice of dining on mantee flesh.
On Vela, tarbeks and wends—unlikely
competitors—have each declared a war of
extermination, though battle has not yet been joined.
On Stepwater, mantee territorial encroachments
and bors reaction threaten to involve wends and
fards as well.

Has John Minder XXIII even noticed? Where are
his poletzai and his warships? Must war threaten
to span the interstellar gulfs before the Arbiter
deploys them? Are his much-vaunted peacekeeping
forces merely tools to maintain his monopoly of
interstellar trade—the monopoly that finances
them?

Ep Tetonak,
Editorial in the *Metok Light*,
Metok, Glaice, Xarafeille 132

Slith Wrasselty shouldered his heavy knapsack. He did
not turn around to look at Valbissag Town's thick sandstone walls as he departed. He had little sentiment for his
birthplace. He did not allow himself to admire its well-
proportioned towers, its arched gateways, or its colorful
crystal fenestrations, because he did not even know, when
he left, if he would be allowed to return—or if he were,
under what imposed conditions. Thus he concentrated on
his own project ahead: geological research in the deep
desert, from which he hoped someday to earn a substantial livelihood.

His dark-irised eyes swept the verdigris expanse of open plain and the gray, rounded line of the distant Vermous Hills, which were his destination and the font of his personal ambition. His hard, glassy nictitating membranes drooped, and their odd refractive properties brought the hills into sharp focus through half of each lens, while the uncovered portion of his pupil passed focused light from nearer objects. A small node on his optic nerve, which was large by non-fard standards, sorted and rationalized the dual images before they reached his brain for interpretation. That ability to look near and far at once had contributed to his race's success on Phyre, for all fards could examine the ground ahead for drumsand and krood burrows without ignoring the cimmerian shadows of nearby rock spires and tumbles where lurked fracts and nimbleteeth. At the same time, they never lost track of the vast scape from near distance to far horizon, but were warned of even slight movements that might represent hostile fards (in Slith's present location, members of the nomadic Wrebek clan) or a plot of groundsnappers seething with hungry excitement brought on by even the slight vibration of a fard's dainty, hopping gait.

Outward bound, he encountered no Wrebeks, no groundsnapper plots, and only a single nimbletooth, which he dodged easily. If he had owned a fine wooden staff with a fork on one end, he could have tried to catch it and milk its fever glands for whatever valuable solutions had accumulated in them—but he had no staff, and he did not expect to find a suitable swarrow root on this trip, the next, or the one thereafter. Wood, on Phyre, grew mostly underground. The tiny fruiting bodies of the swarrow and similar species were never obvious, and appeared in no determinable place or season.

By day's end, Slith neared the first slanting, stratified outcrops of the Vermous Dolomite that made up the hills. Such geological formations reminded him that once, perhaps a billion years past, Phyre had been wet enough for limy magnesian sediments to settle on the bottoms of shallow seas. Now rock columns capped with desiccated limestones and dolomites stood proud of the surrounding sandstone plains because they weathered more slowly than the sandstones, which were weakened by even a touch of quick-frozen dew and abraded by grains driven by the winds.

Interspersed with the dolomites and intermittent sandstone beds of the Vermous formation were occasional thin strata of a rarer rock, a white, coarsely crystalline limestone, almost a marble, made up of the metamorphosed carapaces of microscopic sea worms at least a billion years extinct. The Bright Limes, as geologists named them, appeared only as sinuous lines a few hands wide where they and their dolomite matrix outcropped. Though they represented a vanishingly small portion of the exposed surface of the region, the Bright Limes were of disproportionate interest to Slith Wrasselty because they furnished unusual soluble chemicals—quasi-organic fossil metabolites of the source microorganisms—to the waters that percolated through the porous sandstones around them, chemicals that eventually found their way to springs like Valbissag, to which they imparted much of each spring's characteristic flavor.

At nightfall, Slith made camp atop a relatively unfissured dolomitic crag uninhabited by small, hungry creatures. Nevertheless, he cautiously spread a tightly woven cloth over his chosen sleeping site, then laid a loop of finely braided cord around it, cord saturated with oil extracted from the fat of a krood's tail, which would deter most nocturnal things that crept and bit. Then he ritually sprinkled his hard bed with a pinch of sand drawn up from Valbissag's depths—sand that carried the scent of "home."

He sat within his safe precinct and readied his equipment for the morrow's research. First, he unrolled a cloth sewn with a hundred small pockets and assured himself that none of the glass vials in them had broken and that no precious reagents stained the fabric. Then, unrolling another cloth, he verified that none of his empty specimen vials, each one meticulously numbered, had been damaged. Finally, he examined his tools: his pointed hammer; his small sack of minerals of different hardnesses for scratch-testing specimens; his lenses; his tinted eye-loupes, through which he could observe the color of droplets of dissolved minerals as he held them, in a platinum-wire loop, in the flame of his miniaturized lab burner.

Satisfied that all was in order, he noted his position in a field book, then packed away book and compass. He slept sitting upright, with his eyes wide open but with his nictitating membranes covering them from stray wind-blown sand.

"Boring!" said Parissa, as Sarabet tucked her in bed. "Bo-ring! That story isn't any fun at all."

"It's your own fault," Sarabet responded, concealing her annoyance with difficulty. "You're the one who blabbed to Dad about Robby 'assassinating' him. Now you have to listen to the rest of Slith Wrasselty's story, and if you keep interrupting like you did tonight, Dad will never finish it."

"Daddy says I *have to* innerrupt when I don't understand, or I never will. I *have* to, so it's not my fault."

"I suppose so," Sarabet grudgingly admitted. "Now go to sleep."

"Did you put the rope around my bed? The one with Mommy's perfume on it to keep the bitey-bugs away?"

"Don't you smell it? And there are no bugs in here at all. Now go to sleep."

Not far (as worlds are measured) from the spring Valbissag lay the province of Low Diverness, where Lord Gefke Jandissl ruled. Lord Jandissl was discontent. Just as the security of a tarbek lord's position was strictly contingent upon his status, his status in turn owed much to the number of females who, at any given time, were gravid with the product of his seed, and of late the females of his tribe were producing fewer small Jandissls than was usual.

Paternity, among the other races of man, was often highly conjectural unless an infant was born with some recognizable characteristic or defect that pinpointed the source of its originating seed, but among tarbeks certain chemical complexities borne on a gravid female's breath, and later on her infant's, made any tarbek male who

breathed it aware if the fetus or infant was his own offspring as well.

Of late, however many females Lord Gefke Jandissl
sniffed, few exuded that particular combination of sulfides and pheromones that enlarged his spirit and elevated
his confidence in his dominance and in the stability of his
rule over Low Diverness. He was uneasy about it, but
was not—as yet—panicky. Though he had been able to
find only seven pregnant females in the past month, at
least none of them had been inseminated by another
male's seed. Had any been so, he would have been forced
to assume that the other male had issued challenge, and
that bare-handed battle was imminent. Instead, he concluded that the females had discovered some way to
avoid getting pregnant entirely.

If his semen was still strong, it would consume any foreign male's product deposited in the hot springs scattered
about Low Diverness. Jandissl knew that any young
males who visited the springs in his absence did so for
the thrill of risk and adventure and for the amazingly
pleasurable sensations of ejaculation—which in tarbek
males was brought on not by penetration of a female
(which would have been disgusting and twisted) but by
total immersion in mineral-rich water heated to at least 97
degrees Celsius.

If Jandissl's semen had weakened, or had he failed to
visit each spring in the province at least once a month, at
least some of the pregnant females would have failed to
engender in him the usual pleasurable and elevating sensations only a ruler and a parent could feel. But Lord
Gefke kept a meticulous log of his visits to each spring,
and he knew he had not neglected a single one within the
distance a female could walk without dying of exposure,
mineral deficiencies, and dry skin. He knew also that his
seed was still carnivorous and strong, because he tested it
fortnightly in his small laboratory, observing his cells'
hungry gobbling of lesser men's seed through a huge, ancient binocular microscope made by offworld bors (who
made the finest machinery) with optics cast and ground
by patient wends (who were superior artisans in glass).

Thus if a female had gotten pregnant by another man's

seed, it had been a conscious effort on the other's part, not youthful pleasure-seeking. The challenger would have had first to poison the spring, killing Lord Gefke's superior seed, to have then neutralized the poison, and then finally to have immersed himself in the water and ejaculated therin. Any female whose compulsion to bathe (and thus to remain alive for more than a week or two) drew her to the challenger's deposit would have been impregnated not by her rightful lord, but by the upstart—and that had not happened.

Jandissl had read that certain springs' composition had been known to change with the geological processes that nurtured them, as their aquifers faulted or eroded, shifting the flow past new, unknown, soluble deposits. He had also read that on some worlds there were springs with contraceptive properties or spermicidal ones. He knew, from his frequent visits to his own springs and from the samples he carried back to his lab for testing, that no spring of his was spermicidal, but how could he test for the other, without knowing what exact chemical caused it? His books and datacubes gave no hints at all, but until he found out, he would not sleep well, and his dreams would continue to be of a lonely old age in exile far from the heat and pleasures of Low Diverness's wondrous pools.

CHAPTER 2

The seven human adaptations were designed in laboratories, then evolved far beyond their original conceptions on the diverse worlds of the Xarafeille Stream; yet evolution does not proceed at an even pace, or predictably. Fards' unique experiment, breeding ever-more-clever generations under great stress, has not given them specific advantage over less clever but more ferocious tarbeks—except perhaps in the mixed environments of the cities.

My task, as I see it—and it will be your task as well, in the centuries to come—is not to prevent conflict between the races, which would require oppression like none the universe has witnessed. It is merely to keep one race from exploiting limited and situational evolutionary advantages at the expense of another, and to restrain conflicts within the limits of single solar systems. *Less* might well result in slaughter, in critical losses of genetic diversity all humanity may someday need out there in the vast galaxy beyond the Xarafeille Stream. *More* might result in a tedious blending of the races, a bland, unadaptive folk— and in an equivalent loss.

John Minder I,
Notes for the Next Generations

The metallic clinking of Slith's hammer echoed from the rocky walls of the small canyon. He worked fast, because only when the wind was from the west could he breathe the air there. South and east of him was the volcano

Afkak and tarbek territory. Even a slight easterly breeze pushed heavy volcanic gases into such low places as his canyon. Tarbeks could breathe the stuff, but not fards.

The eastern slopes of the Vermous highlands were thus a no-man's-land between Valbissag and Low Diverness, alternately habitable by fards or tarbeks, but shifting too often and too unpredictably for either race to contemplate settling there. From experience on past trips, Slith anticipated that late afternoon would bring a shift in the breeze that would force him to exit the canyon at its steep, narrow west end when its mouth filled with foul fumes.

He dropped small fragments of Bright Lime rock into a finger-sized vial, and covered them with acid from an eyedropper. The combination foamed and gave off pale yellow smoke. He viewed the gas through a number-five-tint glass, nodded in satisfaction with what he saw, and made small, neat notes in his book. They were written not in Standard or in fardic runes, but in symbols of his own devising, using the grammar and syntax of ancient Universal, a language he had taught himself from old books in his father's library.

Just as he was about to put a droplet of the solution he had just made to the flame test, a clatter of falling rock made him drop everything. His fur stood on end, making him seem twice his real bulk. His nose twitched like a leaf in a gale, and his eyes darted. He had no weapon but his fingernails and his teeth, if the Wrebeks had found him.

"Wherp?" he heard something say. *"Whezz frak madstap."* The words were fardish, but the intonation and pronunciation were odd. He peered through the sifting dust of the rockfall, then breathed a sigh of relief. There was no danger there that would kill him.

"Whar nekit?" he asked. "Who are you? What tribe? And that's *mabstap*, not *madstap*." A fardling. It could not have been more than a few years old, and its speech was infantile. Yet that was no excuse. Words and gestures only functioned when they were precisely used, when two communicants used them the same way. Why think what might have happened had a younger Slith himself raised his left eyebrow at his father without the expected accom-

panying hand gesture! That was a deadly insult. Zip! Slash ... and no more Slith. Evolution in action. No infant who could not tell left eyebrow from right should live to breed more of his defective kind. *Madstap*, indeed! "I am dying of 'yellow'," she had said, not "I am starving."

"Hungry, indeed!" he snapped when the creature did not respond to his questions. Surely, it was a Wrebek infant. His fingers flickered in a gesture of *prektep*, which signified a triviality dismissed. "Go away now," he commanded it. "The wind will shift in midafternoon, and you will die here. Go! Back where you came from." Already, as the trickling breeze brought the creature's scent to him, it carried also slight traces of monoxide, odorless to many humans but distinguishable to a fard's superior chemosensors. Both odors discomfited him. "Be gone!" he squalled in his most ferocious voice, and he hefted a rock fragment as if to throw it, an uncodified gesture none the less clear for that.

Slith's mind and body were the site of a ferocious internal debate. He did not want companionship, and he had only enough food for himself. He did not care if the fardling lived or died, but he fervently wished it would do so elsewhere. The pheromones it emitted made his head feel thick and generated uncomfortable sensations elsewhere. When the fardling did not move away, he threw the rock. The creature yelped piteously and skittered out of sight behind a boulder. He threw another, arcing it over the barrier between them, and was rewarded by a thump, an even more plaintive cry, and the faint sound of departing fardling footsteps. "Now stay away!" he called after it. The canyon wall was a vertical face near the top, and only someone who knew the few handholds could climb out—and there were none in the direction the fardling had run. Ah, well, at least it was far enough away so he could not smell it.

Keeping eyes and ears alert for its inevitable sneaking return, Slith picked up his fallen tools. The specimen vial had shattered, and he had to start over. He hissed angrily, chipped loose another fragment of Bright Lime, and remade his solution. He viewed the flame colors a droplet of it made as it boiled away within his platinum-wire loop, and grunted in satisfaction, then noted his findings in his field book. Because he was sure he had found something significant, he made the extra effort to unpack and assemble his small spectroscope, which he set up on a low, flat boulder.

He heard a slight sound. "Go away!" he snarled, and threw several rocks. The fardling darted silently back out of range. The skin on his chest itched, and his tiny nipples stood up from the white down that surrounded them. He picked up more rocks, and strode stiff-legged toward the small being, throwing one rock after another as he advanced. One found its mark. He did not want to get close enough to verify whether the small, inert fardling was truly dead, so he returned to work. He mounted lens tubes at an angle to each other and placed a stubby glass prism between them at the proper skew. He placed his burner at one end of the assembly and a pad of gridded paper at the other. He draped himself and his apparatus with his sleeping sheet to block the bright rays of Phyre, the sun.

When he held a drop of solution in the burner's flame, the first tube focused the light on the prism, which split it into many colors. The second tube's lenses projected it onto the gridded paper. Slith fiddled with the focus of the tubes until the projected spectrum was clearly defined. Satisfied, he made marks with a pencil corresponding to certain bright lines in the colored swath, and made further notes in ancient Universal in his book.

Periodically, grudgingly, he tossed off his sleeping sheet. His eyes readjusted to the glare almost instantaneously. Twice, he had to chase the fardling off again. Twice, he did not. Once, it had crept up so close that he had actually felt its presence internally even before he divested himself of his covering. That angered him. Did the creature not understand at all? He could not be bothered with a nurseling. He had ambition, and much important work to do.

He reversed the spectroscopic process by focusing a thin beam of sunlight via two mirrors and a filter that passed only a standard "white light" beam through the combustion gases of a solution drop, and was rewarded with a subtly different display. Instead of bright lines, there were dark ones at several places on the spectrum. Elements, when energized by heat, give off light of a particular color—the bright lines he had recorded earlier— but when calibrated light is shined through unheated elements, they absorb certain specific frequencies as well, creating dark lines of no-light in the spectral projection. Although Slith could not determine what exact molecules those elements made up in a particular sample, from long experience he was able to guess what he might find when he made more exhaustive tests in his father's laboratory at Valbissag—provided, of course, that no brother had succeeded in eliminating old Fladth while Slith was away.

He packed up all his gear except his specimen roll and his hammer, then collected samples from the Bright Lime outcrop over an area several acres in extent, though nowhere was the canyon more than twenty meters wide at the bottom. His meanderings took him downward toward the canyon mouth, where the late-afternoon breezes, true to his expectations, were already pushing noxious fumes uphill. That exit from the narrow declivity was already completely blocked. In the other direction, he gathered samples toward the head of the canyon until it petered out in a ten-meter deep cleft. There, the Bright Lime outcrop disappeared, plunging beneath the earth.

Finished, he shouldered his burden, heavier now by the weight of his samples. Then he had a bright idea: he had not spotted the fardling in the last hour, but it was surely lurking somewhere below in the late-afternoon shadows; it could no longer walk out of the valley, so it would have to follow him up through the narrow cleft. But ... If he used his hammer to knock off the few protruding hand-and footholds ...

As he climbed, he reached down between his legs, or far out to one side or the other, and chipped away each possible point of purchase, leaving only useless nubs. The next time, he would have to bring a rope and grappling gear if he wished to depart the canyon in midafternoon or later, but that was a small price to pay for being forever rid of his importunate visitor.

At the top, he peered back whence he had come. He

saw no fardling, no movement in the lengthening shadows. Had the stupid thing already succumbed to the encroaching gas? Soon, at any rate, it would do so, and when he returned, he would find nothing but a few small, scattered, well-gnawed bones. Satisfied, he hiked away, stepping lightly in spite of his burden, and set up camp on the same high pinnacle as the night before.

Prior to settling in for sleep, Slith made notes on his day's work. Perhaps once his conclusions had been carefully edited to safeguard details of knowledge that might result in future profit, he could publish a paper on the interactions of solutes in the Vermous groundwaters. Slith loved seeing his name on the "Contents" pages of scholarly journals, and he submitted articles on diverse subjects: geomorphology, hydrology, and even a few brief anthropological essays based on his visits among the less-hostile of the local desert tribes—after excising any references to particulars he wished personally to exploit.

After all, he sometimes thought, a copyright was a little like a patent, giving him certain controls over what he knew, controls that did not exist unless he wrote it down. The writing and publishing thus satisfied a small part of a strong fardish urge to possess and control as much of the universe as was possible.

Below, and not a great distance from his comfortable camp, small, mewling sounds could have been heard—if anyone had been near enough to hear them.

"Far mebbil mabstap," the tiny voice said. "I do not wish to starve." Her small fingers scrabbled desperately at the broken handholds in the steep bank. Around her feet swirled yet-invisible tendrils of harsh, toxic gases.

The fardling was too young to further articulate her desperate condition. She knew no word for "toxic," for "orphan" or "abandoned" or even "motherless." She felt no anger toward the strange fard who had played with bits of rocks. Had she been old enough to develop a philosophical perspective, she might have reflected that Slith Wrasselty's avoidance of a burden like her was as much a part of the evolutionary dance, of genes striving for advantage, as was her own struggle to ascend the rock face.

But then again, she might not have; she might instead have railed against the cruelty of those genes, against the desperation and cruelty that were part and parcel of the fard female's lifelong condition—with death at the end of any wrong turn for all but the cleverest, the most determined.

"Eft nakrat mabstap!" she cried out loudly enough to cause distant Slith to roll over uncomfortably in his sleep. "I *will* not starve!" Actually, she meant "I will not *die,*" but she was a fardling of limited vocabulary, and as the level of the poisonous air rose higher—reaching her waist now—her words seemed more bravado. She would not have been the first fardling to utter such single-minded and determined words only moments before dying.

"Daddy? What's a fardling?" asked Parissa in a voice much more subdued than was usual for her.

"It's a baby fard," Robby said. "It was bothering Slith, so he got rid of it." His implication—not really serious, from his point of view, but terrifying from Parissa's—was that fards like Slith really knew how to handle obstreperous, annoying children. As soon as Rob said that, he realized he had again gone too far, and rushed to correct it, before Parissa . . .

John Minder, seeing the dismay writ large on his face, raised a hand. "I'll explain, son," he said.

"Remember that fards are not old-humans like us," John Minder said, cupping Parissa's chin in his hand. "Old-human mommies do not abandon little girls as soon as they can walk." Actually, he reflected, not all fard mothers abandoned their female offspring either—unless or until they produced a male, a potential future competitor for tribal rulership. Many female fards produced no male offspring at all, and those women had no incentive to drive off female infants. Yet such distinctions were subtle—too subtle for little girls. Minder sighed. This was terribly hard on Parissa, who saw the world and its examples mostly in terms of herself. Any child, fard or old-human, could be herself. Any frightening event could be happening as well to her as to a nameless fardling. But then, this was not some fantasy created solely to thrill and frighten; it was reality. Fard behaviors were set in their very genes—as were old-human ones—by generations of natural selection. In the fards' case, they were determined also by the efforts of ancient scientists who had combined genes of man with analogues of Earthly kangaroo rats, jerboas, jackals, and other desert creatures. The mix of genes did not always produce what the scientists had hoped for, specialized bors slaves who could cope with the frozen mine pits of one corporate-owned world, tarbek workers to endure the poisoned waters of another, mantees for the swamps, ikuts for the ice, fards for the deserts of others still, but the actions of natural selection upon them produced something that could, and did, survive.

Parissa would have to learn to understand—and thus to forgive—the fards, and others, for the way they were. The universe was full of diversity, of life-adaptations that seemed cruel and disgusting. The long-gone corporations of ancient Earth who had created fards, bors, wends, ikuts, mantees, and tarbeks to exploit the differing conditions of early extrasolar colony worlds had contributed to that diversity; and diversity was strength. Man, in one form or another, now inhabited thousands of worlds like Phyre where original old-humans could thrive only in protective domes or air-conditioned underground caverns.

There was a further aspect of John Minder's callous exposure of his daughter's tender mind: she—or her sister Sarabet or her brother Rober—would someday inherit Minder's own wealth, his position, and his unique burden. He had not yet decided which one of them would be his heir, for they were all still young and incompletely solidified in what would become their adult selves.

Right then—that week, that month—Minder favored Sarabet. No female of his line had ever inherited his particular position, but there was no rule or law to prevent it. Might the next Arbiter of the Xarafeille Stream be not Rober the Ninth, but Sarabet the First? Or might even small Parissa—someday grown tall, wise, and tolerant of the myriad ways of the diverse peoples whose millennial peace she strove to keep—attain the title of Arbiter?

Minder swelled with pride when he considered his children and their future role. Then, as quickly as it had come, his elation vanished. Unless he could solve his very pressing problems, and quickly, there would be no Arbiter's mantle for them to inherit. Unless he could solve them, the interstellar peace that had endured for twelve millennia would collapse, and he might well be the last Arbiter, presiding over the end times of civilization.

There were really only three possible outcomes. The first, of course, was that he would succeed at what he was attempting to do. Then mankind would go on, continuing to grow, develop, and adapt at the slow, not-quite random pace of evolution. The second was that the growing tensions, the planetary wars—brushfire wars, if one took into account the sheer number of human-settled star systems—would escalate beyond all control. At some point, despite his every effort, those wars could spread beyond single planets, beyond the planets of isolated systems; there would be, for the first time, interstellar wars.

John Minder could not currently stop the former, the brushfire wars, at least not by direct intervention. He could, however, prevent the latter—but at what a great cost! He could, if he decided to do it, stop *all* interstellar travel, for he, and he alone, knew the secret of . . . the stardrive.

On Glaice, Xarafeille 132, a dispute between migratory ikut banks and mantee throngs had been brought into his consul's courtroom, where it now precariously remained, but at any moment it could again erupt into the streets of the towns and across the vast, cold planet.

On Stepwater, Xarafeille 578, a mantee-built dam threatened to inundate a bors principality, and the bors contemplated building weapons systems long forbidden. That conflict was not likely to erupt into general, planetwide war—but less likely things had happened.

On Veld, Xarafeille 1029, the very bors engineers whose meddling had started a limited conflict were now selling weapons and logistics support to both combating parties.

On Thald, Xarafeille 1907, wends fought bors over

tracts of forest land and strip-mining rights, and on Carabanderai . . .

"Ah, Rob, Sarabet, Parissa," Minder murmured, "may you never again be required to live through 'interesting' times."

(HAPTER 3

URGENT * EYES ONLY
TO: ARBITER
FROM: OBSERVER, CODENAME "WRATH"
TEXT: The instability on Vela (X-1029)
accelerates at an unprecedented rate. Revise
estimated time-to-crisis from 10 yrs to 4 yrs +18
standard months. Revise intervention class from 5
(diplomatic/economic) to 3 (show of force, war
fleet in orbit).
APPEND: John, this one is out of control! The bors
core-tap stabilized Vela's orogeny at the expense
of tarbek habitat. Tarbeks are currently moving
on traditionally wendish lands. I foresee major
interracial war.

A year or two before young Johnny Minder assumed the
title of Arbiter, his elder brother Shems—or James—had
borrowed a collection of seven ancient data modules from
his father's shelves, and had taken them to a far world
where he could have them translated, because he could
find no computer in the Arbiter's palace that could read
them. Then, when Rober VIII died unexpectedly, Shems
had made himself unavailable to assume his proper position as Arbiter, and that burden fell upon the younger, unprepared Johnny, who later suffered greatly for the lack
of those very crystals the ignorant Shems had removed.

Shems's actions were irresponsible, but in light of his-
torical circumstances and the nature of the Arbiters and
their families, they were forgivable. The first Arbiter,
John Minder (later called John I), had been a physicist,
and had discovered the principle of the "FTL" space

drive. Of course it did not really propel matter faster than light, but when a ship employing it made a round-trip journey between star systems, its passengers, goods, and mechanisms seemed to experience duration, and, upon returning home, voyagers perceived themselves to have aged no more or less than had friends and relatives who had not traveled, and their clocks and watches still kept matching times.

John I, testing his stardrive, visited the six corporate colony planets, and was appalled by the conditions he found. Workers who were no more than indentured serfs had been genetically modified to suit the conditions that prevailed: on icy EE4, white-furred quasi-human slaves herded icebergs containing rare minerals scraped from the surface of a glaciated continent, and they had already coined nineteen separate words for different kinds of ice; on TC3, dugongs and manatees with human hands, faces, and brains combed the weed-choked waterways of a mountainless world for rare plants of pharmaceutical value; elsewhere, broad, stocky men with black fur labored in northern-hemisphere mines through the short summer while their southern counterparts hibernated in unheated caves, costing the corporations nothing for their upkeep through the long, long winter.

None of those modified workers or their children could ever return to Earth, to normalcy. None cherished even slight hope that their descendants' lots would be better than theirs; they were slaves, trapped light-years from human-rights organizations, international laws, indignant citizens, and from even the S.P.C.A. and the Humane Society.

John Minder engineered and led a revolution. It was not violent, and was virtually weaponless. The corporations had weapons, of course, but they had no FTL spaceships to bring weapons to bear on an enemy who stole their workers and transported them to far worlds their slow ramscoop vessels could not reach in a hundred lifetimes—to places beyond the dark dust clouds of the galaxy's Orion Arm, where lay a brilliant, sparkling river of stars the escapees named the Xarafeille Stream.

Among the refugees were unmodified humans also,

corporate folk who did not wish to remain and take the blame for empty workhouses and warehouses when all the workers were gone. Old-humans, they came to be called, and though generations of mantees, bors, and others forgot the nature of their creators and their laboratory origins—and invented new, more palatable legends of independent, convergent evolution to explain themselves— the taint of being old-human remained. Most became interstellar equivalents of ancient Gypsies or Jews, useful and used, but separate, and never wholly trusted or integrated into the societies that evolved.

John Minder felt responsible for the old-humans and, being the sole owner of the stardrive's principles, was able to make a deal with the leaders of the variant human groups: he and his descendants would both protect the old-humans and assure that they never again attained advantage or primacy over the other six races. There was more to the deal: never must bors turn against mantee, tarbek or fard against wend or ikut. One man, one family, would oversee all, and would not allow the inevitable differences between men of different fur, different scents, different racial ambitions, to become general war.

One man, one family, would keep the secret of the stardrive, would maintain a fleet of warships and a body of soldiers called poletzai to enforce the peace of the Xarafeille Stream. And thus arose the seed of Shems Minder's defection: John Minder I volunteered to have his own genes modified. His descendants would not be ordinary old-humans, though they would not have fur, flippers, or other obvious differences. They would, however, be very curious, quite dispassionate (as adults, at least), and singularly lacking in all but purely intellectual ambition. Thus Shems's decision to disappear, to become an anonymous archaeologist on an unknown planet far from the demands of the Arbitorial offices on Newhome, was entirely in character. Many a potential Arbiter had to be dragged to office protesting and refusing; the best rulers were invariably those least content to shoulder the burdens of rule, and the least impressed with the perquisites of office. Shems was unique only in his successful elusion of the searchers sent to find him—and in his choice of "souvenirs" removed from Newhome when he left.

On the seven datacrystals—between them, but not entirely on any one—were the coded location of the Arbiter's war fleet, the formulae and specifications for the stardrive, and the coordinates of the primitive planet where the warlike old-human poletzai dwelt in isolation from the greater polity of the Xarafeille Stream. Without those crystals—which could be read only by an ancient computer locked in the palace's Vault of Worlds, where Shems had never gone—the new Arbiter, John XXIII, was only one man, and powerless. Most Arbiters never needed to use the war fleet or the poletzai that manned the ships, but the implied power of both fleet and poletzai was inherently behind all their decisions and decrees, and the presence of white warships in orbit did much to inspire disputants to seek the conference table for solutions to their problems. But John XXIII had no fleet.

"But I saw the crystals on Daddy's shelf!" Parissa stated emphatically.

"You saw *some* crystals," Sarabet clarified. "Did you count them?" Parissa, she knew, had a unique way of counting from one to twenty: "One, two, free, leben, twenny." There were crystals in some of the padded niches—but not seven of them. And who knew which ones were "real"? One crystal had been placed there only recently. Perhaps, Sarabet speculated, it was only the first or second real one. Perhaps that very crystal had some bearing on the story Dad was telling them, Slith Wrasselty's tale. Or perhaps not. It was too early to tell where Slith's story would lead, and Dad had so many stories. . . .

"Doesn't Daddy have any poleetsies?" Parissa asked.

"Not yet. So far, he has been very lucky. He has been able to resolve disputes without them—but that can't go on forever. Already, people on many worlds are asking questions."

"What questions?"

" 'Where are the Arbiter's white ships?' is one. Obviously, no one has seen any of them since Dad became Arbiter."

"How come?"

"Come on, dear. Think about it, and then you tell *me* why."

"Umm." Parissa made a graphic attempt to "think about it," counting something off on her fingers. Then she smiled. "It's because Daddy needs all the crystals to make the ships work, isn't it?"

"That's it exactly!" Sarabet enthused. "See? You can figure lots of things out for yourself." *And how much easier it will be for me—and Rob—when you do*, she thought.

Slith Wrasselty awakened more slowly than an alert fard should. He awoke with a strange, luxurious, languorous feeling in his very bones. That was quite odd, because his bed was the same hard rock it had been the night before, his last meal had been the same dry, unfilling biscuits, his drink the same dull water—with Valbissag's famous tang and flavor gone all flat. He should have awakened alert and mobile, ready to fight or flee, but instead he looked around himself with vastly disinterested dispassion and irrational contentment.

Even when he realized that he was not alone in his rude bed, he did not jump up or exhibit a single sign of distress. There, in the crook of his arm, was the fardling. There, between his arms, cushioning the small furry creature's head, were his own two enlarged breasts. One, the left, was heavier than the other, which the fardling had nursed on while he slept. A fine trickle of pale milk trickled from his swollen left nipple. Slith Wrasselty moaned then, but it was not an angry sound. The infant's pheromones, working while he slept, had done more than stimulate his mammary glands. Now that he was nursing an infant, he no longer wanted things to be otherwise: he felt too good. For a fard male, no sense of well-being surpassed that of having a well-fed infant in his arms; the languor that followed a rich, generous meal was frantic by comparison. Slith's engorged left breast ached and prickled inside. He instinctively knew to tickle the sleeping fardling's cheek to make it turn its head and lock its lips onto his left nipple. The sucking sensation made him tingle from head to feet, a sensual thrill said to surpass mere sexual release.

A male of another species might have raged when fate dealt him an unfair blow. He might have abandoned an infant, even one he had sired, if it was inconvenient to nurture it. Yet a fard, who could, without much thought, slay a male infant of his own siring, did not—indeed, could not—refuse the biochemical and genetic imperative that a female nurseling engendered in him.

The fardling sucked sleepily—but no less vigorously for that—and Slith Wrasselty contemplated the new situations that faced him. No longer could he venture on two-week expeditions, for his lactating body would demand food enough for two. He would be limited to seven- or eight-day ventures, and his traveling distance would be much shortened unless he could earn cash money to buy a secondhand sand rover and fuel for it. That meant he would have to sell some of whatever he discovered instead of hoarding the knowledge of it for the service of his future plans.

Deep within himself, perhaps, the old Slith Wrasselty may have lingered, howling and spitting mad at the new limitations, but there was not—and there would not be—any outward evidence of it. The new, changed Slith was now the possessor of a more or less permanent companion and a future mate, whose insidious pheromones and other bodily exudations made him feel gloriously happy about it. And that was that.

Besides his chemically induced and genetically programmed happiness, there were other compensations for his new burden. For one, even the slight risk of his being assassinated by his brothers was now a thing of the past. Gleph, Thradz, Splath, or Thplet could no more slay him, a nurse, than they could successfully amputate their own heads, because not only had the nurseling's chemistry affected Slith's, but his own exudations would now form an impregnable shield; other male fards would be unable even to think violent thoughts in his presence.

For another compensation, when the fardling stopped nursing at about four years of age (and Slith estimated it was almost one, at present) it would be sexually mature as well, and would then offer him the lesser pleasure of sexual coupling with it whenever and wherever he wished, in exchange for the greater joy of nursing it, which he would never again experience.

"What's your name?" he cooed at his small charge.

"Smack," she replied without removing her greedy mouth from his nipple. "Bd'eth."

"Biddeth? Is that it?"

"No. Bleth," she said more clearly. "Bleth. I used to be Bleth Wrebeltee, but ... What's your name?"

"Slith Wrasselty."

"Then I am Bleth Wrasselty, now," she said with firm conviction and full understanding of what their relationship had become. She returned to her sucking. Slith observed that she had, as if along with his milk, imbibed a certain command of the Wrasselty way of speaking, which was far superior to the way her blood kin had taught her to talk. Fardlings were impressionable; their small, agile brains were fresh books with many empty pages waiting to be filled—with attitudes, opinions, and moral standards as well as proper modes of speech. It was said that the adoptive nurse of a fardling had no one to blame but himself, should his sometime mate prove less than satisfactory to him.

Slith noticed also that his left breast was now flaccid, but already the right one had begun to fill. He revised downward his earlier estimate of how long he could stay in the field. If tiny Bleth continued to nurse so fiercely, he would be lucky to carry four days' enhanced rations. But then, how long had she been alone and without nutriment since her mother—and likely her male sibling as well—had chased her out of the Wrebek camp with snarls, hisses, and clawed fingernails? Perhaps once she was sated, her demands would lessen somewhat.

That train of thought reminded him that he would have to return to Valbissag immediately, and not only because of the acute pangs of hunger he was even then experi-

encing—though even before Bleth's lips fell open in sleep
he had planned a much larger breakfast than he usually
ate. He would, he suspected, have to drink almost all his
limited supply of water just to replenish what he had already given her.

Carefully, without disturbing her sleep, he rose. She no
longer had cause to awaken anxiously whenever he
moved. She, as well as he, knew their new mutual status.
He wondered how had he ever considered her ugly. In his
eyes she was now a lovely child, though her fur was
clumpy and bedraggled as if she had been dipped in oil
and rolled in the dust of the desert. That observation triggered another new, unfamiliar urge. His hunger forgotten,
Slith hunkered down on knees and elbows and began
licking her. He licked her legs, her arms, all those parts of
her body that were uppermost, and then he turned her
over. She did not awaken, but she squeaked softly. Her
tiny voice was sweet and musical. How had he ever considered it shrill?

Her fur, where he licked it, became soft and glossy. His
own fur stood on end, and his skin tingled with ecstatic,
not-quite-erotic sensations. When he finished giving
Bleth her bath, he sniffed her all over, discovered several
small, intimate places he had missed before, and remedied the omissions with intense enthusiasm. Only then
did his own hunger pangs return.

Slith shouldered his pack only to discover that the
straps interfered painfully with his sore breasts. He fiddled with the straps, adjusting and positioning them, and
finally decided he could not carry the pack at all without
severe discomfort. Little Bleth scampered around his
knees, chatting engagingly. He could not bring himself to
feel frustrated with her, or with his problem. Instead, entirely philosophically, he wrapped all but his specimen
roll and his notebook in the sleeping sheet, and buried
them next to the pinnacle where he could find them again
when he returned there.

Without a backward look he abandoned the precious
equipment, carrying the specimen roll beneath one arm

and the book in that hand, and offering his free hand to
his tiny companion, who grasped it possessively. Slith
again experienced the visceral thrill of contact. He was
not, however, so entirely lost in the joys of nursedom that
he was not grateful that young fards possess great stam-
ina. He would not have to carry her on his shoulders, at
least for the first hour or two. With light and happy steps
Slith and Bleth Wrasselty set off on the long day's walk
home to Valbissag.

"I like Slith now," Parissa announced. "He's a *nice*
fard."

"He's a stupid fard, if you ask me," grumbled Rober.
"A stupid, *perverted* one. Nursing, eeyuck!"

"Why, Robby!" exclaimed his mother, sounding quite
offended. "You don't think of *me* like that, do you? Stupid? Perverted?"

Rober stammered an apology, then tried to explain.
"You're my *mother*," he said. "You were *supposed* to
nurse me. And Slith Wrasselty is the *hero* of the story,
isn't he? Heroes don't have . . . breasts."

"Oh?" Janna Minder queried archly. "Can't women be
heroes, then? Or heroines, if you prefer?"

Rob had dug his verbal hole, and he found himself unable to climb out. "Aw, Mom," he said at last. "You know
what I mean."

"I think I do, Robby. You wanted—no, you *expected*—
Slith to be a Robby Minder, not a fard. Or, you wanted
him to be a 'perverted' fard, an unnatural one whose instincts were all wrong for him, but were like your own."

"Well, I don't want to nurse anybody, ever," he grumbled, forcing himself to keep his baleful glare from falling
on Parissa.

"Of course not. If you did, then by old-human standards, *you* would be 'perverted,' wouldn't you? As 'perverted' as Slith would have been if he had *not* nursed
little Bleth. You see?"

Robby saw. He understood, but he did not like it. He
did not *have* to like it. Parissa's words, repeated by
Sarabet days earlier, returned to him then: "Boring! Bo-

ring!" Now that he could no longer identify with Slith, the hero, who had turned out to be a nursing mother, or father, or whatever he was, he was sure that the rest of Slith's story was going to be a long, boring tale indeed. He would later, much later, admit just how wrong he was.

CHAPTER 4

Fard males are not the only ones who can nurse infants. Solitary wends, upon the death of a lactating mate, have been known to do so, as have old-human males, under the right conditions of privation and emotional stress. Fards are, however, the only humans among whom male lactation is an integral adaptation. A surfeit of hungry males was an unaffordable luxury except for defense, and a single male could impregnate many females. Fards' murderous inheritance struggles served the community by eliminating all but superior protectors—and their bloodlines. Yet those males who were compelled to nurse young females contributed by relieving mothers of the burden of caring for them, and themselves acquired future mates, guaranteeing the transmission of their own "altruistic" natures to future generations.

Such contradictory adaptive strategies—breeding for homicidal males and nurturing ones—is inefficient, but remember: the long-term, evolutionary, success of a species lies in the preservation of just such diverse options, against some future when one or the other alone may better serve the race.

Polarities:
Studies in the Diverse Roles of the Male among Mankind,
University of Salith Press,
Salith, Xarafeille 957, 12022 R.L.

"Ah, Slith," said old Fladth, eyeing his son's most recent acquisition. The old fard's nostrils flared a fractional

amount, indicating *threpth,* which signified a pleasant
sensory memory. Had his nostrils movement been accompanied by other subtle movements of eye or pinna, by a
tilt of the head or a flicker of fingers, it might have—
would have—meant something else entirely. Yet Slith understood it, and was pleased. "You are a fard after my
own fashion indeed," said Fladth. "It was just so that I
found your mother. She, too, was a Wrebek."

Fladth's chamber was a masterpiece of late-colonial
fardish architecture. Its double row of thin, flanking columns were of chemically hardened azurite with ornate
capitals of the ancient Karintian order, stylized dewspot
petals enwrapping globes engraved with the continents of
a fanciful homeworld. Curtained niches behind the columns could hide bodyguards in time of need. One entire
wall was a sheet of creamy, translucent chalcedony, iron-streaked; when it was exposed from outside to the full
sun of afternoon, it seemed to glow with an internal light.
Fladth sat with his back to the chalcedony wall, across
the room from the younger fard and the fardling—for in
spite of his and Slith's mutual affection he was cautious,
and had, thus far, lived long enough for the short fur on
his face to whiten, which was rare indeed among males.
"Now, then. What else did you find?"

Slith grinned and lifted his left shoulder. "The outcrop
has many patches of soluble organics. X-ray crystallography indicates that at least two of them are proteinlike and
have ... interesting ... affinities for human cells." Slith
was purposefully vague. He knew the relationship between caution and success; there was no need for Fladth
to know details.

He changed the subject. "You seem no worse for wear.
Did my brothers sleep the whole time I was gone?"

Fladth snorted scornfully. His entire body shivered—or
so it would have seemed to anyone not a fard. To Slith,
it was not a single shiver, but a whole series of discrete
signs and gestures that elaborated upon Fladth's simple,
unequivocal expulsion of breath. "I found a broody female krood beneath my bed, but there was no burrow between the stones of my walls or floor. The krood did not
crawl in through a window."

"Thradz, you think? Didn't Gleph already try that, once?"

"He did, and I gave the krood back to him—in his soup. It was either Thradz, or one of the young ones. As for Gleph, he plays with poisons of late, but I am immune to his efforts thus far." Again, he made a scornful noise. "I sometimes think I will die of exhaustion in my sleep, worn out by the sheer number of their attempts. Their skills grow slowly, if at all. They do not deserve much of an inheritance even if by accident they succeed in killing me."

The subject of the inheritor's reward was of interest to Slith. Fladth's assassination would not determine which brother acquired Valbissag and its assets; it would merely trigger the next phase of the successional struggle. Only when one brother had slain the others or had personally accepted their fealty—glass jars containing their amputated and pickled generative organs—would he inherit not only palpable assets like the spring, the stones that were Valbissag Town, and the ground which all occupied, but the investments kept in banks and brokerages in Thember, a spaceport city six days south by road.

Those investments were the product of Fladth's work, and his forefathers', resulting from the licensing or sale of chemical processes and of rare crystalline compounds grown in cleverly mixed solutions from Valbissag itself and from small subsidiary wells and seeps the Wrasselty clan laid claim to. Each well, depending on the mountain-country aquifer that supplied it, had a unique chemistry. Fards, long dependent on what other humans called "bad" water, had developed innate abilities to sense the pollutants and poisons in their water and to manipulate them through distillation, precipitation, mixing, and compounding. The wisest fards, like Fladth, obtained patents on their processes and their unique products.

In Thember, in the banking district, were three edifices built on the grand scale that only governments could afford: the Patent Office, the Fardic History Division and Archive, and the Registry. The Registry, which covered twenty acres to a height of fifteen stories, held all manner of deeds, contracts, treaties, leases, court proceedings and judgments, and more. The Archive housed copies of Registry documents of historic import, old diaries of Phyre's settlers, collections of anecdotes, tales, myths and folk songs, paintings, photographs, and holographs of Fellenbrath as it once was. Some records were so ancient they were said to have been brought from the far side of the coal-black cloud of velvet dust that formed the display cloth upon which the jewels of the Xarafeille Stream were laid. The History Division and Archive covered thirty acres, but was only ten stories high. The Patent Office occupied forty acres and had twenty-two stories, and very little of its vast space held offices. Most of it held, of course, patents.

Fards' need to patent things perhaps sprang from the impact of water chemistry upon their survival. It extended through that to all things; it was said that a fard would patent his individual fingernail parings if there were no hard-nosed officials to dismiss his effort as frivolous and then to refund his filing fee.

The University was a lesser complex of offices and classrooms, none over four stories, separated by picturesque cobble paths and dust pools, by colorful lichen beds and low serpentine walls that often served as benches. Befitting its function of furnishing graduates to the three greater institutions—greater, if one judged by height, not acreage—and by its need to draw upon the resources of all of them, the University grounds were like the matrix of a limestone conglomerate, the Registry a granitic pebble within it, the Archive a quartz fragment, the Patent Office red jasper, and the University's own buildings a scattering of grains of coarse sand of no particular color or importance.

By far the greatest portion of the non-fard and non-tarbek population of Phyre lived in Thember, which possessed the single largest distillation and water-purification plant on the planet and a supply of groundwater sufficient to supply such people with water in the vast quantities they ordinarily consumed. Too, in Thember were several places of employment whose positions were not automatically filled by fards or tarbeks. As fards were not by nature interested in history (though they understood the need for keeping track of such things, and understood the Arbiter's decree that they do so), they had early on hired wends as custodians of their racial history. Some highly placed wends among those who worked in the History Division traced their ancestries to those original employees a thousand and more years in the past. Wends, by their very natures, never lost track of their own histories and genealogies, even on minor planets like Phyre.

If fards had run the Patent Office, every fallen whisker and every desiccated scat that dropped upon the desert sand would have had a number and a data file. Traditionally, the Patent Office was run by bors. The stocky, black-furred bors were by nature trogloditic, were inventive, mechanically inclined, no-nonsense men, and were ideal foils for the enthusiastic fards. They were methodical and slow-moving (as all other folk seemed to the quick, graceful, and lissome fards), and they suffered no frivolous applications. They were sometimes known to refuse to return application fees if they grew sufficiently annoyed.

The Registry had fard employees, but also wends and bors, each working at tasks to which his temperament and racial proclivities best suited him.

The Patent Office held what was of greatest interest to both Fladth and Slith. "A3207A expired yesterday," Fladth commented conversationally, "and YB-948C will expire at noon today."

"Ah," said Slith. "Has Gleph noticed?"

"Him?" Fladth chuckled. "He is too busy making new poisons to bother to go to Thember and patent his own inventions, let along to keep track of anything else. He collects his own formulae in a metal box which he buries nightly, always in a different place. He thinks—as do his brothers—that the wires those bors contractors trenched between here and the city carry only electricity to light his laboratory!" Fladth eyed a wall niche covered with a hanging dust cover. Slith had seen the late-model terminal his father kept there. He had used it, on occasion, to check on patents filed in the Patent Office in Thember.

"So how many patents are left?" Slith asked.

"There are one hundred and eighty-seven still unexpired. The last of them will expire within the year. I will," he chuckled, "attempt to remain alive until then."

"And much longer, I hope," said Slith. "I enjoy our 'unnatural' relationship and do not wish it to end."

"I too," agreed his father, the fingers of his left hand clenching momentarily, his prominent ears flattening just a trifle, "but the odds—four to one—are against me. Sooner or later one of them will get me."

"I sometimes think we fards are, as a subspecies, 'unnatural,' and that bors and wends have a better way."

"Ach, no!" said Fladth, shaking his head. "If sons did not kill fathers and slay or castrate their brothers, the world would be overrun with useless males who would gobble all the food and would drink our wells dry. Oh, don't get me wrong; as I said, I enjoy your company, but overall, your brothers are far better fards than either of us." Slith politely agreed, but privately he had several reservations about that.

"I must move to Thember soon," he said, changing the subject.

"Ah," his father said. "For the fardling's sake?"

"If I am to sustain her, and to continue my research too, I will need revenue. In Thember, I can create pharmaceuticals for the offworld trade without having to trade my patent rights for food. Besides, I think Thradz is becoming suspicious of all the time I spend in your laboratory. I need one of my own—away from my brothers' eyes."

"You can't afford equipment like mine," stated Fladth.

"I won't need it. From this point on, I will need only growth tanks for crystals, some glassware, and a large retort. And for all I know now, the final seed crystals of my masterpiece may have to be grown in microgravity—in orbit. It makes sense for me to be in Thember, near the spaceport."

"I suppose so," his father replied grudgingly, "though I would prefer things to be otherwise." Such circumlocution was required by the Fardic tongue, in which there was no way to say "I'll miss you." The closest approximation to that, between male relatives, was "I don't trust you out of my sight."

"What's that?" Rob Minder demanded, seeing the ugly, gnarled, and contorted stick in his father's hand.

"Swarrow root from Phyre," John Minder replied. "It is quite rare and is considered good luck to find. High fard and tarbek officials carry staffs made of it."

"It's ugly," Rob said.

"It doesn't have to remain so. Fard staffs are often ornately carved, and the wood takes a high russet sheen." Minder smiled ruefully. "Tarbek staffs, on the other hand ... Mostly, they only remove the bark."

Rob brightened. "Can I carve it? I can use the new tools the bors delegate from Paramot brought me." He reached for the future "staff"—ugly and gnarled and bark-covered as it was.

"I expect you to clean up after yourself," Rob's mother insisted. "It isn't fair to expect the maids to ..."

"Aw, Mom! I won't make any messes." His mother's expression hinted that she was reserving judgment on that. "Where's Sarabet?" Rob asked. "I want to show her."

"She is at a friend's for the day."

"Show me!" Parissa squealed. "Can I help you carve it?"

"Oh, no! You aren't old enough to use sharp tools. And if you even watch, you'll talk all the time, and I'll cut myself."

"Rob!" his mother cautioned.

"Oh, all right. C'mon, Priss. *Fled rackety nong!*" said Robby Minder to his little sister, as he left the room. His fingers curled under, but Parissa did not notice that.

"What does that mean?" Parissa demanded, pulling on Robby's sleeve, and consequently being led away with him.

Their father's eyebrow lifted, but he said nothing.

"He'll grow out of it," Janna Minder assured her husband. "Both of them will." She, like all the family except

Parissa, knew all the major languages of the human races, and several dialects of each. "I'll miss you," was what Robby had said, in Old High Fardic. His clumsy imitation of the fard hand sign would have been recognized by a fard as an urge to scratch, suggesting the just-realized acquisition of a new strain of biting parasitic mite.

Down the hall, Minder heard Parissa's high-pitched giggle. "*Fled rackety nong* to you too," she chortled.

An Arbiter was many things to many people. Among the less educated masses he was often pictured as a nebulous being, not a man at all, except perhaps an all-knowing bogeyman. In some places "Only the Arbiter knows" was said in the same way other folks might say "God only knows," though if pressed, they would admit that they did not really think of him as a deity.

Those folks who lived on Newhome and had a chance to visit the Arbiter's hearing rooms—or offworlders who came seeking justice, who often found only arbitration—would forever envision him as a robed and hooded figure unseen except for the red glow of his all-seeing eyes. Of course that was all merely tradition, and showmanship. The "eyes" glow was merely a manifestation of the bio-sign scanners every one of his many assistants wore in the courtrooms, to help them discern who was, or was not, being entirely truthful while under oath.

The Arbiter John Minder XXIII thought of himself as a rather ordinary man with a very difficult job—that of quelling individual ambitions without quelling individuality, of balancing the trends toward a unity of all mankind against the needs for continued diversity, for the maintenance of the varied evolutionary options that it allowed, all the while struggling to prevent that very diversity from spinning out of control and destroying the polity he watched over.

It would have been easier to have been a god, John Minder sometimes grumbled.

Bleth—now Bleth Wrasselty—was quite happy to be alive, and to be full of milk, but her happiness was tempered by the realization that her new nurse was not exactly as she might have wished him to be.

Many men, unable to inherit a town, a spring, or even a nomadic chieftainship, would have been glad to have a fardling, a future mate, a guarantee that their precious genetic heritage would not die when they died. Not so Slith Wrasselty. Though he had quickly and philosophically adapted to their new relationship, he did not seem to want progeny now or in the future. Bleth pictured herself being set aside at the very moment her need to nurse ended.

Ah, well; she would cling to him—to the nourishment he provided—for now. If their differences proved too great, she had one option that he did not. If a more suitable male presented himself to her, she could leave Slith.

(HAPTER 5

It is highly unlikely that the tarbek race shares
a common genetic structure with the legendary *frufly,*
the familiar of those ancient witches who created
the races of man in dim antiquity. Yet it is said
that the female *frufly*—which is probably based upon
some real creature—would die if inseminated by
more than a few males, an unhappy result of
toxins in their semen, toxins evolved to destroy
the sperm of other males.

Perhaps the total avoidance of physical contact
between tarbek males and females is based in
some similar chemical incompatibility resulting
from convergent evolution. Yet even *fruflys* required
coitus to reproduce their kind, and tarbeks have done
away with that entirely.

Fruflys, Geniepigs, and other Mythical Beasts
Penteralimin Keteritifen, PhD,
New Age Press,
Faltera, Xarafeille 55, 12002 R.L.

The journey to Thember took eight days. Slith and Bleth
walked the first sixty miles—or rather, Slith did. Bleth
walked fifteen, then rode in a makeshift sling across his
chest. Where the trail crossed a highway they caught a
ride to Krat, an industrial town on the edge of a dusty
playa, and then paid commercial fare (one and one-half
persons) the rest of the way.

During their trip, twelve more Wrasselty patents expired unrenewed. That was Fladth's gift to his son; whoever succeeded Fladth would inherit only real estate, and
when Slith attained his majority at twenty-five, a year

hence, he could patent all the expired formulae in his own name. Until then they would remain unowned, with the risk that someone else might independently discover a formula and quite innocently patent it. There was risk, also, that someone might actually discover that Wrasselty patents had lapsed. It was a chance Slith was willing to take, because he would otherwise inherit nothing at all.

In Thember, he leased a storefront with an apartment over it, on Colony Boulevard, a street that had perhaps been pleasantly respectable an eon or so in the past, when Thember was new. Now the fanciful gargoyles guarding the doorways were mere sand-worn nubs, the windows were mostly frosted by blown sand, and the street was high-crowned with the compacted dust of crumbling buildings. Thember was an odd place, by the standards of the desert; it was odd by the standards of the great polity of the Xarafeille Stream as well; it was a place where electric carts were poor men's taxis, where carriages drawn by clawed beasts, thribbets, denoted wealth and status. Fine houses with intelligent computerized doors lined wide streets that resembled rock gardens, streets that were only a turn and a gateway from disheveled tenements where a single hydrant served a hundred families. Electric vapor lights illuminated the streets at night, brighter than the greasy candles within the houses of both rich and poor.

Slith bought laboratory glassware, a furnace, several crucibles, and a half-dozen salvaged glass-lined drums to use as crystal-growing vats. Bleth, uninterested in his new business, found a cool place in the cellar to play during the day, and a warm spot beside Slith to sleep at night. Her lowered activity level reduced her demand for sustenance, which meant that Slith did not have to work with one hand while carrying her with him in the lab.

His ordinary work entailed the formulation of sun salves, love potions, and mild narcotics for the lower-class wends and bors of Thember; those brought in enough cash for rent, food, supplies, and a small overage from which he bought toys and bright trinkets for Bleth. Her glee was all the reward he craved for his generosity. She was now an attractive, bright-eyed fardling with glossy fur, and she had learned to bathe herself—though Slith's driving instincts sometimes made him salivate when he saw that she had picked up a speck of dust, and a ritual bath was a nightly event.

Life, thought Slith Wrasselty, was good. He eagerly awaited his twenty-fifty birthday, when he anticipated, it would get better still; as a legal adult, he could acquire the expired Valbissag patents. Periodically, tiring of the city, he would place Bleth across his chest in a leather infant carrier, and they would travel by fast commercial rail to the end of the line, not far from Valbissag. The fare for such luxuriously fast travel was exorbitant, but Slith felt he had to visit certain sites in the hill country now and then, usually before the regular rains that fell only on the high ground. He gathered only a few samples on each trip, but he often scattered pellets of tracer compounds that would indicate which low-country wells were fed by the particular aquifer he salted.

Slith ordered letterhead stationery, and commissioned a brochure extolling his products. The latter he sent to customers and to potential customers on a purchased mailing list. One such brochure arrived in the hands of Lord Gefke Jandissl, in Low Diverness, who was about to throw it away when a blue card fell out, attracting his attention. Tarbek brains and eyes have a hardwired affinity for a particular shade of the color blue, perhaps because it is the color of certain copper ores containing sulfur, and tarbeks crave sulfur in all its forms.

FERTILITY PROBLEMS?

It came to our attention last year that lava flows and landslides in North Adderlong have disrupted groundwater patterns along the Damplag Trench, which has changed the composition of wells, springs, and seeps as far away as West Diverness.

If you have been experiencing diminished fertility because of those changes, our Additive 3A can restore the potency of your wells and bathing holes. Additive 3A is specifically formulated to replace compounds found only in the Damplag Formation rocks of the Adderlong plateau which may no longer find their way via groundwater flow to your wells, owing to the changed conditions at the source.

Please use our standard order form (page 5 of our brochure) and enclose a prepaid money order or certified check. Your purchase will be shipped to you in a plain brown wrapper.

Slith opened the envelope and gazed wide-eyed at the check, in the amount of twelve thousand standard creds. Lord Jandissl, he surmised, was quite desperate. He wished to purchase enough Additive 3A to restore his fertility, to boost it, and to maintain it at an unprecedented level. The population of Low Diverness, Slith guessed, was about to expand rapidly. What would Jandissl do with the excess population? It would mature rapidly and increase the stress of crowding.

Bleth, who had grown rapidly of late and could now see over the top of the lab bench, helped him pack eight kilos of Additive 3A for shipment to Low Diverness. If any other orders for it came in, Slith would have to buy the raw materials to make more of it in order to fill them.

Slith's small brother Thplet visited the apartment on Colony Boulevard on several occasions. Bleth thought Slith's cavalier treatment of him was unwarranted—ignoring him for hours at a time while Slith puttered in his laboratory below. Bleth found herself entertaining Thplet until Slith was ready to see him. She did not at all mind that, because Thplet had a keen eye and mind, and an acerbic sense of humor—while Slith seemed to lack humor entirely. Yet, she reflected, they are obviously brothers. That observation inspired her to study Thplet quite closely; after all, being full siblings, they shared a common heritage, one that *her* infants would inherit as well. By examining Thplet as well as Slith, she opened a larger window on the future that awaited her as mother of future Wrasseltys.

Thplet, for his part, also enjoyed those hours before Slith condescended to join them. Bleth, despite her tender years, was good company—an endless fount of questions, many of which seemed astute enough for an adult to have uttered, and all of which were flattering to Thplet, who allowed himself to ramble on endlessly, feeling quite wise, and enjoying the sound his own voice made, resonating within the large sinuses of his short fardish snout.

When Slith did arrive, there was no time for such pleasant pastimes. Slith was all business, wanting to know everything that went on at Valbissag. He quizzed Thplet harshly, so much so that Bleth wondered why Thplet continued to visit at all. Once Slith arrived, Thplet's conversation was limited to curt, precise answers to his brother's questions, and it seemed as though he became soon anxious to satisfy Slith and to depart.

With the windfall from Low Diverness, Slith and Bleth were able to move into larger quarters in Varamin Park, a stylish neighborhood mostly occupied by midlevel officials and offworld traders, and to afford carriage fare between the shop, now wholly a manufactory, the new house, and a new retail outlet in a fine, prestigious location.

The large single houses of Varamin Park presented only their ornate doorways and wrought-iron gates to the street. Each one enclosed an interior court with cool, shaded cobbles, columned arcades, and reflecting pools of water or mercury. The street was barred to vehicles and was planted with meandering rows of boxwood hedges and beds of flowering madge. Tradesmen and caterers used balcony-hung alleys behind and beside the houses.

Thplet only visited there once. Bleth, returning from an errand, found him sitting on the front steps. "Thplet!" she exclaimed. "Why are you sitting there?"

"You new doorman, or butler, will not let me inside, and Slith is not here to identify me."

"Well, I can. You must come in!"

"I do not like wends, and they do not like me!" Thplet spat. "I will chat with you awhile, then be on my way. And where *is* Slith?"

Bleth giggled. "Our wendish servants do not seem to like *any* of us. 'Just so they like the money we pay them, and strive hard to earn it,' Slith says. And Slith is out in the dry middens today. I do not know what he is doing there."

"Ah," said Thplet. "And what have *you* been up to?"

"I visited an orphanage for fardlings less lucky than me."

"Why did you do that?" asked Thplet, quite astounded.

"I donate part of the money Slith gives me for trinkets and household things. There but for the purest luck, I would also be—if I had not died on the way to the city."

"There but for your own cleverness, you mean. Slith had told me how you crept up on him in the night. He still wonders how you got out of that canyon alive."

"And he might continue to wonder," she said firmly. "I am not about to reveal my secrets to Slith. Is he angry with me still?" Bleth asked, sounding almost fearful.

"I think that deep inside, Slith still rages, not at being entrapped as much as at discovering that there exists someone cleverer than him—someone who outsmarted him."

"I am afraid, then," said Bleth. "I do not wish to starve, or to drink the artificial milk those orphans are given. It tastes like white mud, and makes my stomach ache."

Thplet laughed indulgently. "Can a female tarbek stay away from water?" he asked. "Can a bors grow feathers instead of fur? Do not concern yourself, small one. Slith is well and truly trapped by his own nature, and by the endorphins that now circulate in his blood. He will not abandon you. You are safe . . . and that is more than I can say for myself."

"What is wrong?" Bleth asked, now ashamed of her self-centeredness.

"I suspect that Fladth nears his end," Thplet said. "And that mine will be soon after."

"Oh, no, Thplet! You must not die. There are ways . . ."

"Ways? You mean I should castrate myself and present my organs to the winner of the succession struggle in a jar?"

"Would that be worse than death?" asked Bleth. "Is *anything* worse than never again being able to strive?"

"You are not male," Thplet said, stating what was obvious. "You could not understand."

Bleth put a hand on the disconsolate fard's knee. "Surely there is a way," she said. "I have heard Slith say there are old-human shamans in the dry middens who can perform such tasks quite painlessly. . . . "

In the evenings, when all Varamin Park was in shadow, Slith walked hand in hand with the fast-growing Bleth, who grew too heavy to be carried with ease. They joined the other residents of Varamin and neighboring streets in sociable promenade. "Good evening, Sar Slith," said plump bors matrons, smiling, indulgently tweaking Bleth's soft ear tufts while out of the corners of their eyes assuring themselves that their own black-furred progeny did not approach too closely. Young bors played rough-and-tumble, and their mothers did not wish to offend the daughter of such an up-and-coming young merchant. Slith did not disabuse them of their belief in his kinship with Bleth. He usually wore a silky duster that covered his now-much-reduced breasts; he was not sure how bors felt about fards' unique adaptation, though as a fard living among other races, Slith had learned how to accommodate to their slow reflexes and unobservant eyes. When he spoke with a bors, he consciously forced his body into uncommunicative stillness, his face into a rigid mold. He kept his nose from twitching—or tried to—and made his ears point only forward. He kept his eyes wide open as if he were an infant who had never stared into the desert's glare. It would have been hard for him to accept that for the bors—or wend or old-human—his efforts made him seem only slightly less twitchy than other fards; yet it was an invaluable edge in his social and commercial dealings.

"Ah, Wrasselty," said an elderly wend scholar from the History Division. "I've been meaning to stop by your new emporium. Hammady Wheln—you'll remember him, the documentarian from over on Flower Court—suggests I try your new memory-enhancing formula. But forgive me . . . promenade is no time for business. Will you be in at your posted hour?"

Slith's new shop, with a fine green-and-gold sign identifying it as PARK STREET APOTHECARY, was just off Port Street. Offworld traders and tourists seeking the renowned products of Phyre's wells and springs—substances extracted, distilled, and precipitated from the planet's unusual waters, then mixed with krood-skin oils, blackwort dust, and other exotic organics by smart-nosed fards, according to exacting formulae and procedures—would see advertisements for Slith's establishment the moment they left the spaceport. It was a busy and profitable operation, and Slith need only keep limited hours there meeting with wealthy notables and bulk traders who refused to deal with his many clerks, assistants, and underlings.

The tarbek metabolite Additive 3A now accounted for only a small part of Slith's sales, though it had given him the initial wherewithal to leap for commercial success. Yet to give him his due, Slith was not lazy and was a clever and original researcher. He did not use formulae developed by his father and forefathers, the former Wrasselty patents, for fear that some clever analyst would duplicate them before he could legally claim both the process and the ingredients as his own. The products he sold were either original creations—which he thoroughly and diligently tested on indigent bors and wends before selling them—or standard products much in demand, made more cheaply according to Slith's streamlined processing than elsewhere, and thus sold for less than his competitors could afford to do.

Slith now spent more time than ever away from Thember, extending the area of his geological research radially. Bleth of course accompanied him. The sector where lay Valbissag and Low Diverness was only a thin sliver of his pie. He bought crystals, precipitates, and supersaturated hot-spring solutions from tribes, clans, and principalities formerly only known as names on maps, and he explored the high-country aquifers that charged springs and damps all the way to Phyre's dry equatorial seabeds. He mapped and he tested.

Upon his return to the city, or before leaving it, he occupied himself for extensive periods in the Registry and the Patent Office. In the Registry's Deeds Rooms were documents concerning the lands that interested him. Whenever Slith did fieldwork, he did so with full knowledge of the land he surveyed: Who held title to it? Had mineral rights been granted, or was it otherwise encumbered? Were there use or passage easements that would hinder or help him?

While Slith was so occupied, Bleth—who was with the exception of her nursing quite an independent fardling—explored the city on her own or visited with her friends, people she had met through Slith's business associations. Slith, always busy, was mostly incurious about her activities.

The Registry also kept well-drilling logs from which Slith could determine much of the underlying nature of the strata in his chosen research areas. By the time he actually walked an area, he was as fully informed as possible about what lay hundreds, even thousands of feet beneath him.

The Registry did not keep paper copies of deeds, restrictions, or easements, of course, just as it did not physically store the actual stone drill cores from which its stratigraphic data were derived. All information was stored in multiterabyte datacrystals, which were locked in shelved cabinets. There were, or so Slith was told, many rooms lined with such cabinets, but Slith never saw those. From a terminal carrel in the outer rooms, he ordered what he wished to see, and particular crystals were brought forth by wendish datakeepers. Often he ordered printouts, which he was required to pay for before leaving the room. He resented that, for though he was becoming wealthy now, he retained the frugal habits of an impoverished youth. "I can print these myself at no cost but paper! Why must I pay you five creds to print them?"

"To do that, you would have to remove the crystal containing the data from this room—which is not permitted," a clerk responded. "Not The Valbissag himself can do that," he continued, referring to Slith's eminent father in the formal manner.

Bakh! Slith complained subvocally as he paid for his maps. *I could simply throw the data module from one of those windows when the clerk's back was turned, recover it outside, and copy it at my leisure.* Yet being essentially law-abiding, he did no more than contemplate that.

Security measures at the Patent Office were even more stringent. There, one was required to submit a list of patents one wished to view, and a clerk was sent to fetch them. There, a customer never even saw a datacrystal, only phosphors on a screen, or paper copies—which cost even more than those at the Registry. Yet some men walked into the Patent Office datarooms as if they owned them! There! That tarbek lord with the twisted bitternut staff, for example. Or the finely dressed wend carrying the elaborately inlaid flute denoting his rank in the wendish community.

"The tarbek is Lord Mfabek Salicot, from the Barmin Dells," a clerk explained. "And the wend you describe was probably Chief Clerk Elemerimen, who would be allowed to peruse crystals at will because he is Adjudicator of the Westland District wend community—even if he were not also my superior in this very office."

"Ah! Then I am Slith Wrasselty of Valbissag, favored son of Fladth. Stand aside and let me pass."

"I cannot. If you were Fladth, The Valbissag, and carrying your staff, it would be a different matter."

Slith complained to his father about the restrictions upon him. Fladth then gave him a note designating him Agent Plenipotentiary for Valbissag—but that had no effect at all on the wendish clerk. "When you succeed to the seat of Valbissag itself you may pass within," he said, "but not before." As Slith had no intention of becoming The Valbissag, he resigned himself to enduring the more cumbersome and expensive procedures.

"Even when I was granted access to the crystal rooms," Fladth reflected during a subsequent visit, "I contemplated hiding a crystal in my document case and printing its contents at my convenience. After all, the crystals I wanted held Valbissag patent information, and Valbissag itself is mine. It would not have been theft, not exactly."

"Why didn't you?" asked Slith.

"Have you noticed those little grilles by the doors to the outside, there?" Fladth inquired. Slith had not. "Behind them are sniffsnakes trained to react to the ozone given off by a datacrystal's charge. The constable at the door would have apprehended me immediately."

The next time Slith visited the Patent Office, he did see the inconspicuous grilles, though he could discern no sniffsnakes behind them. The constable at the door, noting that Slith's eyes lingered overlong on the grilles, took a step forward. He was alert to such things. Slith, not wishing to become an object of serious suspicion, hurried on inside.

In spite of the officious clerks and suspicious constables, Slith's was a good life, and he could no longer contemplate it improving very much. He was rich without having use of the Wrasselty formulae. He had enough money that he could not outspend his income unless he wished to purchase an in-system interplanetary spaceship (he dreaded the dark cold of space, which he thought of as being similar to a dark well, but never-ending) or a palace (but he was content in his house, which was always exactly cool enough, or warm enough, without mechanical augmentation). As his twenty-fifth birthday neared, he considered what he should do about the expired patents. Of course he would register them; his father's honor and effort on his behalf would not allow him to do otherwise. He was not sure whether he would manufacture some profitable substances, or license them to other, less original, fards.

One area where life would improve was that of Slith's personal serenity. Once everything—the Wrasselty patents and his own formulae—were properly registered, he would no longer have to keep the knowledge of them in a steel-doored vault beneath his shop or, as with the most valuable of them, in his head as well. The latter ones he reviewed often, refreshing his encyclopedic memory in the quiet hours of the night when both the ecstasy of Bleth's last nursing and the exigencies of daytime business had faded, when his mind was most clear.

Bleth—when she herself did not fall immediately asleep—listened to Slith's almost-inaudible murmurs. Her feelings, at such times, were quite mixed. She felt a strong affection for her nurse, an affection that was surely not entirely biochemically engendered, but she was less than content with his single-minded obsession with wealth and control. Of course she understood the connection between patents and the licensing fees they generated, and the relationship between a healthy bank account and starvation—even then, warm and sated, a small, sleepy mew escaped her throat, remembering—but there were so *many* suffering people.

Just a day or so earlier she had spotted a fardling lurking in the thornbushes outside the gate to Varamin Park. The gatekeeper would have chased her away, had he seen her—it was not the kind of neighborhood where derelict criminals or fardlings were ignored. It was not Colony Boulevard.

"You must not stay here," she whispered to the youngling. "The guard will beat you."

"Mar stepak?" it replied. "Where can I go?" Bleth remembered the dingy orphanage. "What is an 'orphanage'?" the fardling had asked.

"It is a place where fardlings are fed artificial milk," she said.

Bleth tried to describe it to the child but, not having nursed, not having learned much speech, it displayed a blank uncomprehending stare. "Never mind. I will take you there." The fardling only made it part of the way. It had been too weak for even a moderate walk, and Bleth was too small herself to have carried it. She left the small body in the doorway of a fan maker's shop. Perhaps the child's small, flexible ribs and delicate sinews would outlast her frail flesh and would have some small utility, as parts of decorative fans, that they had not had during her short life.

Bleth did not, at that time, understand how the evolutionary process worked. She did not understand that pain was sometimes desirable—it warned of danger to one's body, and created a powerful aversion to the practices that caused it. Depression, grief, and anger functioned similarly, modifying the future behavior, enhancing the survival of those who experienced them. The subjective experiences, the discomfort of those who hurt, grieved, and raged, was of no real account in that ongoing process; if an individual survived long enough to breed, to reproduce its genes in sufficient quantity, and if those off-spring themselves survived, it was enough.

There was, Bleth might have thought then—as she did much later in her life—no countering evolutionary advantage to joy, to complacent satisfaction, or to happiness. The carrot, had there been carrots on Phyre, was a less effective motivation than the stick, of which her planet had a few, mostly hard and knobby like swarrow, or thorny, or covered with dry, toxic bark.

Pain worked. Bleth was determined to avoid it. Sadness worked too. She grieved over the fardling's shrunken corpse—but only momentarily, because she was determined to do everything in her power to prevent a similar fate from overtaking her. But there was not much that a nurseling could do ... was there?

CHAPTER 6

Though the male progeny of a surviving fard male tend to inherit his strength, speed, and cleverness, his male seed does not partake of those qualities, but is weaker and slower than its female counterpart. The tails of fards' Y chromosome-carrying sperm have only half the mass—and energy storage capacity—of those carrying X chromosomes. That insures that far less than half his offspring will be male.

The selective advantage is obvious, and parallels that of siblings' parricidal, fratricidal behaviors; the community is saved the burden of raising large numbers of young males whose destinies, upon the death of their sire, are the rendering pot first and the soap jar later.

Polarities:
Studies in the Diverse Roles of the Male among Mankind,
University of Salith Press,
Salith, Xarafeille 957, 12022 R.L.

Slith seldom visited Valbissag, though he treasured the rare moments with Fladth, his sire. Out of sight of his brothers, he believed, might really be out of mind, and he nursed the hope that the eventual survivor of the succession war might forget him entirely, and not importune him, glass jar full of brine and sharp knife in hand, before Bleth came of age, before he had experienced the allegedly lesser, but much different, joy of mating with her when her nursing days were past. He expressed that thought to Fladth during one surreptitious visit.

"You have indeed experienced the greater pleasure, nursing her," said his father, "and the cost of *that* has been only a few extra groceries, which you yourself had the enjoyment of consuming, plus a few scraps of clothing for her, and a handful of trinkets that jingle. Have you considered the costs of sexual fulfillment?" Slith had not. "First, of course, are the expenses of maintaining your brood. With only one mate, those will not be as steep as for Valbissag's inheritor, who will sire hundreds. Still, a half-dozen sprats . . ."

"Will not cost enough to be noticed," said Slith proudly. "And my profits grow. Who knows how many I will be able to subsidize, when the time comes?"

Fladth nodded, not wishing to puncture such confident pride with carping and howevering. Still, even with his eyes dazzled by his own self-importance, Slith wondered what the sad look in his father's eyes might portend. But Fladth changed the subject before Slith could ask. "How does your masterpiece progress?" he asked. "Have you tested it on tarbeks yet?"

"I haven't dared dose a whole tribe. If someone guesses what I have invented before I am old enough to patent it . . ." He shrugged. "I have given it to a mixed group of tarbeks and old-humans who inhabit the dry middens north of Thember. What they may guess hardly matters."

The dry middens were a vast acreage of heaped refuse deemed unsuitable for reprocessing after its water was removed. There exiles, jobless ex-criminals, defectives, and old-humans congregated, sifting the various dusts and slags for items and fragments overlooked by the recyclers, which they could sell for a morsel of bread or a sip of water. "The results of my informal tests are optimistic," said Slith. "I expect to become the richest man on Phyre, once I eliminate the side effects."

"Ahh . . . and what might they be?"

Slith shrugged again. "Currently, only mouth boils. I have eliminated the possibility of obvious birth defects; of course, the tarbek wench I tested was pregnant by an old-human, so the chemistry is not exact, but . . ."

Slith's masterpiece was a crystal grown from a mixture of rare solutes collected from a total of forty-two widely separated springs. He had mapped hundreds of springs, and had in most cases traced their aquifers either to or from their respective recharging grounds in the mountains, and he now knew the exact times in the weather cycles when the specific waters he desired were produced. He had bored hidden wells of his own, usually on marginal land unclaimed by fard or tarbek, and thus had what he considered safe supplies of all his ingredients. The process by which he combined them was known to him alone—as was the substance's utility.

His tests so far indicated that any water treated with a single grain of his crystalline pièce de résistance rendered that water palatable to tarbeks—as the lip smacking and broad grins of his test subjects proved. Perhaps the dry-midden dwellers were less picky than some tarbeks might be—Lord Jandissl, and his like—but still, whether the water was tasty or merely drinkable, the result would be the same.

He had not eliminated the crystal's contraceptive effect, but that was not a problem. It would merely stimulate sales of a lagging product—Additive 3A.

"Exactly how much money do you think you will make?" Fladth asked.

"How much will tarbeks pay for the free use of one full third of Phyre's land?" Slith asked, by way of reply. "Now, much land is useless to fards and tarbeks alike; we fards cannot tolerate vagrant volcanic fumes, and tarbeks—who can—wither, sicken, and become morose because the water in such places is not foul enough for them. Since an antidote for the gases has eluded the best fard chemists, I feel no guilt over making all such marginal land available to the tarbeks instead."

"As well you should not. Patriotism must never interfere with business." With that Slith agreed. Being fards—and being in business—both men chose to ignore the greater implications of Slith's discovery: that a chemical compound capable of polluting wells in the Vermous Hills could also pollute lakes, rivers . . . and, in sufficient

quantities, even oceans, making their water unusable by
anyone *except* tarbeks. Even had he considered that, Slith
would probably have discounted the possibility—the formula was his alone, and it depended entirely upon the
specific content of Valbissag's wells. Even with access to
the wells, no one could manufacture his formula without
knowing just which waters to choose, how to treat each
one, how to mix them, and in what particular order; even
should such a one know *how* to manufacture it, they
needed access to those wells—which would not be given
cheaply by whoever was the Valbissag at the time, if at
all. No, Slith was not concerned with the potential consequences of his discovery, only with the wealth it would
bring him. He would only sell the finished product, and
would control its use.

Father and son then discussed the continuing efforts to
assassinate Fladth, and Slith observed that Fladth's scorn
now seemed less hearty than before. Were the brothers
improving their skills that much? He did not ask, but he
resolved to visit the old man more frequently, to savor the
friendship they shared while it lasted.

The orphanage door was open, but Bleth hesitated, because a tall figure stood in its shadow. It was not a fard,
a bors, a wend . . . It was entirely shrouded in rough robes
of some coarse undyed homespun cloth; even its face was
concealed, except for a pair of strange eyes—blue eyes,
like crystals of celestine. "Do not be afraid, small one,"
it said. "You may pass within."

"Are you . . . an old-human?" she asked, not coming
forward.

"Who else would be so robed?" he replied—it was a
male, judging by its deep voice. Old-humans, it was said,
exuded fumes and pheromones that had strange, arousing
effects upon members of the other human races—
especially those of the opposite sex. "I am a physician of
sorts, here to examine the health of the poor children
within. But you . . . you are not seeking charity, are
you?"

"Feh!" spat Bleth. "I was lucky enough—or clever

enough, some say—to acquire a nurse. But do not look upon me as a coddled child. I have my own problems."

"Ah," said the old-human, squatting until his eyes were level with hers. "And what might those be?"

"I live in fear. My nurse is not like the hopeful males who come here seeking a future mate and progeny. He wishes no children. I am a burden he has—so far—put up with, and that is all."

"But can he break the nursing bond? I have not heard of that happening."

"I do not know if he *can*—but if he could do so, he would, and I live in fear of it. I want to protect myself against that, but the laws will not allow it."

"Is that so? What is it you wish to do?"

Bleth did not, at that moment, think it strange that she was confiding in a complete stranger—indeed, a stranger of particularly shabby and disreputable mien. Later, she would consider that, and attribute it in equal parts to her deep-seated need for reassurance and to the effects of old-human biochemical effusions. But now, she talked. "I wish to be secure. I want to buy stocks in the Minip and Dujong Overland Railway, and a mining company and . . ."

"Stocks? How odd! You are but a child!"

"And that, Sar Old-human, is my problem! I am a *child*. I cannot buy stock, or apply for patents, or even rent a house! I am entirely dependent on the goodwill of Slith Wrasselty, who *himself* is underage and cannot claim his *own* due!"

"I see," said the robed man. "Have you considered a trust fund?"

"Trust? Hah! I trust no one except to follow their own interests with diligence. I am a fardling. When I was starving in the Vermous Hills . . . When my mother spat and clawed at me, and drove me away . . . "

The old-human was a good listener, and quite obviously had strong knee joints. He remained squatting, silently attentive, while Bleth's entire sad tale spilled from her lips. Only when she at last began to run down did he raise a hand to silence her.

"An irrevocable trust is a legal instrument," he said, "by which assets—like railroad stocks—can be bought and held for your benefit. The trustee can be a banker, a friend—or even, in your case, the Arbiter's consul, here in Thember, who has a fondness for charities such as this orphanage. . . ."

Bleth had learned much, and quickly, by listening to Slith and his customers. She had learned more still in the marketplace cafés and sitting quietly on the stone bench outside the tall doors of the Thember Stock Exchange. Now, listening to the old-human, her horizons widened further still. "Very well," she said, surreptitiously clutching her small purse full of carefully saved credits. "I will visit the consul, and will see what can be done. But enough talk of me—I am curious about your presence here. . . ."

"Me? Oh, I have an affection for the young of all species. I have volunteered to handle certain matters of accounting for the orphanage. Every year, they are required to file an audited financial statement with the Regional Charities Board. As I am a certified accountant . . . But what is that sour face for, child?"

Bleth explained her sudden frown. She had, she said, donated a tithe of her hard-won cash to the orphanage, thinking of it as a hedge against her uncertain future. Yet she was not happy about it. The nurses dressed well, and took the eastbound Park Street trolley when they went off shift. There were only fine residential neighborhoods in that direction. And the orphanage's director arrived each morning in a long, green-lacquered carriage. Bleth suspected that not a tithe of her tithe actually trickled down to benefit the poor fardlings within.

"You are quite right," said the old-human accountant. "But you are wrong, too. Skilled nurses are worth their pay—and many of them donate extra time without recompense. As for the director, he is a skilled fund-raiser, and many wealthy behinds have warmed the seats of his elegant carriage—and their owners have donated large sums to maintain this building, to buy medical supplies and equipment. Yet, perhaps it is wasted. Some would say that the true function of charity is to benefit not the waifs whose genetic and evolutionary vigor is made questionable by their very presence here, but to enhance the success of the best of the fard race—the clever director and his offspring, and the hard-working, intelligent nurses."

Bleth, considering her own success—however wobbly a foundation it sometimes seemed to be built on—secretly agreed. She was not yet well educated, though she read and studied everything she could, but she was thoroughly imbued with fardish ideals, among which was a concern for the vigor of the race. Perhaps that concern was an artifact of the harshness of desert life—only the fit deserved to survive. Perhaps, though the engineered origins of the races was lost in antiquity, a deep and abiding sense of the tenuous nature of fards' adaptation remained. "That may explain one of my doubts," she said. "I have often thought that such things as orphanages seemed contrary to our fardish nature—and for all the fardlings that starve, there is only this *one* orphanage."

"Just so. If indeed you visit the Arbiter's consul to set up a trust, as we have discussed, you might ask *him* what he thinks. It seems as though the Arbiter himself might agree—that the function of laws and organizations should be to maintain a level playing field alone, where the game of evolution can continue to be played out in all its efficient cruelty."

"Do you really think so?"

"Oh, I don't know. Perhaps I merely feel helpless to do enough."

"As do I," Bleth admitted, no longer concealing her purse. "My few creds can hardly make as much difference to the orphanage as they might for me, if I just save them."

"You *will* visit the consul?" asked the old-human.

"Perhaps—but not until I have saved enough money to make it worthwhile." At that moment, having had enough of talk, she took her leave—without having entered the orphanage at all.

* * *

Slith's plans to visit Fladth again were not to be. Only a week after, late in the evening just as the last brittle rays of sunset shattered themselves against leaded windows up and down the street, a wendish servant, Fenethelem, entered Slith's sitting room and announced a visitor. "He claims to be . . . your brother," said the elderly wend with an air of finicky distaste. "Perhaps you should view him through the pinch-nose?"

Between the outer wrought-iron gate and the inner door to the secure house was a small entryway. The gate was seldom locked. Beside the door was a tiny window with a weighted sash, all metal and no glass, that was too small for a child to crawl through. The pinch-nose provided a good view of visitor and anteroom. Slith's quick glance gave him a wealth of information unavailable to Fenethelem—he was able to read much of the other fard's state of health and mental well-being, as well as its lack of murderous intent. "That is Thplet," Slith said, "and he looks quite miserable. Let him in."

"Thplet," he addressed the smaller, younger fard, "are you unwell?"

"I am alive, which is more than some can say. Our family has shrunk, Slith."

"Who?" asked Slith, feeling dread.

"Gleph, wearying of subterfuge, hired mercenary bors with grenade-guns to storm Fladth's chambers in the night. They slew him. When the bors were gone, and while Gleph gloated, Thradz rolled an unexploded grenade under Gleph's chair, unmanning and laming him. Thradz then ran down little Splath in the courtyard, carried him into Valbissag, and held his head beneath the water until he drank too much and died. It was all nasty and unfardlike, with no subtlety, no honor to the Wrasselty name."

Slith, too numb to begin grieving for his father, agreed. Mercenaries? Bors feet thudding in the streets and corridors of Valbissag? Gleph had involved non-fards in that most uniquely fardish struggle, and the result—his accession, however brief—would not have contributed subtlety or cleverness to future Wrasselty generations. Happily, none of Gleph's unsubtle genes would pass on, but Thradz's solitary grenade was no more fardlike, subtle, or clever. His opportunity had sprung, so Thplet explained further, from generalized confusion and Gleph's disorganization before he had been able to replace Fladth's defenses, which the bors had blown up. Thradz was thus no proper heir either. The young fard seemed to burn with indignation. The brutal drowning of young Splath also reflected poorly on Thradz's mentality and his genes; were future Wrasselty generations to be judged superior only in brute strength and the accuracy of their grenade-throwing arms?

"And you?" Slith asked, already suspecting from Thplet's dull fur and downcast demeanor what had happened to him.

"There was a brine jar on my threshold, and a small, sharp knife. Thradz is now no longer concerned about any threat to his inheritance that I might pose."

"Ah, Thplet. I am sorry."

"Do not be. It is not as terrible a fate as you might think. Already, I begin to examine my future with a gusto never before known, a future without Thradz's baleful eye on me." Thplet did not, however, meet Slith's eye. Instead, he rummaged in his suitcase. "Ah, here it is," he said, reaching deep with both hands. He then stood straight, and turned to face Slith. "Here," he said, proffering his discovery, "is our elder brother's gift to you."

Slith stared. The jar was ordinary clear glass, a commercial vessel with molding scars, bubbles, and an off-yellow tinge that owed nothing to the brine it contained. Its lid was green-painted metal, not even new: the stamped knurlings were worn bare. The knife in Thplet's other hand was no more notable: a single strip of drop-forged steel with faint grooves patterning its handle; a quarter-cred knife, a cheap tool. Its small, sickle-curved blade, though, gleamed with acute, honed menace. "For me?" Slith squeaked. "But no! *I* do not threaten Thradz. *I* have no ambition to inherit. Put it away! Give it back to him!"

"I will do so, as he instructed me, when the level of brine in the jar is ever-so-slightly higher than now, but not before." Obviously Thplet, who had already suffered the fate he proposed for Slith, was not overly sympathetic to his brother's qualms and fears.

"You do not understand, Thplet! I am already a rich man. Look around! See this house? It is mine. It is paid for, not rented. See the gold chandelier, the leather benches? Mine. What is Valbissag to me? Nothing! I spurn it! I waive all claim to it. Who wants dusty Valbissag? Not me! Explain that to Thradz."

"I will do that. Only seal your sincere words and good intentions with a small donation"—he tapped the jar's lid with the knife—"and I will be on my way, and will give Thradz your well-wishes."

Slith shook his head, but it was hard to notice that, because he was also shivering violently. His well-groomed fur stood stiffly away from his body and moved in waves with each twitch and shudder. "I am nursing a child!" he ventured, addressing the impassive Thplet, who for obvious reasons might identify with his horror, but could not sympathize with his plight. "The hormonal change alone . . . my milk would dry up, and poor Bleth . . ."

"There are many males about who have no heritage in dispute. She will find a new teat to suck. It is of no moment. Merely take the knife. Whish! One quick, precise slash, a plop in the jar, a passing agony, and you will be free of all such concerns forever, free to enjoy your riches without fear of kroods in your bedroom or arrows in the night—or of future sons who would surely slay you."

Slith drew himself up to his full height. "No!" he squalled, and with a sweeping gesture swept the knife across the room and the jar to the floor, where it shattered dully. Brine darkened the fine slates, and the tinkling echo of the knife's fall lingered momentarily.

"You are either a brave or a foolish man, brother," said Thplet, with what seemed genuine regret, as he turned to close his suitcase. "Spend great wads of your creds on barred doors, then, on guards, and on a suit of body armor with no chinks where a poison bug might get in." Pulling his luggage, he moved to the door. "I will give Thradz all your words. Perhaps he will consider them, and the security your riches can buy you, and will judge the threat you pose to be less damaging than the expense of countering your defenses, since you are here in far Thember, and not in Valbissag."

Fenethelem, the wend, had observed the exchange between brothers with no little curiosity, and no comprehension at all; the discussion had all been in the high Fardic dialect of Valbissag, which to a wend was a clatter of unmusical hacks, coughs, squeals, and sputters without meaning, style, or panache. He knew only three things: that his employer was quite distraught, that the task of mopping spilled brine and sweeping up shattered glass would fall upon him, and that the small, unsavory fard now waited to be let out—which pleased him, while the other things did not. He unlocked the portal, and neither bowed nor nodded as Thplet passed through it.

The heavy door closed with a secure thud and a clatter of latch bolts. For the first time since Slith had hired Fenethelem, the outer gate was also locked. The old wend sensed a change in the air.

Slith considered: it would take a while for Thplet to get word of his failure to Thradz, and a bit longer for the heir to mobilize assassins here in Thember. Slith would be able to sleep safely this night (even if never again) without fear—if, that is, he was able to sleep at all.

Rousing Bleth, he ascended to the highest corner room of the house and curled up with her in a blanket, on the hard floor. The heavy tile roof above them no longer seemed much of a barrier. The stone walls of the fine house were thick, but ah! how many windows! And that honeyleaf vine—its leaves brushed the window, and its thick stem was surely strong enough to take the weight of a climbing man. . . .

Slith lay awake. Bleth had nursed fitfully, and he could not remember any pleasure from it. Perhaps the chemicals of fear had tainted his milk, causing her to suck less enthusiastically than was her wont. Perhaps he was, as Thplet suggested, a fool not to have given Thradz his token, despite the immediate pain it would have caused. He was not, as the other half of Thplet's speculation had proposed, a brave man. He was, he knew full well as the hours marched slowly and wakefully toward dawn, not brave at all.

CHAPTER 7

While in Fabundi make sure to visit the Berjab
tarbek bazaar in the city's old quarter, where one
may purchase rare red desert spice by the vial
or the truckload. Though tarbeks across the
Xarafeille Stream produce such spices—which are
often a tribe's only source of cash income—only
in Fabundi Old Quarter will you *experience* the
heady spice, walking among open barrels, cases,
and baskets of rubbed or ground spice, among
towering bales of spice fiber that will sell for no
less than ten million creds each.

Unlike fards, tarbeks are not inclined to
secrecy about their product; Bcrjab merchants will
gladly explain in detail the fascinating processes
by which the red spice is derived from roots,
insect carapaces, and the water of caustic
springs—they have no need of secrecy, for none
but they can endure the conditions under which spice
is gathered and processed.

> *Parkoon's Guide to the Dry Worlds,*
> Volume 7 (Phyre, Brefth, Aloglis, El Jab Al),
> Parkoon and Parkoon, Newhome, 12118 R.L.

Life went on, and to a casual observer no change would
have been apparent except for a brief flurry of activity at
the Wrasselty house in Thember. For half a month, tradesmen's vans were often seen in the alleyway behind it,
where trucks delivered stacks of wood, pallets of cut stone,
spools of thick wire, and many unmarked boxes, all of
which were winched up from balcony to balcony, and then
carried inside.

Technicians strung wires behind walls, beneath floors, and within ceilings. They installed relays, snap-contact switches, holocams, motion-, vibration-, weight-, sound-, and heat-sensing devices in every room and hallway. Masons constructed a thick-walled vault in the cellar and drilled holes in the foundation of the house. Engineers with a vibrating conduit-shooter ran shielded tubes from the cellar to a communications trunk in the street without disturbing the boxwood hedges, the beds of flowering madge, or the artfully laid cobblestone paths.

In the vault was a computer, seven days' worth of backup batteries, a terminal, and a chair from which Slith could monitor all that went on within and around his house. For the first week after it was set running, the computer registered every footstep, every voice, heat signature, face, silhouette, and mannerism, and built its database. Slith was recorded sleeping, pacing, speaking, voiding. . . . So was Bleth, and so were the two maids and the cook (bonded and certified by the finest agency), and so was Fenethelem, who had been majordomo to many high officials in his long career, whose credentials were unimpeachable, and whose loyalty went beyond his high salary.

If the computer detected an unfamiliar tread, a voice made off-key by heavy negotiations at the shop, a shape too tall or too short, a body made even slightly too heavy by overeating at lunch, or any other changes beyond what its programs had come to accept, alarms would sound inside the house and out, on screens at the precinct police headquarters, and in the offices of a very exclusive, very expensive, very anonymous security firm.

The broad windows opening onto the balconies were bricked in, leaving only narrow slits that allowed nothing thicker or more substantial than a ray of sunlight to enter. The balconies themselves were removed. The walls were stripped of the honeyleaf vines that had shaded them, and the honeyleaf roots were poisoned. The fertile beds that had nurtured them were replaced with colored gravels.

The carriage that called for Slith each morning was heavily sprung to carry its unobtrusive armor and, though it was still pulled by a matched pair of black-legged thribbets, the whiffletree contained an explosive decoupling device by which the vehicle could shed beasts and harnesses; within the coachwork was a seven-hundred-thribbetpower engine that could whisk coach and passenger away at the slightest suspicion of danger.

Slith's offices, his manufactory, and his elegant apothecary were similarly, unobtrusively protected as well. For a week or two he was acutely conscious of the changes, and the very extent of the precautions his consultants recommended enhanced his level of anxiety. Then, before a month had elapsed, he began to inure himself to them; he stopped noticing every time he looked sidelong at some unfamiliar face; he became used to the presence of furtive men from the security firm who lurked in the shadows, thus making the darkness unavailable to other lurkers less well intentioned; he even stopped thinking of Thradz for whole hours at a time.

Then Slith had time to grieve. He did not weep or mope, because fards did not ordinarily grieve a father's passing. More usually, once they were no longer busy securing their own positions by collecting the private parts or the entire, lifeless bodies of their male siblings, they were too busy inseminating their father's widows, their female cousins, and their half-sisters (who together comprised almost the entire female population of their inherited realms).

Since Slith had not inherited, and since as a fard he had no ready behavior pattern to express his unusual grief, he immersed himself in work and diligently prepared for the day he turned twenty-five. His sole consolation was that he, not the despicable Thradz, would "inherit" the meat of his father's estate, the real creation of the Wrasselty line: the patents. He did not, as he had explained to Thplet, need any of Valbissag's wealth, but (as he had not said) he intended to take it. Effort and success would substitute for the tears he could not shed.

Slith compartmentalized his objective into three parts with varying significance: of sentimental importance were the Wrasselty patents, which he would hold in honor of his late father; those procedures of his own devising were the background of his present success and would be patented to insure that his prosperity, the result of his genius, could not be snatched away from him; finally, the one concoction he treasured above all else, the self-replicating crystal that rendered pure water foul and thus palatable to tarbeks, stood alone in his estimation. Its introduction would cause waves of change in the real-estate markets of Phyre, and matching ripples across the entire Xarafeille Stream; wherever conditions obtained that made land otherwise ideal for tarbeks unusable only because the water was not suitable for them, he would profit from it. He would profit, and no one would be harmed by that, because the crystal represented not an advantage to tarbeks at the expense of neighboring fards, but a new and pure thing comparable to the discovery of an unsullied, unoccupied planet tarbeks could colonize without displacing anyone else.

Slith awaited the day of his majority with excitement and no little trepidation, and planned each step he would then take. There were several areas of vulnerability to consider between the instant he opened the secret vault in the cellar of the apothecary shop—a twin to the one under the house—to the moment he locked up the signed and sealed copies of his new patents again. Too, now he kept the procedures for his self-replicating molecule in his head alone, and no one could take it from him, but the patent office would demand it be written down, and the proper forms filled out, and his experiments documented. Once it was written, it would no longer be secure.

Finally, the day arrived. All was in readiness, and the chief patent officer awaited him at three fingers past sunrise. From vault to front door of the shop would be the first step. He ordered all his clerks to take the morning off, then checked the status of the security monitor in his office. He verified each departure, and was at last assured he was entirely alone. He then opened the vault and carried the thick sheaf of documents upstairs and to the front door. He verified that the carriage outside was hard against the sliding armored glass doors, so close that no one could step between. He peered through the doors, and saw that the street held no idlers, opened the door, and leaped into the carriage, pulling its door shut and locking it. With a clatter of thribbet claws and a creak of harness that he could not hear through the armor and glass, the carriage began moving with a jerk. Slith and his treasures were under way.

By the time the Patent Office loomed huge in the carriage's windows, his eyes were tired from straining, looking for lurkers between parked vehicles. Slith skeptically eyed the low stone wall around the complex, a wall that enclosed a small, watered green with imported orange trees in full fruit. He eyed the open gate and the lackadaisical guards leaning against its pilasters. Was he expected to walk all the way from the street?

He imagined snipers in windows. He was about to signal the driver to turn around and take him back to the shop when he saw the squad of armed men wearing his security firm's patches. They surrounded the carriage and, when he opened the door, crowded around him, a human shield of black-furred bors. They hustled him and his documents inside. He had little sense of the corridors he traveled, but the security corporal had obviously done his homework: the squad escorted him swiftly to the door of an airy, spacious office on an upper floor.

"Ah, Sar Wrasselty," the chief patent officer greeted him. "Please sit here. Will you have tea?" Slith, who was anxious to have the work done with, the patents safe, declined. "What have we here?" the bors official asked, eyeing the stack of documentation.

Slith proffered the top page only, a précis of his most important invention, the water-soluble crystalline molecule. The CPO reviewed it. "You can support these claims, of course?" he asked, as the realization of the formula's economic potential sunk in. Slith could almost read his thoughts: to speak with a land broker as soon as he was alone, and to buy certain worthless, marginal lands that would soon be in great demand—if only a few people controlled them all. He would be one of the few.

Slith nodded. Subject to testing and confirmation in the official labs, his own experiments, as listed and described, were entirely duplicable. Still, Slith had been cautious; where possible, he had referred only to source waters and to mechanics: "Three deciliters of the product of the Shambalag seep collected in the second weeks of the months Liss, Pret, or Arr, diluted by half with that of Valbissag, the whole evaporated, and the remainder mixed dry with . . . " There was much he knew—exact molecular constituents and the strata from which each were dissolved—that he did not write down.

The official agreed that all seemed in order and he called for an aide to take the documents and chemical samples to the labs. He returned the cover sheet to Slith; it was now emblazoned with his office's seal and his signature, as a receipt. He then nodded toward Slith's remaining stack, hardly diminished, as yet. "It looks like we are far from finished," he commented.

"These should be simpler," said Slith. "They are existing patents of my father's, now expired. It was his wish that I re-register them in my own name."

"The procedure for them is different," the official said, "but unfortunately, it is no simpler." He filled in a simple form with Slith's name and address, and attached Slith's list of all the Wrasselty patent numbers. Slith signed the form, acknowledging his submission, and then initialed each page of the list. He passed them across the officer's desk, and the bors again pushed his call button.

When the office door opened this time, no aide came through; instead, three massive bors wearing the yellow sambrowne belts of Thember policemen entered and marched, with heavy, thudding treads, to where Slith sat. "Arrest this man," said the chief patent officer. "Book him for patent fraud." He waved the document Slith had just signed. "Here is the evidence. These patents belong to another. They were registered months ago."

The troopers lifted Slith by his arms—skinny arms, next to their thick borrish ones—and marched him toward the door, his toes dancing on the floor, his heels never nearing it. "Wait! What is this?" he squalled. "They are my patents. My father wished me to have them." He could not understand. How had Thradz known? And why was it a crime to try to patent them? Even if Thradz owned them in truth he, Slith, had committed no crime . . . had he?

"They are mine!" he squalled even as he was carried out. "And my formula! What of my precious formula?"

"That remains to be seen," said the official to his receding back. "Such a momentous discovery . . . in the hands of a proven fraud like you . . . economic repercussions . . ." The door swung shut on his words.

Slith's passage out of the patent office was as swift as his entrance and was no clearer to him. He was aware of lights at the intersections of corridors, of great doors that thudded shut behind him, of toes stubbing against rough tile and heels that never felt the ground at all. His eyes reacted to momentary bright light as an exterior door opened and he was hustled out. Then he was in total darkness; the metal door of the police wagon had crashed shut after he was bodily thrown in. The wagon had no windows; he traveled in swaying, rumbling darkness all the way to the Thember Retentory, a low, gray structure he had never paid attention to before.

"Did you have something to do with that, Dad?" asked Rober Minder.

"With Slith's arrest? Why, no. I did not become directly involved in Slith's affairs until much later."

"*Directly?*" Rober asked astutely. "How about *indirectly?*"

His father chuckled. "I can't fool you anymore, can I?" he said. He added, "Slith's arrest was a consequence of his own actions. My involvement was at that time so indirect that I myself did not yet know of it. As for just *what* that involvement was—I will let you discover that for yourself."

Rob knew better than to waste effort pursuing that line of questioning further. "I can see how dangerous Slith's compound was, but I fail to see *why* anyone would use it to destroy other people's water supplies. And tarbeks? They are the least developed of the races, and are not usually inclined to combat."

"That is so," John Minder agreed. "But ask yourself *why* it is so."

Rob did so. For several moments he was silent. His father knew when he had it figured out, because Rob's face grew quite pale. "They are not technologically inclined because they are ordinarily limited to the areas around active volcanoes, areas where unique conditions of alkaline and acidic groundwater and concentrations of carbon monoxide and sulfurous gases are all present at once. They do not *need* to breathe such contaminated air, but they *do* need the polluted water to breed and to bathe in. If they could breed anywhere they wished, given their prolific natures . . ."

"Exactly," Minder said. "Population growth. If they move into areas where the air is clean enough to allow plants other than thornbushes to grow, air clean enough for prey more nourishing than sandsnappers and scorpions, they would not only be well fed enough to breed more prolifically, but more offspring would survive, and they would then need still more land . . . and if the only land available was already owned by someone else . . ."

"Then that 'someone else' would soon die when their own wells were poisoned," Rob said. "And if they did not die right away . . ." He envisioned a great horde of adult male tarbeks swarming through a village of small, helpless wends, their wattles swollen, flared out like bright vermilion ruffs, brandishing knobby blackthorn and swarrow-root clubs set with sharp flints and obsidian fragments. "War," Rob said. "Everywhere there were tarbeks, thousands of others—millions, even—might die."

"Exactly. As if I do not have enough problems maintaining the tenuous peace between such diverse peoples anyway. If I *had* known about Slith's formula then, I would have had to do something about it. But *that* part of the story has not yet been told. We are still with Slith, now in his prison cell. . . ."

CHAPTER 8

The months of Phyre are based on an old fardic calendar. Its periods are supposedly those of the lost racial homeworld, which was perhaps called Sand, Dry, or Desert. It has thirty eighteen-day months and a 540-day year, yet Phyre's orbital year has almost exactly two hundred and one-half days.

Fards on Phyre give eleven months in one Phyre orbit the old names, and follow them with a one-nine-month hiatus, called Summerspell even when it falls in the coldest season. During Summerspell, fards sleep overtime, avoid work, and the lucky ones who have the opportunity to do so have sex often. The next orbital period encompasses eleven months (with different names) and another hiatus, called Winterspell, in which fards sleep, avoid both work and sex, and become quite combative. Over seventy-five percent of all male deaths occur during Lant and Trit, the two months preceding Winterspell. Phyre's third orbit in the three-year calendar cycle is composed of the last six months of the Sand calendar, plus five months named simply First through Fifth, and a one-ninth-month holiday, Yearend, in which no work is done, no food eaten, no sexual desires fulfilled. Every second year cycle (once in every six Phyre orbits) Yearend has three additional days, a leap year to adjust for the odd half-day in every orbital year.

Parkoon's Guide to the Dry Worlds,

Volume 7 (Phyre, Aloglis, El Jab Al),
Parkoon and Parkoon, Newhome, 12118 R.L.

For all Thember's cosmopolitan interstellar modernity, its
facilities for incarceration of miscreants were modeled on
those of an earlier, more primitive age. Slith's cell walls
were stone. Perhaps the floor was also, but he had no
urge to discover what was under the dusty blackness that
covered it, that crunched where he walked as if it were
composed of equal parts soot and insect carapaces. He
kept his feet up on the stone shelf that was his bunk, his
table, and the limit of his new environment. Sometimes
the blackness below moved, as if living things indeed
burrowed in it.

"Where is my attorney?" he shrieked until his voice
broke and his squalls were reduced to guttural croaks. "I
am thirsty. Is there no water?" was his next refrain, when
his voice returned. It brought no more result. Was he entirely alone? Did no one listen? Would he die here, and
would his bones rattle and crunch beneath the feet of the
cell's next occupant?

There was a window high above, but the dry-laid stone
was well fitted and impossible to climb; besides, the window seemed too small for an adult fard. The door was a
stone slab, a hairline rectangle of unknown mechanism.
The door was the only thing to hold his interest; he could
speculate and wonder about what was on the other side.
It could open. It might not, he admitted, but it was physically capable of it, and that was the closest thing to hope
he allowed himself.

Slith was aware that time passed, though he could not
guess how many minutes, hours, even days wore on. He
became aware of a sickness in his gut, but he did not immediately associate it with hunger or thirst. Fards, well
adapted to going without food or drink for long periods,
did not suffer deprivation in the way other men did; the
symptoms of physical suffering would only have distracted a primal, primitive fard from the business of survival in a milieu where one was always hungry, always
thirsty. Eventually, though, some time before death was
imminent, even fards experienced distress.

"Slith!" he heard, in his dying dreams. "Slith! Here is water. Take it. Here is food." He lay on the cool stone slab, so far gone in internal misery that it no longer seemed hard or felt rough. He ignored the delusion, the soft, sweet voice, and kept his eyes on the thin, dark rectangle of the door's seams. He knew there was no food and no water, though his mind created the scent of sausages spiced with karrow seed, of clear water with the distinctively pure aroma of Thember's distilled product, that even finicky bors and wends could drink. After a while, when he continued to ignore the taunts of small voices and the torments of imaginary scents, both went away.

Perhaps much time passed. The window's glow—which he could not identify as sunlight or electric, but which was too yellow to be either of the planet Phyre's satellites—came and went many times. He had lost track of its fadings and glowings long ago. "Slith, are you in there? Take the food. Drink! Tell me if it's you. Slith!" He was lying on his right side, facing the door. The dream voice seemed to come from above, affecting his left ear alone. He rotated his ear. The voice was unchanged. Dream voices, he decided, were undirectional. How odd. Laboriously, forsaking his door-watching vigil, he rolled over. The dim light from above flickered. Did a day pass in a moment of his slow, starved perception? It flickered again. Daylight did not flicker and Thember's generators, powered by starship engines, never faltered. Reproaching himself for his foolishness, he rolled onto his back, and looked up. A roundness blocked part of the tiny rectangle of light. "Slith!" he heard, from that direction.

"Eggh!" he croaked, unable to speak. "Urwey. Au'her."

"Of course you're thirsty. And here is water. You'll have to reach for it, perhaps. I can't see down there. Drink some, then you can speak to me, and I will know I'm not wasting my bribe on the wrong prisoner."

Water? Other prisoner? Madness. There was no other, only him. He would have heard moans, or breathing. The shadow continued to block the light, blurring as it moved about in the opening. He struggled to focus his encrusted eyes. What was that, in front of his face? A flask? How odd. He perceived a laboratory flask floating in the air over his head. He perceived printing etched in its base: MARD CHEMICAL SUPPLY, THEMBER. With great effort, he raised his hand until it blocked the illusion, which made a dull clunk against the back of his hand.

With a great moan, even still chiding himself for wasting his last reserve of energy chasing a dream, he reached for the flask. It resisted, as all dream things do, but then seemed to come free. A cord dangled from it, from his hand. It was not corked, so he drank immediately. Not until his third or fourth gulp did he dare admit that it was not dream water at all. "Arrr! Good!" he grated when he had emptied the bottle. "More?"

"Slith, is it you? I can't tell."

"S'me. Hungry. Thirsty. Attorney."

"I have no more water. There is food, which I will let down when I know it is you, when you prove it."

"Prove? Thirsty. Hungry. Need attorney, now."

"Tell me the combination to the vault beneath the shop. Then I will know."

"Frad brablit! Ngor emmerits falt! Begn sorrap!" Obscenities, all. The combination to his vault? A trick! "You have my crystal! You took Fladth's patents, and I will not give you mine!"

The voice from above broke into abrupt fragments, not words: laughter. "It *is* you!" Bleth exclaimed joyfully. "No other would react so, though your voice is still strange. I am coming down." The shadow filled the opening and emitted high-pitched grunts. Had Bleth been larger, she could not have squeezed through. In the clear, weak light of the window, Slith watched her lower herself down a yellow rope. Her little work smock, a present, bulged oddly: its pockets were full. He could smell the sausages, the smoked rock mullet fillets he had planned to eat while celebrating his new patents. Bleth!

The next hour remained forever as diffuse in Slith's mind as the days that had preceded it. Slith ate every crumb from Bleth's pockets. He remained thirsty, but she assured him she would bring more water soon.

"Get me out!" he demanded. She explained that that was impossible. The window was a tight squeeze for her small bones; even starved, he would not fit through it. "I will bring you food and drink. You will survive, and you will be freed, someday."

Once the food was gone and Slith was coherent enough to ask questions framed simply enough for an intelligent fardling, he learned much about his situation. It was the eleventh of Slib. As he had been arrested on the seventeenth of Plet, just before the two-day Summerspell interval, he had been imprisoned for fifteen days. (No wonder the fardling's fur was dull, and her manner phlegmatic. She was as starved as he himself.) He was imprisoned for fraud. His brother had renewed the Wrasselty patents long before he, Slith, came of age. Slith conceded that Thradz was not as stupid as he had seemed. He had known, had guessed, that Slith's disdain for Fladth's estate was more than it had been meant to seem. He had guessed or turned up hints of the nature of Slith's masterwork and its world-shaking value, and he had devised a plan to get that too. Surely the chief patent officer had been in on it—or had it been just an unlucky chance that Slith had offered the self-replicating molecule first? If the molecule's documentation had not been forthcoming, and if he had tried to repatent his father's discoveries first, would the officer have cried fraud immediately or would he have waited until Slith had submitted the crystal, too? Perhaps indeed Thradz had worked alone, or the officer would have tried to winkle his other formulae from him, the ones still in the vault.

Slith was to be imprisoned for two years, Bleth told him, beginning with his arrest. He would be freed on the eighteenth of Fifth. The Wrasselty patents were gone. The crystal patent had been awarded as damages to another—whom, Bleth did not say. "The factory?" Slith bleated. "The shop?"

"Closed," Bleth told him. "The constables have boarded them up."

"The house?"

"They did not take it. I live there still. The servants are gone. The security people took back their alarms and the computer from the vault there."

"Those were mine!" Slith protested. "I paid for them."

"Your brother—the little one, Thplet, not Thradz—had me sell them back to them. I have nothing worth stealing, anyway. Everything was sold to pay the taxes for this year and next, because your bank accounts were confiscated also. You will at least have a house, when you get out."

"Thplet, you said. Is he here, in Thember?"

"He comes and goes as Thradz orders him. He whispers advice to me through the pinch-nose off the rear alley. He is afraid Thradz's spies will see him."

"Thradz's other spies, you mean," Slith muttered. "Do not trust him."

"Did he advise me wrongly?"

"Well, no, but . . ."

"The house is still yours, and the vault is still sealed."

"There is nothing in it! Not if the computer is gone."

"I mean the vault under the shop."

Slith jerked back, his eyes suddenly wide. Had he told her about that? The store's vault had come with a fifty-year unconditional warranty that no one but he, Slith Wrasselty, could open it, a warranty backed with a million-cred insurance policy on any contents, their nature not specified. Slith realized that he was not entirely destitute; the house would proved a nest egg to begin again; the vault would make him wealthy even if it had been emptied—if his patentable discoveries were safe, they were worth millions, but if the vault was opened by anyone not him, the insurance settlement was his. He relaxed ever so slightly, and considered the future he had so recently given up on.

He could not escape, Bleth assured him, but she could pass in and out, and there were few restrictions on what goods she could bring to him. One limit was the rope itself, which she had to rent from the jailer each time, and which would not hold anything much heavier than herself. Another was the window's aperture, and of course, the jailer kept watch over the courtyard and the cell windows. He charged extra every time she lingered more than an hour, and in future she would have to be swifter than today, or her limited savings after the taxes were paid would soon evaporate. Now, in fact, she had to go. She assured Slith that she would return with more water and food.

"And an oil lamp, and paper, and . . ." All those things, too, she assured him—though each time she was only allowed to bring in what she could carry in her hands and pockets.

Slith's imprisonment was bleak, but less so than had Bleth not still required nursing. Had she been a bit older, able to survive without the vital substances his adult body was able to synthesize, she might have been less willing to make the effort of supplying him. Had she been younger, requiring nursing for three more years instead of two, she might have sought another male, and abandoned him to the dark.

The nursing bond was strong and was reflected in many aspects of fard culture, even the architecture of prisons. Consider that nursing fardlings grew only to a certain size, concentrating their development effort on adapting themselves to the complex chemistry, the "poisons," of their environments. From the end of their first growth spurt until puberty, at age four, they remained half their adult size and one-fourth the weight; thus any nursing fardling could crawl through small prison windows like the one in Slith's cell. Outside, all the windows were at ground level, though the cell floors were well below. Nursing fards survived prison in order that their fardlings would. Most others did not.

The mechanical, biologically determined and pragmatic nature of his relationship with Bleth was not lost upon Slith. He had nursed her only after she had trapped him. He had continued because his mind and body required him to; there had been nothing in it for him except the fleeting joy his glands doled out to him. Bleth's concern for him was similarly rigid and self-serving.

Things important to the species, Slith reflected, often produce ecstasy. Bors, before the advent of modern biochemistry and drugs, craved sexual release only with the female they imprinted on during their first copulation. Perhaps the rough nature of their ancestral habitats, the scarcity of food, and the chill of their primal caves required one parent to hunt while another huddled with the infant pair—all bors infants came in pairs, one male, one female.

Tarbeks found similar joy only in steaming, reeking seeps at the margins of volcanoes. Only old-human males experienced assorted ecstasies (or so Slith had heard, or read, because he had never conversed closely with an old-human himself) with females, males, with nonsapient beasts, or all alone. If it were true, as some iconoclastic scientists claimed, that old-humans were ancestral to all the human types, then had tarbeks—happy solitary ejaculators all—evolved from old-humans under some strange environmental pressure that made it dangerous for more than one of them to enjoy their pools of muck at a single time?

During Slith's two-year imprisonment, the stone door of his cell was opened only three times. The first was on the third of Slib, shortly after Bleth's second visit. When Slith heard the grinding of stone on stone he did not have to squint to see the hairline seam widen: his new lamp, fueled by compressed gas, made his cell bright, if not exactly cheery. When the door opened, Slith pressed back against the far wall. He could not imagine anything good coming through it. He had no hope of a reprieve.

When he saw who it was, it took him many moments to create an appearance of false aplomb. Happily, his new light glared more brightly than the unseen passageway beyond, and Thradz's eyes did not adjust to it immediately. Thradz! His fur glistened, licked and groomed by females—and no few males, too—who vied for the privilege. His eyes gleamed with the health that good food, good sex, and Valbissag's waters promoted. His clawed nails were long and smooth without cracks or chips, and his ear tufts were as fluffy as a well-fed fardling's.

With the confidence of undisputed rule his high, mobile ears did not rotate; he did not seek dangers all around with radarlike sweeps; his pinnae remained fixed on ... Slith. "Brother!" he exclaimed, grinning. His teeth were clean and shiny white. "Valbissag greets you."

"I greet you," Slith responded.

Thradz frowned. The proper response was "I greet Valbissag," which referred not to the spring, but to its personification, its master. "So that's how it's to be, eha?" he said, scowling now. "I had hoped your plight would have helped you to see sense. You still deny my hegemony?"

With a cool calm he did not feel—after all, Thradz was much larger than he, and was an experienced fighter— Slith replied. "I deny nothing. I do not care. Valbissag is of no interest to me whether you, or Thplet, or a complete stranger rule it. Our interests do not coincide. They do not conflict. Why are you here?"

Thradz emitted a long, laborious sigh. "Don't you want to get out of here?"

Slith, suspecting what was coming next—and suspecting what it was that Thradz held concealed behind his back—merely shrugged. "I will get out by Yearend," said Slith, making the sign of a madman, crossed index fingers against his nose. That was a fardish nonverbal pun: it was a leap year, and the five-day holiday at Yearend was then called Madness. Slith's sentence began with his arrest just before Summerspell and continued until the eighteenth of Fifth, the day before Yearend. Slith did not intend to be insane at that time. His prison cell, as Thradz had noted with no satisfaction, was clean, well lit, and furnished with every comfort of a nonelectrical nature that a fardling could carry in pockets and two hands.

"In the meantime," Slith continued, "I am writing an ethnography of the fardic tribes of the Western Wells, and a comparative study of the sexual adaptations of the races of man."

Thradz frowned. "Ethnography? Sexual adaptations? Those are wendish things. What makes you an expert in them?"

"Oh, I am not. I have worked among the Western Well folk, though, and as my sentence is two civil years—

twenty-two months—of which one and eight-ninths[1] have elapsed, I have time to learn. Bleth brings me books and scholarly works from the History Division. I am sorry that displeases you. I am sure you would prefer me to write down my formulae instead."

That was exactly what Thradz had hoped, of course. He had no way to get into Slith's vault; in fact, he did not know of it, but he did know that Slith's financial success had not been due to the Wrasselty patents. Because of what he believed Slith kept in his head alone, he had not brought a weapon or poison with him, though the jailer might have allowed it. He was, after all, Thradz, The Valbissag. "Brahk!" he spat, revealing his hidden burden and setting it carefully on the floor. "Study this! It may make you wise." He spun about and departed. The door ground shut after him.

Later, Slith asked Bleth to pour out the vinegar and salt from Thradz's jar outside in the courtyard, and he used the jar for a chamber pot. The cheap knife he employed to pare his toenails, but it quickly dulled, and he had her throw that away too.

---

[1] Fards count in nines. Those who accept that the races of man were products of animal genetic grafts on old-human stock suggest that early defective fards lacked a finger. Indeed, the fifth finger on the left hand of some inbred present-day fards is shorter than its counterpart on the right.

CHAPTER 9

I sometimes wonder if my illustrious ancestor and namesake made a grievous error, allowing men of more than one variety to settle any one individual world. The agendas of the seven subspecies progress apace in the countrysides where borders between them are clearly delineated, but the cities of the Xarafeille Stream are hotbeds of conflict and confusion.

I suspect that the first John Minder had too little time to think things out, and far too little time to explore the Stream itself; knowing of worlds with climates and conditions as diverse as those of Earth, it was surely easier to locate colonies of bors in the mountains, wends in forests that seemed vast, and fards in the dessicated high plains— "one-stop" colonization.

John Minder III,
Unpublished manuscript,
Newhome Public Archive

The second time Slith's cell door opened, it admitted another brother, Thplet. Thplet was not the miserable, bedraggled creature he had been when last Slith had seen him in the anteroom of the house in Varamin Park, though the stylized clipping of his ear tufts announced to all that another part of his anatomy, a portion that unlike ear tufts would not grow back, had also been docked. He seemed to have recovered from that trauma. Thplet wore a fine travel smock of Densivil linen, unsmudged with road dust. His waist purse bulged, so full of crystalline cred disks that it did not rattle at all when he moved. He was now urbane and self-assured. "As you see," he said to Slith, "I am not only free, but I am content. Are you?"

Slith snorted. Something about Thplet brought out the worst in him. Perhaps it was the castration. At any rate, he felt no need to be polite. "I eat, I nurse Bleth, I receive letters from scholars, masters, and offworld dons, and am becoming a scholar of note myself; Winterspell is past, and in eleven months less a day I also will be free." He nodded toward the plastic box Thplet carried. "If that contains another of Thradz's specimen jars, do not open it. As you can see"—he gestured toward the corner of his cell—"I already have a glass chamber pot."

"As long as you retain your useless purse and its unspendable stones," Thplet said, shaking his head and expressing cool amazement, "Thradz will continue to demonstrate his concern for his inheritance. Have you no fear?"

"I fear that should I submit to Thradz's authority one time, I will be compelled to do so again and again. 'Do this, Slith,' he will say. 'Do that. Give me your silly formulae. You do not need them. I, Thradz, love you and will see to all your needs. Such things are rightly Valbissag's, anyway, and should go to my heir. Would you see them scattered in the next generation?' Hah!" said Slith. "I will risk Thradz's disfavor."

"I admire your courage, brother," Thplet admitted ruefully. "Even if I had such wealth as yours in my head, I might not dare decide as you did." He shook his head again. "Still, you may be wise; Thradz is indeed a hard master. I would much prefer to serve one like you."

"Me? I am what you see, a prisoner, a scholar of some small but growing repute. I have no need of retainers. Even freed, I will require only hired clerks—wends—to sell my products, and a few fard chemists to make them. I will have no employment for a messenger boy."

Thplet ignored his brother's condescending manner. No doubt it was mild, compared to Thradz's broad scorn. "Still," Thplet pressed, "when you are out and about again, you may find me useful."

"At what risk? And why?" Thplet's humble air had triggered involuntary cascades of hormones in Slith's undocked body. He felt strong and wise. He felt potent, powerful, and in control of everything within the borders of his tiny domain. "Aha," he said to himself, becoming aware of his behavior, "so this is what Thradz feels all the time. I like being the dominant male. Perhaps I will indeed wish my little brother to visit from time to time."

It was a fact of fard behavior that just as the scents and pheromones clinging to the fur of dominant males caused females to consider raising their behinds to them and inspired lesser males and neutered ones to shrink and cringe, even to wet the pavement, so the shy fawning of females and the cringing of sycophants enhanced the unaltered male's sense of self, his wit, his confidence, and his monstrous libido (except, of course, in nursing males, who had no libido to speak of). Slith's studies had suggested that, and his scholarly papers documenting the biochemical basis of such behavior generated approving replies from professors far and wide, who uniformly reported that their own double-blind experiments confirmed his hypothesis.

Thus Slith understood that the threat he posed to Thradz was not only that he was his father's descendant and a rival heir, should Thradz die without adult sons; he threatened Thradz merely by remaining in full possession of his testicles, by his ability to draw strength from the adulation of those like Thplet, who even now reacted both to him and upon him. "Ah, Thplet," he said softly when his brother did not reply, "never mind. When I am free and above ground, come visit me, and we will discuss the many futures that may unfold."

With that promise, his mission unfulfilled, but without the desire (or indeed the capacity) to press Thradz's cause further, Thplet departed. He and Slith would not meet again for quite some time.

On the third of Hek, Slith's cell door, opening, shed distorted rectangular shadows upon his clean, polished stone floor for the last time before he was to be freed one hundred and twenty days hence.

The first man to enter his cell was a fard wearing a full-length white laboratory smock. It was not a "work-

ing" garment in the usual sense, being unstained by mineral solutions or reagents and uneaten by acids or strong
bases; it was a formal smock, an academician's robe. No
prefect or stentor stood by the tiny doorway to announce
him, but had there been one, he would have said, "His
Cognizance Al'mith, Catalyst of the First Water, Peer of
the Keeper of Patents, Supervisor of the Laboratories, and
Preeminent Emeritus of the Schools and Universities of
all Phyre." Slith recognized him by his insignia, an un-
symmetrical test tube that bulged as if soft; its rounded
bottom sloshed with cerulean fluid that represented the final, unattainable end: the universal solvent. Slith stood
for him, but did not bow.

The second man was a wend, rounder of ear and fea-
ture, with uniformly brindled fur beneath his black garment. "His Hindsight the Curator of Days, Years, and
Times Immemorable, Prethelerimen, Archivist of the
Stacks and the Histories." That was how a stentor might
have announced him, but Slith did not need an announcement to recognize such an eminent man.

Slith had been expecting someone from the History Division or the University to confer his degree upon him,
but he was surprised that two men should come, and more
surprised by their high rank. Had his dissertation been
that well received?

It might seem improbable for a man to earn an advanced degree in less than two years, while in prison and
unable to perform research. It might seem unlikely for
such a man to qualify himself in a field of endeavor so
different from that of his earlier successes, too. It would
perhaps seem strange to some that the most estimable
dons of the highest institutions of learning would visit a
man in his confinement in order to confer upon him a
high degree. To Slith, all those were one and the same—
his talents, his work, and now, judging by the rolled document His Cognizance Al'mith proffered, his reward.

Slith had approached his studies with the same zeal and
intellect he had earlier bestowed on the chemistry of
groundwater and the production of nostrums. Too, his
carefully chosen dissertation topics related, in an offhand
manner, to his earlier work, and it is the nature of the in-

ventive, creative mind to make logical connections, to discern relationships between disparate events and phenomena. Finally, too few doctoral dissertations were grand syntheses; most were carefully researched footnotes documenting or supporting the grander theories of tenured academicians.

Slith's ethnography compared and contrasted various Western Wells fard tribes' various cultural adaptations to their differing water sources, which he had studied and mapped in what seemed another life altogether. His premise was small, yet sweeping: that the diverse waters of Phyre's wells, resulting from complex organic chemicals encapsulated in the planet's soluble limestones, tended to isolate the tribes adapted to each well, to reduce exogamy and thus cultural transferrals that might otherwise have led to the development of sophisticated urban cultures. It was one of those things everyone knew—that fards were tribal and did not create cities or great literature—but that no one had ever bothered to explain.

Slith's comparison of sexual adaptations among the races of man was no more world-shaking. Of course, men said, the avenues by which the pleasure centers of human brains were stimulated were determined in no small part by adaptive considerations. Everyone knew that fards futtered their aunts and sisters, and seldom the same ones twice, by preference; everyone had a working impression of why, too. They knew that bors seldom raised speculative eyebrows at more than one female in a lifetime, and that a male mantee got to top his throngmother—the only fertile female in his tribe—only once in his entire life. "So what?" men asked. "Ah," wrote Slith, "there are *reasons* why it is so . . ." and he proceeded to explain them, to relate them, to trace their origins into the mists of the millennia. His work would make a fine footnote in some don's more sweeping study, and would lend spice to that academician's wide, thick, heavily illustrated popularization of his work. Such a fine book would adorn tables in salons and ostentatious private libraries, and would pay for the author's summer cottage or bathing pool, his collection of primitive art, his holidays at the shore or in the mountains. . . .

That night, no longer merely Prisoner #7345-2 but Dr. Slith Wrasselty, PhD, Slith would sleep better than ever before. Too, one less day remained of his incarceration.

"Well, he took the diploma," said His Hindsight the Curator, ascending the steep, worn stone stairway from the underground cells, "but he did not exactly snap up our job offer. What do we do now?"

"Perhaps when he is freed," speculated His Cognizance, Catalyst and Peer, "he will reconsider, once he sorts through the wreckage of his past success. I am comforted that he merely skimmed over the fine print of the contract we offered him. If he does so again, then . . . "

"I will make sure he is distracted," said another person whose face could not be seen in the shadows of the dim corridor.

"He will have no choice," said a fourth voice from the depth of the passageway, some distance back. "The doors behind him are all closed, and we stand guard at the ones ahead. Only the Arbiter himself could force us to stand aside for him."

"The Arbiter, indeed," scoffed Prethelerimen. "Happily, this new, young Arbiter remains on Newhome and does not meddle much in the affairs of the Xarafeille Stream."

"And fortunately so," agreed Al'mith, "but I sometimes wonder why. The stars seethe with plots and unrest, yet no white warships have been reported at all since his father's death, and no black-armored *poletzai* have been seen, either."

"Oh, hi, Dad," said Rob Minder, laying down a delicate number-two sweep gouge. Before him lay the swarrowroot staff, its wood gleaming redly now that the warty bark had been removed.

"It's looking much better now," his father commented. "What's that you're carving?"

"I thought since it's kind of a fard thing, I would make scenes from the story you're telling us. That one will be Slith and Bleth in Slith's prison cell."

"I see. Then that half circle will be the window? Very good. I can visualize it already."

"Just wait. I'm getting pretty good at this, Dad.

"Dad?" he said a moment later. "Speaking of fards and that story—what about those university types? Why did they care whether or not you were ... meddling? Were they planning something you wouldn't have allowed?"

John Minder sighed. "All men have their own interests," he said, "and in a universe of men and interests, a lack of conflict between them is the true rarity."

"If you had the datablocks, the keys to your fleet, would you have used them, then?"

"On Phyre? Not then. There was no overt problem, and I did not yet know about Slith's masterpiece, his self-replicating crystal molecule. I found out about that much later."

"Tell me!"

"Your sisters aren't here. I'd only have to repeat everything for them, later."

"Please? They're gone for the day, swimming. That's why I want you to tell me, and not water it down for P'riss."

John Minder sighed again, and reflected silently on self-interest and conflicts, and upon how his family was a microcosm of the universe at large just as was Newhome, the only planet where all seven human races dwelled together. "Very well," he said. "On the morning of the eighteenth of Fifth, Slith Wrasselty was a free man...."

CHAPTER 10

It is interesting to reflect that the graveyards of
Earth's early cities were rife with broken heads.
Only as centuries and millennia passed did rural
folk evolve an other-directedness that reduced
violence to lesser levels by making people aware
of their own impacts on others—and the consequences
of them.

There, as here and now, the newest arrivals
from the "bush" often found themselves confined
to shantytowns and aging "foreign quarters" where
they could experience the new pressures of urban
life in relative isolation from the staid, older
populace, to places where those most susceptible
to violent interaction could slay each other, hopefully
before reaching breeding age, without disturbing
the quiet lawns and gardens, the placid nights,
of the established urbs.

John Minder III,
Unpublished manuscript,
Newhome Public Archives

Slith eyed the empty hulk he had once considered his
home. Where sand-and-glue paintings by Fratteth of
Balsivy had hung were pale, square places on the walls,
and where cerulean blue curtains once kept out the glare,
only bare windows remained; some were broken and kept
out nothing at all. Bleth, cringing with fear that Slith's
displeasure would turn to blame, said, "I did not know
about insurance for the glass. Thplet did not tell me to
pay the premiums."

"No matter," Slith replied, to her relief. "There are

more important things than broken glass and dusty floors. As soon as I have patented a few of my formulae and licensed them, I will get Blant and Nuggam, the bors security firm, to reinstall our alarms. I will not sleep well until that is done."

Bleth led him to her humble bedroom, the only furnished chamber in the house. Perhaps "furnished" was too strong a word: there was a sort of mattress on the floor, a canvas sack that contained what Bleth owned, and a gas lamp—the house power had been off for two years. Slith felt sudden guilt: while he, in jail, had slept on a soft mattress with a lertskin coverlet, Bleth had enjoyed only a moldy tick stuffed with crumbly grass for a bed. "But no!" he told himself. "Without me, she would have starved in the Vermous Hills. Without me, she would have been forced to beg a teat from some back-alley ne'er-do-well, and later bear his scrofulous brats. Ehh!" As always, the mere thought of infants gave him a strange, uneasy twinge in his groin. Perhaps, he thought, his subconscious mind was reminding him of the procreative pleasures he would enjoy with Bleth someday. Perhaps—but the twinge was not the same as the one he felt when, after being parted from Bleth all day, he anticipated her nursing. It was more like the genital twitch he felt when he thought of Thradz, his glass jars and little curved knives.

After breakfast Slith examined the house. "They pulled all the wires!" he complained. "It will cost more to replace them again than what the ones they took were worth!"

"I did not know!" Bleth cried. "They said, 'We bought everything, and we will take everything.' " Slith's homecoming was not as she had imagined it would be. She had not realized how everything that was wrong would redound upon her, his only companion and scapegoat. "Thplet did not say, 'Make them leave the wires.' He said, 'Sell everything back to them.' " Thplet, she thought, had been much kinder than this new, free, ungrateful Slith. Perhaps Slith would have been nicer if he too had used Thradz's jar for its intended purpose.

His inspection finished, Slith said, "Now! I will go to the shop and retrieve my formulae."

"It is not your shop anymore," said Bleth.

"The vault and its contents are," he replied. "I cannot be denied what is mine." He began walking—there would be no carriages until he set things right, until there was money. Bleth followed him uneasily.

Reaching the corner of Port and Park, Slith stood as if transfixed. "That is not my shop!" he stated unnecessarily.

"It is the shop of Slem Banto, Dealer in Home Convenience® Residential Systems," said Bleth, reading the red and yellow sign.

Slith burst in, roughly pushing aside the glass door. "What is this?" he said, confused. Nothing was as it had been. Partitions had been installed, showcases moved. He could not find where the door to the cellar had been hidden. "Where is my cellar?"

An enormous bors behind the counter scowled at him. "As to your first question, this is a shop whose door may already have been damaged by your impetuous entrance. Be more careful on your way out. As to your second, I have no idea where your cellar is. You will not find it in my building." He eyed the fard with unconcealed displeasure. Slith's smock was worn. His fur was knotty and clumped—the jail cell had boasted no sonic cleanser, and there was no power to the ones in the house. This fard, the bors had decided, did not intend to buy a Home Convenience® Residential System. "Your questions have been answered. Leave now, and be careful of my door as you depart."

"I am not satisfied! I wish to retrieve my possessions from the vault in the basement."

"*Your* possessions, you say? In *my* vault? Whatever do you mean? What is in my basement is, by very definition, mine. What is in the vault in my basement—my vault—is thus mine also, and does not concern you at all."

"The vault is nontransferable! I paid for it, registered it, and insured it! Only I can open it."

"Have you seen my sign?" asked the bors. "It says

'Slem Banto.' As I am Slem Banto, and Slem Banto is
not some nameless fard, this is my ..."

"My formulae are in the vault. They do you no good.
I will remove them. You may keep the vault." Slith was
about to push past the bors and seek the cellar door, but
suddenly his feet were not touching the ground. That had
happened once before, he remembered, and he had not
been pleased with what had followed. He was not pleased
this time, either. The bors guided him to the door and
opened it by pushing with Slith's nose; then Slith decorated the rough pavement with small patches of fard fur
and skin as he bumped and skidded across it.

"You are lucky he did not call a constable," Bleth commented as she helped Slith limp away. "You are a felon.
A repeat offense ..."

"I am not a felon! I have committed no *first* offense! I
was wronged!" His angry gesticulation knocked Bleth
aside. She eyed Slith skeptically, and did not offer to support him again. Her eyes suggested that he had committed
a grave offense indeed: he had truly frightened her.

"I will find an attorney," Slith said. "I will get a warrant, and will recover my formulae. Come! There is a law
shop this way."

"Wait, Slith! You cannot go there today!"

"Cannot? I cannot? I will. I can."

"It is Madness. You cannot."

"Am I mad? You think so? Then perhaps you do not
want to suck a madman's teat tonight!"

In spite of that deadly threat—which struck her with
the force of a terrible blow—Bleth persevered. "Madness! Yesterday was the eighteenth of Fifth, and it is now
Yearend. It is leap year, so this Yearend is Madness. The
law shops and most others are closed. Even Slem Banto
merely kept his door ajar for air. He was not doing business. I am sorry, Slith. Your business will have to wait
five days."

Slith, who should have apologized, did not. "*Bahk*! I
had forgotten. Then let us go home. I am hungry. Is there
food?" Happily for Bleth's already shaken peace of mind,

there was. Slith ate, and Bleth nursed; then they both slept. Slith tossed and turned all night.

"Madness," he said in the morning. "Must I dither and fret for four more days without recourse?" Bleth did not respond. "Each Madness, when I was nine, fifteen, and twenty-one," he mused, "Thradz took his holiday at Boiling Mud Seep. I remember Fladth complaining of the cost. Surely this first Madness since his inheritance, he will go there again. Valbissag will be unguarded."

"What does it matter?" Bleth asked.

"Ah! I encoded copies of my formulae in Fladth's terminal there. Even Fladth did not know it. I will recover them, and will not need the copies in the vault."

Bleth did not think it was a good idea. Besides the danger to Slith—if Thradz was not at Boiling Mud Seep but at Valbissag—there was not much money left, and the property taxes would come due at the end of Madness. She had husbanded the money from the security firm carefully, had resisted Slith's most exorbitant demands while in prison, but now that he was no longer confined, she felt less able to resist. She bought tickets as he instructed her, and then rented a half terabyte of computer memory in the Archives, via a public terminal. When that was done, there was little money left—enough for a few meals, perhaps. Shortly later, she followed Slith to the transportation hub. Buses, trains, and sandcars did not stop for Madness. Soon, they were under way.

Valbissag. It would be pleasant to report that Slith saw his homeland's hills standing bleak and strong, as he remembered them, that the town Valbissag's stone walls and edifices gleamed white in clear sunlight, and that tasty fungi nestled in every shadow. It was not so. In the years he had been gone, Slith had explored taller, darker hills whose strong shoulders reared skyward in bleaker, sterner majesty, and gentler ones covered with sandfern and water root. He had visited towns whose walls were bleached whiter, whose iron gates were more polished or painted with bright blue enamel. He had experienced bright equatorial sunlight, darker shadows, and tastier lichens than Valbissag provided, and he was no longer impressed. It was a small and dingy place.

At some distance from the town wall, Slith unpacked geologist's tools from his knapsack and hung them from his work belt, filled a net pouch with spurious samples—common stones—and considered himself disguised. Bleth posed no problem; he had not nursed her for very long while at Valbissag and few, if any, would associate her with the long-gone younger brother of their lord.

Slith planned to beg use of his father's terminal to send a message to fictional superiors in Thember. Travelers had often done so, when Fladth had ruled Valbissag. It was the only terminal in the town. A simple code, entered as part of an address, would dump his personal files into his rented memory space in Thember, and no one would be the wiser.

No one stopped them as they hiked into the stone warren that was Valbissag Town, though sharp eyes noted their passage, peering from alleys no wider than a man's shoulders, from windows set at ground level and rising no higher than his knees—windows uncomfortably like Slith's cell's. Eyes gazed through shuttered balcony screens above.

"See there?" murmured Slith. "That street leads to Valbissag, the spring. Only Thradz would be so crass as to install a tollgate. Was not the donation pot full enough? Could he not stand for a few poor widows to sneak a free dipperful, once in a while?" A few blocks father on, he again spoke. "Ahead is my father's palace, now Thradz's. We will knock at the side entrance."

Slith knocked. A pinch-nose snapped open immediately. Obviously, his approach had been noted in advance. "Yar?" said a gruff voice.

"I wish to use your terminal," Slith replied.

"There is no terminal here. Go to Thember. There are many terminals there."

"Thember? I wish to send a message to Thember, not go there. Come now! I am Fenth Paslittik, of the Geologic Survey. I have used Fladth's terminal often, in the past."

"Oh, it is *Fladth's* terminal you want? That is different. Go two blocks the way you came, then right to a small street with fruit vendors on all corners. Follow it to its end. Fladth's terminal is there, among other things of interest. You will not miss it." The pinch nose clapped shut, almost catching Slith's stubby proboscis in it and living up to its name.

" 'Right to a small street . . .' How odd," Slith mused as he and Bleth retraced their steps. "My memory must be failing. I remember nothing at the end of the fruit-market street but an old cemetery." He shrugged, thinking of the tollgate that blocked access to the spring Valbissag; he guessed that Thradz, discovering the terminal, had put it to profitable use. He, Slith, would find it behind a gate, with a gaudy sign listing prices for various services. "How much money do we have?" he asked Bleth.

"Thirty creds. We must save it for return passage."

"That will be twenty creds. Surely even Thradz will not charge more than five to use the terminal, which is double the Thember rate." The intersection with the fruit merchants' street was at hand. Slith turned down it. Ahead, fresh light painted dark stone walls. "You can see the clear place ahead," Slith said. "It is the old cemetery. I cannot imagine where the terminal is."

As he approached, as the light from the open space intensified, it became hard to see inside the unlighted windows of the shops they passed. "I can't miss it, eha? I see no terminal, no sign, no arrows or toll-taker. Where is it? Did you see anything, Bleth?"

"I saw a cobbler's shop, a currier's, a wholesaler of dried mealworms, and . . ."

"A terminal! Did you see a terminal?"

"No."

Slith swore angrily. Bleth cringed. "Here is the cemetery," he said as they reached the end of the street. An area the size of a goalball park stretched out, surrounded by faceless stone walls. The motionless ballplayers were knobby burial mounds, blocky cut-stone cairns, and scattered gravestones. Few were decorated with blue cloth or bunches of dried flowers because it was an old cemetery, mostly full for a long time, and surely its occupants' sons and daughters were too old and decrepit to pay respect to long-gone parents. "I see no terminal," Slith said, and turned to examine the storefronts again. Bleth did not follow. Instead, she passed through the cemetery gate.

"Where are you going?" Slith called out.

"The terminal," she replied.

"What? Where?" His eyes traced her direction of travel. There was a new burial mound, a heap of trash only partly covered with dirt. A few flutters of indigo fabric draped it. A large stone was atop it. The name HEVELTEEK had been rudely hacked at and partly effaced. In its place, someone had painted a new name, in black letters with runs and dribbles: FLADTH WRASSELTY.

"Fladth? Here, in this paupers' field?" Slith thought of the fine mausoleum on the edge of town where his father's father's fathers rested in splendid glass-faced drawers. He looked closely. The gravestone, at his eye level, could be reached by a short, worn path up the mound. The stone was encrusted with ocher dust, stains, and tiny crystalline efflorescences, the kind that form on the wood of stables, near the ground, urine crystallized by the slow action of dew. "That krood Thradz!" he snarled. "He befouls his father's grave." Slith hardly noticed the blue flutters, the bunches of colored weeds, the tokens of others' esteem: here a worn, brown book, there a copper chain with a rusty iron locket. Those were tokens from folk who had loved Fladth—who had been a kind man and a considerate ruler.

"The terminal?" Bleth reminded him timorously.

"What? Oh. It is not here, of course. The doorkeeper at the palace enjoyed a pun. Fladth's terminal? No, his *terminus*, his end. I will go back and remonstrate with the wretch."

"But the terminal *is* here!"

Slith looked. His gullet spasmed. A terminal indeed, Fladth's terminal, lay among the broken pots and shreds of cloth left by widows, cousins, and sisters. It lay unconnected, on its side, and it was as encrusted with nitrogenous crystals as was the stone above it. It had not been functional for a long time. With dragging steps and a forlorn slump of his shoulders, Slith looked closely. He nicked dust and ocherous efflorescence from its identification plate. "It is Fladth's," he said.

"It is broken," Bleth observed. "Can we go home now?"

"Home? Without my formulae?" Slith spoke harshly, shrilly. "We must take this with us."

"But it is broken. It is too heavy. The conductor charges extra for baggage."

"The datacrystal inside it will not have dissolved in Thradz's effluents! A bors electronicist can remove that, and install it in another machine. Here, help me pick it up." It was an unwieldy armful. Bleth was too short to help him carry it. She hung back uncomfortably as Slith staggered toward the cemetery gate. There were strong taboos against robbing graves.

"Here! What is this?" an old voice called out. The graveyard caretaker had returned from his dinner break. "Thieves! Thieves robbing the dead! They desecrate Fladth's grave!" Though there had been few signs of life in the streets before, now people swarmed from every doorway: old men with sticks and canes, children with throwing-stones, women brandishing cleavers, kitchen knives, and brooms. A stone bounced off Slith's head, stunning him. The terminal crashed to the pavement.

"I recognize him!" croaked the oldster who jabbed Slith with his cane. "It is that rascal Slith, who did not contest Thradz's inheritance. Fladth favored him, and he, ingrate, abandoned us! Give him another blow!"

Slith leaped away, into the path of a broomstick that cracked across his shins, a stoneroot walking stick that tripped him, and a volley of rocks. Slith moaned, and sunk to the dusty cobbles. The blows did not stop, though Slith was soon unaware of them.

He awoke—and immediately wished he had not. He could not open his encrusted eyes. It hurt to breathe. He moaned, and it hurt to moan, too. "Slith! Slith!" he heard a small voice calling. It hurt even to listen, he thought. But he could not keep from breathing or listening. He could not even suppress his low moans, so shortly he became inured to those pains—and was then able to appreciate more fully his other injuries.

Bleth, who had been saying his name, recited a list of the damages she had been able to find: "Three broken fingers and a thumb, and two cracked ribs, I think. A torn ear. Two black eyes, from concussion. One eyetooth gone, and two incisors broken. . . ."

"Stop! Enough!" Slith snarled, and immediately regretted it. "Owww!" He did not howl, but merely grunted, almost subvocally. Grunting hurt less than moaning or vituperating, and he decided to grunt from then on.

He picked fur, dust, and unspeakable grit from his eyes. From the odors that rose from his fur, he deduced that he had been treated by the common folk much as Thradz had treated Fladth's grave—though Thradz's ritual urinations had been less frequent, less copious, and less varied by diet and metabolism. Slith had a hard time remembering just who he was, where he was, and why he was there. The blows to his head did not aid clear thinking, and because he was covered in the scents of dozens of people his nose insisted he could be any one of them. He was an old man (who had eaten nettleberries for breakfast), he was a woman (who had licked dew from stones with a high sulfur content). He was this one and that, and only marginally Slith Wrasselty.

"Where are we?" he asked as he slowly recovered his wits. He saw low hills, black dust unadorned with a single living thing.

"The midden," Bleth informed him. "Outside Valbissag Town."

Thrown out like trash! Slith raged. Urinated upon, then discarded. A thought crossed his mind: "Why am I still alive? Did Thradz stop them from killing me?" He thought perhaps Thradz, not having obtained his formulae, wanted him to remain alive.

"Thradz was not there. He is vacationing at Boiling Mud Seep as you suspected, and will return tomorrow. We must be gone before then." Prodded by Slith, she ex-

plained that the folk who had beaten him were not
Thradz's admirers, but Fladth's. He remembered one
man's words, to that effect. Of course: Fladth had been
wise; Thradz, as anyone could see, gave the people of
Valbissag nothing, charged them for everything, and had
allowed the city to fall into disrepair.

Bleth explained that it had taken her some time to talk
sense to Slith's assailants. They had been truly incensed.

"Where is the computer?" he demanded.

"They put it back."

"You let them? I must have it!"

"The datablock is not in it. Thradz kept it. He may
have sent it to Thember with Thplet."

"Oh." That blow was no less painful than what he had
already endured. Could some hired expert break his en-
cryption? "What now?" he asked himself.

"We must go," Bleth said, as if he had spoken aloud.

"I suppose so. It would not do to have Thradz catch
me here." He got to his feet slowly, and after orienting
himself by the shapes of the distant hills, began to
walk.

"Not that way," Bleth protested.

"Why not? The railhead is over those hills."

"It is shorter if we cross over the Crumbles, by way of
Bilous Seep."

"That is wrong! We will miss the train entirely!" An
unwelcome premonition crossed his mind. "The money?
Have you lost our fare?"

"I paid the citizens for a memorial to Fladth," she explained. "They had a collection pot for it. Otherwise, they
would have killed you for robbing Fladth's tomb."

"I was not robbing Fladth!" he protested angrily, then
realized how ridiculous it was, defending himself before
Bleth. "You gave them *all* our money?" he whined. "Our
ticket money?" Bleth nodded. "Couldn't you have paid
less? Ten creds, perhaps?"

Bleth's face became impassive. Slith was not himself,
she argued silently, concealing her hurt. He would be
nicer when he realized that thirty creds or a thousand
would have been cheap, for his life.

As the miles between the travelers and Valbissag

stretched out behind them, Slith indeed decided that thirty creds—and his knapsack, with his tools, and all their food and water—had been cheap enough, provided they survived their journey.

PART TWO

SEDIMENTATION
Sand, Clay, and Lime

CHAPTER 11

Arbitorial policy does not demand that people live in peace and contentment. It does not require that they love each other, play fair, or even refrain from murdering each other. Such are matters of municipal, regional, or planetary concern.

That is not to say, however, that I have no interest in such things; they are the meat of my ordinary work. When all ordinary avenues have been explored, my office is the court of last resort: few discontents are ambitious enough, determined enough, or angry enough to cross my threshhold; those who do are often exactly the ones I *must* meet, for such ambition, determination, and anger, directed elsewhere, are the seeds of chaos.

James Minder IV,
Unpublished diary,
Erne Museo, Newhome, 4321 R.L.

It took them thirteen days to walk all the way to Thember, via the old road that skirted the depths of the Damplag Trench. Water was no difficulty. "See this reddish efflorescence?" Slith often pointed such things out to Bleth. "Gather a handful of it, and fold it in the hem of your smock. It neutralizes the organotoxins that thrive in the public wells of Flednast Playa." Public wells within the highway right of way did not benefit from government attention, or from any obligation to provide potable water. The wells were as they were, and each traveler's risk was his own. Knowing each source as if it were an old friend, Slith collected substances to neutralize the worst of them.

Food was a problem, because where people lived there was not much forage, and where people did not the desert was not generous. Bleth, however, was an excellent beggar, being small and pathetic, and it was against fardish nature to refuse food to a nursing fardling—or rather, to the man who nursed her: if Slith did not eat, he would not lactate. That fact encouraged those folk whom Bleth importuned to give scraps of old mushroom bread, dry handfuls of seeds, twists of bitter root. It also inspired Bleth to heights of histrionics she could not have attained in less pressing circumstances. "I die," she howled, causing chance passersby to cover their ears. "I waste away! His teats are empty sacks, and give no milk! Will no one feed him? Is there no offal to be had, no foul scraps, mold-covered and sour?"

"You need not *insist* that what they offer me be corrupted," Slith remonstrated, when none could hear. "Why not ask for fresh trufflids and hot fritters?" He sighed. "When we reach home," he decided, "I will eat everything in the cupboard. My teats will swell like kerbit eggs. Then we will both sleep for two days and two nights."

"What is this?" Slith demanded, dismayed. The doors of his house were covered with thick, rough boards. Bleth hung back and said nothing. A notice was nailed to the front door: FOR SALE

" 'For sale'? Bleth! Did you order this? Why? We did not discuss selling the house!" Bleth remained several paces away, and did not explain. Slith read the paragraph of small printing below the announcement. "Taxes? A tax sale? Bleth! You said you paid the taxes!"

"I paid them when you went to prison, at the end of Summerspell. I paid again at Winterspell. It is now past Yearend, and another payment is owed. I told you before we left for Valbissag. You said, 'Don't bother me with that, now,' You said, 'Soon, we will have the money.' "

Slith examined the boards, and tested one that seemed loose. Bleth approached, and read from the sale notice: "Tampering with this seal is a felony punishable by . . ." She did not have to finish reading the sentence. Slith had backed away as if the planks were red-hot iron. The law was hard on repeat offenders.

That night they drank from a leaky dew trap in the alley, and slept on hard cobblestones. By morning they were sore, hungry, and angry. Slith was angry with Bleth for what he considered her many oversights. Bleth was equally upset with Slith for blaming her. After all, she was not yet four years old, and though such fardlings as she seemed to absorb knowledge at a great rate, as if with the milk they imbibed, she was not an adult. Besides, she had unarguably saved his life several times, and she was in no way responsible for his misfortunes.

There was only one option left that Slith could think of, one untraveled avenue that might have good fortune at its end: the insurance money.

"Has the bors—this Slem Banto—broken into your vault?" asked the insurance agent.

"How should I know?" Slith replied. "The vault is in the cellar, and I was not allowed past the main floor."

"Then your papers may be safe and secure," the agent said. "Bring me photographs or holos of a broken vault, of a door forcibly breached. Bring a list of all that is missing. Then I will issue a check to you."

"A list? The contents are insured. What they are, or should be, is not specified. See? There, in your contract copy: ' . . . insured against loss.' I have lost them. I want my money."

"If they are in the vault, then you know where they are, and they are not lost."

"Then show me! Prove that your vault is secure! Demonstrate that my papers are safe, and I will take them, and we will be done with this."

"Get permission from this Banto, or a warrant for us to enter his shop, and we will examine your vault. If the contents are gone, we will pay."

"The bors will not allow it! I cannot get a warrant where no crime is suspected."

"No crime? No warrant? No permission? Well, then. There you are! What more can I do or say? It is all quite problematical, isn't it?"

Days passed slowly. Slith and Bleth ate and drank what and when and where they could. They made a bed of sand where the house's gardens had once been; it was softer than the cobble pavement. Bleth dutifully sought scraps of blowing waste paper for Slith, who, using discarded pencil stubs, attempted to write down what he could remember of his formulae, then hid the marked scraps beneath paving stones. For once, his vaunted memory seemed to have failed him. When his life had been good, when he had slept in his soft bed in the fine house, he had recited them each night, and kept them fresh in his mind. In prison—first in misery, and later as his thoughts had turned to ethnographies and anthropological topics—he had neglected that ritual, and now . . . he could not remember them. He wrote down what he could remember, but as he had no laboratory to test his memories, he could not be sure they were right, and being unsure, could not apply for patents on them. If the Patent Office's labs failed to reproduce his claims, they would be denied. Besides, he had no money for application fees. Still, he persevered.

To survive, to buy food, Slith and Bleth collected mineral efflorescences that occasional dews drew from the dry middens and dungheaps outside Thember. Those they sold for fractions of a cred per bushel to wholesalers, ungrateful men who cut their promised prices in half over the smallest scattering of useless sand grains in a bushel of nitrate.

Slith continued to press his claim with the insurance firm, with no clear result, until one day two months into the new year.

"Here," the agent said, offering Slith a two-cred chip.

It was more money than Slith had seen in a long time. Slith's fingers itched for it, but he shook his head. "What? You think to settle so cheaply?" he snapped. "Am I a fool? I want one half million creds. Take back your coin!"

"I am not offering a settlement. You saw me reach in my pocket for the coin. It is not from the firm's funds, but is a gift from me. I want you to pay a magistrate to rule on your claim. I am paying two creds for you to hear, from an authority, what I have told you all along. I am paying two creds to reclaim the peace of mind which fled during your first visit here, and which had not returned since." Because the chip was not from the petty cash drawer, and since the agent did not require Slith to sign a receipt, he took the money.

"The agent is correct," said the magistrate, a silver-whiskered bors. "Reveal the violated vault, and you may have a claim. Otherwise you have none." Slith, thoroughly broken in spirit, rose to depart. "Wait!" commanded the bors. "I am not finished. I have examined all the records concerning you, and I have found irregularities."

His words terrified Slith, who had only approached a government official with trepidation in the first place. Irregularities? Would this magistrate find yet another "crime"? Would he discover that Slith's sentence was three years, not two, and send him back to jail, to some new cell, dark, cold, and dirty, where Bleth might never find him to succor him?

"The chief patent officer who ordered your arrest has since retired under strange circumstances," the magistrate explained. "There was a charge of bribery, never resolved. Are you absolutely sure you did not claim to be acting as an agent for your family's estate when you attempted to patent the Wrasselty formulae? The holo recording of your appointment at the Patent Office, which should have proved guilt or innocence, is oddly blank. Without it, I do not understand how you were convicted in the first place." But Slith understood. He had seen the avaricious speculation in the CPO's eyes. He said that to the magistrate. "Then you are, at least in the eyes of the law, innocent of fraud. And your own discovery, this mysterious crystal now licensed to Lord Jandissl of Low Diverness ..."

"Jandissl! Jandissl? Lord Gefke Jandissl? What does he have to do with this? My crystal patent was taken as a fine. How does Jandissl come to control it?"

"It says here that it was awarded as partial reparation in another, related court action. Lord Jandissl seemingly paid you several hundred thousand creds for a useless placebo called Additive Three-A."

"Not true! Not true at all! My Additive Three-A restored the fertility of Jandissl's wells. It it not my fault that he remained anxious and continued to buy all that I could produce, even after the normal groundwater flow from Adderlong and through the Damplag Formation was restored by a subsequent earthquake."

"Hmm. Did you inform him of that change in circumstance?" asked the magistrate.

"I did not!" Slith stated indignantly. "Was I his hired consultant? Did he pay me a retainer? Did my office door have a plaque naming me Low Diverness's geologist in residence? No. None of that. He required Additive Three-A; I produced Additive Three-A. Perhaps he spiced his soup with it, or dusted his fragrant sand bed, or used its gritty crystals to polish his toenails, or . . ."

"Enough!" the magistrate protested. "If there was a misdeed on your part, it was a minor one of omission, not one worth . . . How much did you say?"

"Millions! Billions, even. One-third of a planet—what is that worth?"

The magistrate sighed. "This is all too complex for me. I am only an attorney, paid by the city case by case, and with two-cred fees like yours. I am not the Arbiter. I do not settle the fates of worlds, even thirds of worlds. This matter of your crystal may go beyond Thember and Low Diverness, beyond Phyre. I cannot resolve it, but it must be examined. The Arbiter himself should hear of it."

"The Arbiter is on Newhome, a thousand light-years from Phyre. Star-travel fares exceed the revenue of cities, and I no longer have even the two creds I came in with. Besides, what could the Arbiter do? And why would it be so important to him?" Lurking not far below the level of Slith's consciousness was the fear that just as one official had jailed him for two years over his crystal, so a greater one—an Arbiter, for instance—might jail him for an eternity.

"The Arbiter's representative recently announced a new policy. I think I have a copy somewhere. . . ." The magistrate rummaged in a desk drawer. "Ah, yes. Here. Read this." He passed a stiff plastic sheet across his desk.

A New Broom!

The Arbiter John Minder XXIII, newly ascended to that position, has reviewed the costs of his office, among them maintenance of his ten thousand armed ships of the line, supply and regulation of the remote, secret world where his savage *poletzai* are recruited, and the training, supply, and disciplining of those ferocious troops, twenty million men-at-arms.

The Arbiter points out that every cred not spent on those things will remain in the pockets of ordinary folk, enhancing their well-being and mitigating their dissatisfactions. To that end, he has established consulates in every major city of every world of the Xarafeille Stream. He urges: bring them your unresolvable grievances. Peasants, shopkeeps, overlords and princes: before you take action against your fellow man, against foreign nations or offending worlds, appeal to your consul, who speaks with the voice of John Minder himself.

The Arbiter points out that the cost of his service is the fare to his consul's office, for prince or bricklayer. The profit of conflict, even to the victor, is lost when ships and troops are called, when inevitable fines and reparations are assessed.

Maintain the peace of your neighborhood, your community, your world, and the Xarafeille Stream! Save yourself the burden of paying for the launching of white warships, the mobilization of marching men! In Thember, call 45-ARBITER or visit the new consulate on Park Street at the corner of Booksellers' Way.

"That was a good idea, Daddy," Sarabet said, leaning her blond head against her father's knee. John Minder had just returned from offworld, and his daughter had confronted him with the newssheet clipping. He stroked her hair absently, then shifted his weight on his uncomfortable seat. For once, Parissa was quiet, dozing in a persistent sunbeam. Rob—perhaps coincidentally—was also silent.

They were on the high balcony of the country palace in the Duchy of Erne, and before them spread a landscape that was representative of all Newhome. To the left spread the Rhend marshes, where mantees colonized the waters and the hammocks, and wends the dry ground. Ahead were the Sofal Hills, where the smoke of human occupancy arose from villages and from the city of Nort, where lived mantees, wends, fards, and a few tarbeks. Beyond a vast savanna on the right, the Meridite Aridity stretched almost to the far horizon. There, on the edge of visibility, towered the Skybreak Range, riddled with bors tunnels and enclosing a vast bowl of glacial ice where dwelt a few migrant ikuts, far from the polar floes they preferred.

Sometimes the Rhend mantees fought the wends, and sometimes mantee fought mantee. Sometimes they came to John Minder instead, and submitted to his arbitration. Ikuts and bors conflicted. One lost, one won—for the moment. Sometimes, when they submitted to arbitration instead, both departed with something, and the quarrel did not arise again.

What John Minder did on the large scale, he did on the small. His poletzai were silent because he had lost the codes to summon them, so he retired the Newhome constables to their barracks. If he could maintain peace on Newhome without them, perhaps he could maintain it in the Xarafeille Stream, even without his crystals, his codekeys, his troops, or his fleet. He had to—or the stars would erupt in the flames of war.

Just as the scope of what the family viewed was a microcosm of the planet, a patchwork of peoples, municipalities, industries, and endeavors, so Newhome mirrored all the worlds, and it was said that from his lofty balcony the Arbiter could see all the worlds, all the cities, and every man who walked and toiled there.

Again, John Minder shifted his buttocks to relieve their tingling. Sarabet, her repose disturbed by his wiggling, asked, "Daddy, why don't you throw away that old barrel, and have someone put a real chair up here?"

"Because just as what you see below this balcony evokes all the worlds, so this little wooden barrel reminds me of my position and responsibility."

"I know it's an antique," Sarabet stated ambiguously, "but why not put it in a showcase with the other old things—like George Washington's ax?"

"It isn't much of an antique," Minder said. "Several staves crumbled over the years, and my father, or his father, had them replaced. And when Dad was little, he crawled inside the barrel and rolled down a hill. Two of those iron hoops had to be replaced, after that." He shrugged. "The barrel has no value, really. It's the idea behind it."

"What is that?"

"You have read about wooden sailing boats, in the ancient days on Old Earth, haven't you?"

"Yes. De Ruiter, Nelson, and Jones. The Golden Hind and the Constitution, Trafalgar, Salamis, Lake Erie . . ."

"And pirates!" Parissa broke in. When had she awakened? "Bluetooth and Blackbeard and La Feet! Hook and Smee!"

"Parissa, don't interrupt me!"

"It's all right, Sarabet. Yes, Parissa, pirates too, though I remember their names differently, except for Lafitte. Any of the men mentioned would know what my barrel is. Can you guess?"

Parrisa thought long and hard. Sarabet had no idea at all, nor did Rob. Finally, Parissa brightened. "I know what it is!"

"What, dear?"

"It's a powder keg!"

Indeed it was. Sarabet then understood. She murmured something inaudible except to Rob, who grinned irreverently.

"Share the joke?" their father asked.

"Johnny-on-the-spot," said Sarabet.

Later, alone—as Arbiter, he was really always alone—Minder reviewed his most recent voyage, fingering a small tear in his trouser cuff he had acquired on Tembrod, Xarafeille 15. It was an old world, settled in the first millennium of the great human diaspora. It was blessed with almost limitless resources—thick, rich agricultural soils, oceans teeming with protein-compatible life, and not one but two belts of asteroids where metals and organic base chemicals abounded.

Tembrod was a major assembler of spaceships, a manufacturer of the specialized hull plates that starships required. Structural frames were made elsewhere, and were imported unassembled. Control systems—all the myriad components—were produced in bors' underground industrial warrens on worlds widely scattered, no one bors enterprise knowing exactly what they made or why, or where it would be shipped. The origins of stardrives themselves were even more carefully obscured, and one of Minder's more tedious duties was personally to oversee each engine's final installation, and to enter the final codes on a small keypad he carried on a chain around his neck, a keypad that jacked into an obscure, unnoticeable socket exactly like a hundred others, a socket that would—during the stardrive's functional lifetime—serve another function entirely, as the input from a waveguide's feedback coil. Once coded, the engine would function as expected—as long as no one meddled with it.

As long as no one meddled with it . . . as the Meripol shipyard on Tembrod had. The tear in Minder's cuff had been made by a jagged curl of metal—a burst blast door a half kilometer from the exploding starship. Minder assumed that the Meripol engineers had attempted to convert the erstwhile cargo ship into a weapons platform. There had been secondary explosions; one bomb, thrown free in the initial blast, had obliterated a wendish suburb—there were twenty thousand dead there alone.

On Barrenbeck, Xarafeille 2411, only seven light-years distant, eight ships stood in an urban spaceport. They had been there, out of service, for far too long, and Minder's agents had noticed them. There did not seem to be any significant activity around or within them, but who could tell? Was it because Barrenbeck's engineers had not figured out how to override their safety interlocks or because they had done so, and did not dare trust their handiwork until it was absolutely needed? Minder had no doubt at all that the Meripol vessel had been intended to take out the Barrenbeck ships. The explosion had saved them from that. But what would save the city of Feiropoli, when—and if, always if—even one of those eight vessels destroyed itself in a planetary-orbit-altering fireball?

Not for the first time, Minder asked himself why his ancestors could not have found a less destructive way to maintain their hegemony and control. He had seen Meripol's shattered residences, the charred corpses of innocents—old men and women long retired, schoolchildren in their charred classrooms, husbands, wives. . . .

But Minder had also seen the destruction of actual war. No inhabitable planet was *small*. A planetary surface was an immense theater for a war, and the slaughter of a planetary population was an incalculable loss to the species that begot it. What suffering! Which unique ideas— sprung from that world's unique interplay of climate, geography, and politics, and the specific interrelationships between races and individuals—would not reoccur in a thousand years, or ever again?

His task, his all-too-limited duty, was to prevent the spread of all-out, high-technology war *between* star systems. One world, however precious, was only a single experiment in the vast human laboratory. Its loss would be a tragedy, but not the end of all things. Interstellar war, however, was a fire spreading through the human edifice, a fire that burned experimenters and experiments alike, and that left nothing but dead ashes in its smoldering wake.

On one of these many worlds a spark would ignite. Somewhere, in the ferment of ideas, the secret of the stardrive would be rediscovered or a new technology would emerge. It had happened before. But before, Arbiters had sent war fleets to isolate the incipient conflagrations, troops to take over the factories and laboratories, accountants and scientists to sift through the records and ferret out every trace of the discovery, every last glowing ember.

Now there were no ships, no troops. Now, he thought, for the first time, an Arbiter was forced wholly to live up to his name: to arbitrate, to depend on his wit, sensitivity, and concern to nip war in the bud, before it could spread, because once begun, there was no way he could stop it.

He was not entirely bereft of hope. Even now, on Stepwater, far away, across the Xarafeille Stream, an agent reported that one of the seven data modules, holding a vital portion of the missing codes, had been located in the wendish archives there. Now, if only it could safely be gotten off-planet, and to Newhome.

Another module had been traced to Glaice, Xarafeille 132, but that one, his source informed him, might be forever lost at the bottom of some deep oceanic trench. If so, he mused darkly, there was no hope at all; others might still safely reside in the homeworld archives of the bors race, the tarbeks, the mantees, but two, three, or six of them were not enough. To reactivate his warships, to locate his *poletzai's* hidden world, he needed . . . all of them. All seven.

CHAPTER 12

TO: All consuls
FROM: Arbiter John Minder XXIII
TEXT: Be alert for disputes whose potential
resolution can reinforce the utility of your offices
and which can generate positive publicity for our
program. The eventual success of our efforts will
depend entirely on the public support we are able
to muster. Do not hesitate to refer cases with
Potential Rating of 3c or higher directly to me,
or to issue travel vouchers liberally to disputants
whose cases are both reasonable and of high profile.

The consul was an old-human. Since Slith had resided in
Thember he had seen several of those odd men, always
heavily robed and veiled. It was said that old-humans exuded pheromones that had unsettling effects upon the li-
bidos of other races. Slith had even heard that the robes
and veils they wore were filters of absorbers that neutralized their effluvia. That was what tarbek robes were; of
course tarbeks never wore them on their own lands, only
in towns, and tarbek emissions produced only nausea,
sneezing fits, and effluxions of the bowel, not strange
sexual behaviors.

Since this old-human wore no robes, and since Slith
felt no odd urges, he decided that either the man's filters
were hidden, or the air-conditioning of the building was
superb, or he had been told fairy tales. He would have
preferred the old-human to be robed and veiled, though,
because he was the ugliest thing Slith had ever seen. His
nose was pink and pointy, not black and soft. His ears
were like clusters of pink worms and were close to the

sides of his head, and immobile. Did he have no fur at all—anywhere?

The man—George Van Dam—wore a crimson tunic and trousers, tall shiny boots of offworld leather, and a shiny black cap, and he possessed a dry, pedantic demeanor. He indicated a chair for Slith. "I have studied your case, Sar Wrasselty," he began, "and I am completely intrigued. Your conviction for fraud was either a mistake or part of a vicious plot. The production rights licensed to Lord Jandissl reek of collusion, conspiracy, and other crookedness. The prompt foreclosure on your house was irregular, too. Ordinarily Thember grants an automatic extension of a hundred days to pay the tax—though in your case that might not have sufficed. I considered ordering the house withdrawn from the market, but that might have alerted the culprits to my inquiries. I am sad to say your house was sold yesterday to a fard from out of town."

The news was a crushing blow to Slith, coming on the heels of the consul's earlier words that had restored his hopes. "Even your doctorate was irregularly granted," said the consul, peering curiously at the supplicant. "You have two legs of a length, arms of a size, and eyes that match," he reflected, "but evidently what I see on the outside is all that is regular about you. Ah . . . one teat is smaller than the other, isn't it? But that is temporary. It is the one your little companion—Bleth, is it?—nursed on most recently."

Slith added shame and embarrassment to his sum of misery. To be examined so, and to hear it spoken, was humiliating. Yet he replied. "I *earned* my degree. I worked for it," he stated emphatically. "I am respected by scholars."

"Of course. I do not doubt it. Yet how many first-school graduates obtain doctorates without completing years of study, classroom hours, the master's thesis . . ."

"Work credit! My years of fieldwork, my travels, were applied to those things."

"How true. Yet how . . . irregular. Do you still have the contract the two dons offered you? No, of course not. All was lost with the house. Yet I managed to download a copy last night—just before the datablock that held it was blackened and shattered by a current surge. Heat lightning passing through an atmospheric dust flurry, I was told.

"But that may or may not be relevant to your case. I draw your attention to clause 4 (a) on the eighth page— 'intellectual properties.' Had you signed the contract, all your discoveries, patents, copyrights written and unwritten, even unspoken *concepts* would have become University property. Does that suggest anything to you?"

"I did not sign," bellowed Slith. To a fard, it would have been a roar; to the old-human, it was a shriek at the high margin of audibility. Slith now feared a forged signature and the loss of everything—but then, he had nothing, did he? He was hurt and angry that the consul thought his doctorate a ploy and probably undeserved.

"You did not, indeed—and good for you. What you owned, you still own. You have only to recover it. Not the house, of course, but . . . "

"My formulae!"

"Just so. Exactly. I am getting to that. Be calm, be patient, and all will out." Slith repressed an urge to squeeze the round, ugly head, to force out the information that was stopped up in it like a fur plug in the bowel, like a krood in a flooded whek burrow—though when Slith realized that the man's shiny cap was actually fur held down with perfumed grease, he abandoned all thought of touching it.

"Here is what I want you to do," the consul said. "I need copies of documents. First, from the registry, the deeds to your house, your shop on Park Street, and your factory on Colony Boulevard. Facsimiles will do."

"I have no money!" Slith protested. "I would need thirty creds for that."

"Here," the old-human said, tossing a packet to Slith. "A hundred creds. Buy yourself and your little ward good meals, and take a hotel room. Only do not say where the money came from. Say you found a fat beryl concretion in the dry middens, instead."

"I will do as you say," Slith asserted fervently.

"Next," said the consul, "I will need copies of all the Wrasselty patents. Fifty creds should suffice for that, leaving you twenty for necessities." Slith abruptly downscaled the size and opulence of the hotel room he would take. There must remain enough for sweetthorn pith pudding, offworld hen's eggs, toast with bird-liver paste—and that was only for breakfast. Lunches and suppers . . .

As if a mentalist, the consul sighed and tossed Slith another packet. "Do not deny yourself. You must be well fed, well rested, and alert to the slightest suspicion of irregularity wherever you go." Slith agreed that was wise. He would have liked to hire a squad of bors mercenaries, too, but he realized how ostentatious it would have been.

"One final thing. There should be a record in the Patent Office of Lord Gefke's license to use your molecule's formula, which seems otherwise lost."

"I will get it! Jandissl! I fume! He is a hack, a shaman, a road-camp cook let loose in a laboratory. He may follow directions well enough to use my formula, but he cannot understand what he does. He does not know the hundred strata of differing composition and porosity, the rainfall in the Vermous Hills, the dews in the Sublimation Karsts, the . . ."

"Yes. Indeed. And a thousand vital details known only to you, I am sure." The consul felt overwhelmed.

"And tarbek metabolism, too!" Slith added. "Jandissl does not know a fart from a hiccough."

"There is that, too. Now: are we finished? Have I forgotten anything? No? Then good luck, Slith Wrasselty. Leave by the rearmost door—and when you return here, whisper the word 'Sarabet' into the pinch-nose to effect your entrance."

"Sarabet? Is that a dance? I do not know it. Or is it a kind of bug?"

"It is the Arbiter's youngest child's name. As she was born only recently, no one on Phyre knows it except me—and now you."

"Ah," said Slith, impressed with knowing anything that others did not.

Slith's room had a soft agravitic bed manufactured offworld. He dined on tasty sand pears and a potage of lattice-house fruits. He purchased a new tunic at the hotel outfitter's shop, which catered to rich foreigners new to Phyre. Bleth eloquently—for a fardling—expressed her approval of Slith's sudden means. She became less ebullient when she attempted to nurse. Perhaps as a result of Slith's recent stresses and dejection, there was little milk for her, but, wisely, she kept her dissatisfaction and her hunger to herself and allowed Slith to doze off with his own newfound contentment intact.

All those luxuries should have elevated Slith's confidence to a high level. He should have strutted through the high corridors and out through the great double doors manned by bors uniformed in blue tunics and matching pillbox caps. He should have strode purposefully down the middle of Port Street's sidewalk—but Slith did neither of those things. Instead, he left the posh old Hotel Xarafeille by the shippers' entrance at the rear, and made his way northwest via the alleys, dodging dump-carts and boxes of goods so he would not have to pass in front of Slem Banto's establishment, once his own. He angled due north at the intersection of Port Street and Booksellers' Way, to the wall of the compound that housed University, Patent Office, Archive, and Registry, then stopped at a gate off Booksellers' Way. The last time he had entered that compound he had been forcibly ejected into the maw of a police wagon. He was uneasy, even now. Then, he had been rich and confident, and look how his fortunes had fallen during those few moments inside this very place! Now, he was to enter it again, a pretentious pauper in a silky tunic, with no assets but hope itself. Uneasy? Slith was terrified.

The gate he chose was not near the major buildings inside. It was wide enough for a fiacre or a dray, though, and through it Slith could see the grayish pink granite of the Registry to the right, the creamy quartzite Archives rising above intervening University structures to the left, and the bloodred jasper and carnelian upper stories of the Patent Office lit by low morning sunbeams, straight ahead. At the entrance to the Registry he hesitated uneasily. The watchman, a bors, noted his pause and became suspicious of him. "You there!" he called as Slith made to pass within. "Your papers! Do you have an appointment?" Slith did not. He produced his identification disk—no one carried "papers"; "papers" was merely an intimidating word armed policemen and quasi-officials enjoyed using, a word whose meaning was lost. When the watchman read the disk's contents on his wristband terminal, he grinned and reached for the tangler cords draped from his belt. "A felon, eh? A fraud here to defraud whom? And how? Put out your hands!"

Slith did not present his wrists. His course of action was as if preset by his antecedent terror of the place. He pirouetted, then dashed through the open doorway of a classroom building just ahead of a group of noisy students. The bors guard could not match his speed and agility, and hesitated a moment too long over leaving his post unattended. Slith found his way past busy classrooms to another exit and across the main street, where a flagstone path branched to several other structures. He chose one at random, and entered. A wendish receptionist looked up from her acrostic puzzle at him. Behind her, on the wall, was a directory of those academicians she served.

"I have an appointment with Tutor Chelemerin," Slith announced, reading the name from the directory.

"He is not in," said the wend woman. Slith was, in spite of his fear, a quick thinker still. A tutor. That had colored his choice of names—morning classes had begun, and tutors were busiest early and late, often sleeping during normal University hours. "I will wait," he said. "He will be here momentarily."

"I do not think so," she stated. "He left an hour ago."

"He will return. He is expecting me." Slith settled uninvited into a worn cloth chair in the waiting alcove. The receptionist shrugged and returned to the acrostic whose eventual solution Slith had delayed.

Slith pondered his failure to gain the foyer of the Registry. He had hesitated. That had been his undoing; others had strode right in. Did the watchman know every face among them? Surely not. Slith's anxiety had given him away. He considered the Patent Office and all the terrors it held for him, the memories leading to his imprisonment. He would be less able still to enter *that* place with confidence and aplomb. Had he failed entirely? Was he defeated?

His eye fell on scholars' robes draped from pegs, one ultramarine, one russet, two black, and one crimson with pale azure piping. Each peg was surmounted by a small plaque with a name. M. CHELEMERIN, he read, over a black robe. He sat, and he pondered.

"Tutor Chelemerin is not coming," the wend said again, breaking Slith's train of thought. "Shall I call his home before I take my break?"

"There is no need," Slith replied. "I will wait. If he does not arrive by the time you return, I will ask you to call him. He is probably rushing down Accountants' Way even now, having remembered our appointment."

"Accountants' Way? He lives on Court Street."

"Just so. He mentioned other business. . . . But no matter. By all means enjoy your break now. Ignore me. I am content to wait." The wend rose, picked up her acrostic and stylus, then departed. Slith pondered the imponderable: she had been at work, and getting paid while solving her puzzle; now she would go elsewhere, perhaps drink a cup of rock-apple juice, and continue her struggle to match words, numbers, and phrases for fifteen minutes or a half hour of unpaid time. Then she would return and, again earning her pay, would fill in still more blanks. He wished his own life were so straightforward.

When her footsteps faded and a door closed deeper in the building, Slith snatched Tutor Chelemerin's robe from its peg, wrapped himself in it, and practiced an unfamiliar, firm, purposeful stride as he proceeded westward toward the Patent Office. Confidence, that was the key to success: not a strut, not a soldierly march, but the pace of a busy man deeply involved in his business, expecting no disturbance or interruption of his thoughts.

The watchman at the vermilion gate did not notice him at all. Once inside the building, he punched letters on a touch-screen let into a decorative plinth and found directions to "Copies, Printouts, and Summaries," then pressed on, making sure his deliberate stride did not falter. He resolved to try a different gate to the Registry later, and to try his new demeanor there, but for now he presented a list of the Wrasselty patents, prepared the night before, to a wend clerk, who slid the pages through a scanner one by one. A printer on the far wall sighed, and produced a stream of white sheets that rapidly grew into a stack.

"Seventy creds," the clerk demanded, placing the thick sheaf of documents on the counter. Seventy? Slith and the magistrate had calculated no more than fifty. He drew breath to protest, then reconsidered. He wanted no ruckus in that place of fearful memories. He counted out credit chips and then reached for the documents. "Your identity disk, please," the clerk said.

Slith hesitated. "I . . . I have forgotten it. But no matter. You have seventy creds, which is far too much, and I have these papers." He swept them up under his arm. "Let go of my arm!" he hissed.

"I must insist! I must process the disk!"

"Later, then. I will return. Stop grabbing at me! Let go of my papers!"

"Help!" yelled the clerk, which was a low, hoarse sound to a fard, though shrill to anyone else. "Security to Room Seven-fourteen!" he shouted. Slith tried to back away, to no avail. He tried to spin around, and the papers became a white flurry, then settled to the floor. A door at the far side of the room burst open, and Slith glimpsed yellow sambrowne belts hung with stun rods, tanglers, and threatening, shiny things. He tore free of the wend's grip and fled the way he had come. He heard the thud of heavy feet at his heels.

Slith ran. He did not consciously contemplate his path: all ways were equal, as long as they led him away from the threat. He ran down one hallway, down stairs, making split-second decisions at every intersection: down, and away. Slith's rapid flight was reminiscent of his last exit from that building, in that he remembered only flashes and impressions later, while huddling in a scenic grotto across the street to the east. He remembered corridors, escalators descended in a few quick bounds, lights, turnings, and at last the clear, free air of morning. The pursuing footsteps did not follow him outside.

He crouched in his impromptu lair, recovering his

breath, and considered his accomplishments. He had no deeds, no patents. He had almost been apprehended twice—and for what? He had only the wend patent clerk's blue-and-yellow badge of office, torn off in the scuffle. It was clutched in his still-trembling hand.

Noon came, and the sun beat on his rocky roof. Afternoon followed. Slith discarded the scholar's robe, which was torn, and then again practiced his purposeful stride all the way to the West Port Street gate. Beyond that, making his way through narrow residential corridors paralleling Booksellers' Way, he allowed himself to resume his natural posture. By the time he approached the consulate's rear door, his ordinary slouch had degenerated into a felon's cringing slink. It had all been too much for Slith Wrasselty. He was a thoroughly broken man. His last hope of justice had been lost.

"Sarabände," he said into the pinch-nose. The door did not open. "Seraphim," he said with no better result. "Xarafeille. Serotonin, serration, serif, sara ... Ah ... Sarabet?" He heard the clack of an automatic bolt retracting. The corridor beyond the door was as dark as his future, he thought. Outside, behind him, the streetlights had come on; the consul was surely home with his family, if he had one, or enjoying fresh sandsnappers and white wine somewhere on Commestic Plaza, or ...

(HAPTER 13

There are few genetic differences between the human races. Only about half the added genes on the supernumerary V chromosome, perhaps indeed derived from non-human species of the mythical mother planet, actually differ from race to race. For the most part the differences lie in certain homeobox sequences that determine the way identical genes shared by all men are expressed, and when.

Old-human males experience the admiration of young females as a rise in testosterone and certain brain chemicals; a male chosen and cosseted by females becomes quick, strong, and libidinous; a male scorned by females cannot compete in any arena of life. Among fards, the same gene complex reacts only to specific female-produced pheromones, and is activated only by the sated contentment of a nurseling.

Slith Wrasselty,
"Variations on a Single Theme,"
Natural History Monthly,
Volume CLVII, forthcoming,
Newhome

Having run out of money to keep the hotel room another day, Slith brought Bleth with him when he next visited the Arbiter's representative.

"This is beyond my competence," said George Van Dam, the old-human consul. "Only the Arbiter himself can resolve your difficulties."

Slith slumped dejectedly. He had known it all along.

All night, in the dark corridor, he had waited to hear just those words, ones he had heard before. Who had said them then? "Only the Arbiter . . ." It was a common enough expression, an idiom for a problem without a solution, a hopeless cause. Slith laboriously pulled himself to his feet, and prepared to depart. He still had a few of the consul's creds left. He would spend them on rail fare into the deepest desert, and there he would jump off the train. Bleth? He did not even think of the fardling.

"Wait," demanded the consul. "Where are you going?"

"As you said, only the Arbiter could solve my problem. I will leave Thember. I will perhaps mine dry middens in some far town where I am not known."

"What of Bleth, your child?" He smiled, and tweaked the fardling's chin.

"She is not my child," Slith stated emphatically. "She is a fardling soon to be a fard. She will learn to eat food, herself, or she will find a fresher teat than mine. Someday she will be grateful to have been saved from a disastrous mating with a felon such as me."

For his part, the consul felt sorry for the small, charming fardling. How could her guardian be so cold? "Nonetheless she is human, and thus is the Arbiter's charge," he said, smiling warmly at her. "If there is ever anything I can do for you, child, will you come see me?" Bleth nodded shyly.

Slith's behavior might have been excused by his mental state. He was, of course, thoroughly depressed. If he had not been so immersed in his own despair he might have noticed two things. First, he might have remembered his own studies and realized that his rejection of Bleth expressed a corollary to his thesis about male influence and female admiration in old-humans, and nursing behavior in fards: just as a beaten-down and depressed old-human male might feel no libidinous urges, a fard in similar circumstances felt no compulsion to nurture his fardling. In both cases, he might have pointed out to himself, the species was served: the old-human, inadequate (by definition), would contribute no depressive genes to his tribe, and the depressive fard, by driving off his fardling and refusing to nurse her, would force her to seek nurture from a more adequate male, and would himself pass no genes on to the future through subsequent breeding.

The second point Slith might have caught, had he not been dejected, was a minor one, a matter of grammar, but fraught with significance. The consul apprised him of that one almost immediately: "I did not say 'Only the Arbiter *could* save you.' I said 'Only the Arbiter *can* save you.' That is to say, we have not exhausted all recourse."

"The Arbiter is on Newhome, and I am on Phyre," Slith said needlessly.

"And the Arbiter will not come to you? Well then, I see only one solution: you must go to Newhome."

The suggestion's frivolous impossibility brought Slith partly out of his depths, buoyed by anger at being mocked. "Ah!" he said. "I will mine a basket of saltpeter beneath the midden heaps! I will bring it to the ticket master at the port, and will say 'Here! Apply this half cred of value against my fare. I will pay the rest upon my return from Newhome.' Or I will return every day with another basket, and another, until all is paid. Who knows—perhaps the ticket master's grandchild, or his grandchild's grandchild, will have the honor of issuing me my ticket!"

"Slith, Slith! Listen to me. I am the Arbiter's consul. I will issue your ticket. You will be on your way to Newhome in three days, as soon as a suitable ship is available."

"Why three days?" asked Parissa. "Why can't Slith come right away? And Bleth! I *like* Bleth. I would like to play with her. *She* would not chase me away." She eyed her older siblings accusingly, with deep dissatisfaction.

"All this happened years ago, P'riss!" Rob said. "Slith is probably dead of old age, and Bleth is a grandma by now."

"Daddy? Is it true?"

John Minder, who was still a young man of thirty-odd years, not a gray-haired grandfather, smiled indulgently. "Perhaps it's not that long ago, Parissa; but it's true that you were not yet born. Remember that Sarabet was a newborn baby then."

Parissa lapsed into disappointed silence, which suited Rob perfectly. "Why couldn't Slith have left right away, Dad? Weren't there lots of ships at the port in Thember?"

"There were cargo ships, Rob, not passenger ones."

"Of course!" Rob exclaimed. "I just forgot for a moment." What Rob had forgotten was an essential stratagem devised by an Arbiter long ago, an ancestor dead a millennium or more: there were no passenger ships. It was illegal to construct ships capable of carrying more than four or five passengers. The shipyard that violated the rule, that attempted to convert a ship carrying a few wealthy patrons to one carrying armed troops, could count on being razed, leveled by the weapons of the Arbiter's white ships. Firms, consortiums, or governments that commissioned the conversion of ordinary vessels to weapons platforms or troopships could count on being disbanded, dispersed, and obliterated from history itself by the Arbiter's deadly poletzai. There was no concern that men would build new ships of radically different design than those the Arbiter allowed: he, as had his ancestors back to the first John Minder, kept the secret of the stardrive. Men used his machinery, but when they tried to fathom it, to break the seals on the engines, men and engines erupted in fusion flames.

The Arbiter could not prevent all wars. When a conflagration broke out on one planet, it might be days, weeks, even months before his fleet could arrive to put an end to the conflict, before his consuls and reconciliators could sort through the inequities, grievances, and antipathies that had instigated it. But where there were no ships capable of carrying more men than necessary to crew them, no war could spread from one star system to another.

So far, John Minder's informants had kept him abreast of the few attempts to flaunt his dictum, and he had thwarted the constructors with stock manipulations, strikes, hired saboteurs, and by judicious fomentation of riots among workers who feared for their families and their worlds, should the white ships and the poletzai come.

So far, so good, Rob thought, because until John Minder gathered all seven of the datablocks his brother

Shems had unwittingly stolen, the Arbiter had no ships at all, and no troops, and sooner or later some corporation or government was going to build a fleet of modified freighters and decipher the stardrive's workings before he found out about it, and the Arbiter's impotence would be unmasked. Rob did not like to think of the devastation that would ensue when every resentment, every conflict of interest, caused armed ships to fly among the long-peaceful stars.

"Bleth! Are you here?" asked Slith.

The hotel room door was open. Bleth did not reply—but another voice did: "Eya, Slith! It is me, Thplet."

"Thplet? Why are you here? If you have a package for me, then throw it out that window now. Go back to Thradz! And where is Bleth?"

"I brought nothing, and Bleth is merely downstairs, practicing eating in the dining room."

Slith was nonplused. Practicing *eating*? Or, specifically, practicing the act of eating in dining rooms? "How strange. Why is she doing that?"

"She will someday be required to eat to survive. She will also need to learn manners. She practices both."

"Good," said Slith. "That makes me feel better."

"It does?" From what Thplet had heard of the bliss nursing males experienced, he could not imagine Slith's contemplating its cessation.

"Just so. I am called away to a place Bleth cannot go. It is good she can eat food, because . . ."

"She eats it, but she is not old enough to digest it properly. Slith! If you abandon her . . ."

"She will find another male. Too bad you are not a whole male, and thus capable of lactation. She would make you a fine mate, someday." For the first time since he had discovered the nursing fardling at his breast, in the Vermous Hills, Slith had begun to contemplate a life without her. During his deep depression just past, he had felt no urge to nurse her. His milk had not come in at all. In fact, he had realized one implication of nursing a fardling, perhaps the very one his father Fladth had hinted at during their last visit, the very one that was the source of his frequent disquieting moments when he contemplated future sexual congress. It was this: the natural life span of a fard approximated that of other humans, about ninety years; the abbreviated life span of a mated fard was only fifty, because even with a preponderance of female offspring, eventually most men helped their mates produce ... a son—a son who would someday slay them. Slith Wrasselty did not enjoy the thought of dying at fifty—or at ninety, though ninety was surely preferable. "If I survive this," he had promised himself in the consul's office, "I will get rid of the fardling." And now was the perfect opportunity: the consul had said nothing about *two* tickets. Bleth must stay behind. She would only have to practice a bit harder at her new skill of eating.

Thplet protested vehemently: Slith was cruel; Slith was heartless; Bleth might die. His very protests strengthened Slith's resolve. "Good," Slith said to himself, "Thplet cares for her. He will be sure she finds another male to feed her. I need not feel the slightest guilt." Aloud, he said: "It is good you are here. Now, shut the door. We must talk."

Thplet obeyed, curious. What could his failed brother have discovered to cause him to flit and bubble so? "What is so important?" he asked.

"You are a good brother, as brothers go," Slith stated. "You never planted stinkweed in my sleeping sand, or mocked me in my time of despair. Therefore I wish you to take this." He pointed at a basket draped in cloth that stood beside the door.

Thplet peered under the drape. "Song scorpions? But why?"

Slith did not answer the question. Instead, he said, "I bought them for Bleth, but since you are here ... Take them, and Bleth, into the barrens south of Low Diverness and wait for my return. Then, many things will change. In the meantime, you and she will be safe."

"Safe? That is High Diverness and is a deathplace. Not even kroods live there!"

"Take this map. There are seeps only I know, caves with sweet fungi, and hidden sweetroot beds I planted myself."

"But why? I am content to serve Thradz, and Bleth is not my concern. Besides, she must nurse."

"Bah. She will adapt," said Slith, not without a twinge of guilt. "After all, she is a resourceful fardling—I myself have taught her everything she knows. If she does not cope with changed conditions, then her genes do not deserve to reproduce themselves anyway. Either way, the good of our race is served."

Deep inside, Slith did not feel as callous as his words implied, but if he did not overstate his rejection of Bleth, he would not be able to abandon her so, and he would not go to Newhome at all. That could not be allowed to happen. Too, his current resolve was as much a product of fard biochemistry as his compulsion to nurse Bleth had been; because he had so recently failed in his endeavors he had become dejected and depressed. Levels of serotonin in his brain and of testosterone in his blood had dropped markedly as a result of his depression and he felt less powerful—less male—than before, when he had been at his most confident.

Being less male, less powerful, his bodily messengers told him—on some entirely unconscious level—that he was no longer fit to be a nurse. Thus, in one very real sense, Slith was no more in control of his rejection of Bleth than he had been of his nurturing of her. Still, somewhere deep inside, a very small, hidden Slith Wrasselty grieved for the fardling—and for himself.

With visible effort, Slith pulled himself back to the present moment, and to Thplet. "As for Thradz," he said, "he is less than content with you, Thplet. He suspects you of nefarious plotting; he plans your demise." Slith knew of no such dissatisfaction or plan. He merely wished the fardling to have a companion and guardian in the high desert, to inspire Thplet to hire some indigent male to feed Bleth, and to have some sort of refuge to flee to if things did not work out as he now hoped they would. Still, from Thplet's readiness to accept that Thradz suspected him, Slith guessed that he had accidentally hit on a truth: Thplet indeed plotted something.

There was a sound from the corridor beyond the door.

Slith called out, "Bleth, is that you? Return downstairs at once and practice eating again. I will send for you."

"I wish to nurse!" the fardling cried. "The food is a rock inside me. I want milk to wash it away."

"It will pass," Slith insisted, unaware of ambiguity, steeling himself against further plaintive protest. "Eat more, and your stomach will become inured to it. Or do not eat, as you wish, but do not disturb me now." He listened at the door, and when he heard her small footsteps and dissatisfied snuffling fade, then heard the sound of an elevator descending, he nodded his satisfaction. "If she came in," he explained, "I would be overcome with the desire to nurse her, and all my resolve would depart."

"Where are you going, that you can't take her?" Thplet asked.

"Never mind that. Do you know how song scorpions are used?"

"Am I a fool or a child? The bugs are now dormant. When I place one in wet sand, it soon awakens. I repeat a message three times, until it learns my words, and then I set it free at dusk. It seeks its eggshell, and when that is found it sings my words."

"Close enough, though the part about eggshells in myth. It merely finds its birthing place."

"Whatever," said Thplet. "What else?"

"You must visit the seep located here"—he indicated a spot on the map—"once every week, and listen for a scorpion singing 'Thplet and Bleth, all is well,' and must obey whatever instructions follow. That is all."

"And if Bleth wastes away? If she becomes ill?"

"Find her an unaltered male. Tie him up, if you must, until he lactates and it is too late for him. But now, I must go. I leave it to you to explain all to Bleth. Goodbye."

Thplet nodded pensively, wondering what bug had bitten his strange brother. He did not look forward to weeks in the desert. Even more, he did not look forward to informing Bleth of her nurse's betrayal.

CHAPTER 14

Slith changed hotels that night. Let Thplet get started on
his task. Slith wondered what his brother had been plotting, that was now rendered void by the lie about
Thradz's suspicions of him. But no matter; Thplet, Bleth,
Thradz . . . what did they matter? Each of them had, in
their own ways, manipulated him for their own ends, had
they not? He owed them nothing.

His new lodging was within the port precinct, which
was off limits to casual visitors. Only Slith's boarding
pass for the starship *Long Haul III* had gotten him past
the gate. Once inside, he did not plan to go out again. Inside, he was safe. Even Thradz could ill afford a starship
passenger's ticket, and there was no other way he—or his
assassins—could enter the precinct. Slith pondered the
advantages of wealth beyond counting, the wealth that
would be his when, with the Arbiter's help, he regained
control of his molecule's patent. . . . Would he travel often
on starships, then? Would he visit far, exotic worlds all
the way to the edges of the Xarafeille Stream on the business of still further increasing his wealth? Would he perhaps even travel as a . . . a *tourist*?

Tourist. One who tours, usually for pleasure alone. Over the years and the millennia since the settling of the Xarafeille Stream under the aegis of long-gone Arbiters, the simple word had become loaded with new significance. Tourist: one with the means to tour. Slith contemplated that with great enthusiasm.

Slith did not know the half of it. While he awaited notification that his ship was ready for him to board, while he sampled the exotic fare in the traveler's restaurants within the precinct—all at the consul's and the Arbiter's expense—many other people were working day and night to ready his quarters aboard ship.

Long Haul III stood tall on a reinforced bedrock pad not far away. Had Slith known which ship it was, he could have watched it being prepared to receive him, all from his hotel room's window. First the hull plates were stripped from a belt around the ship's midsection, providing access to the inside, and its cargo—huge crates of mineral salts destined for a refractory on Beldger Ace, four hundred light-years distant—were removed. The cargo had only been loaded some days before, but now, to accommodate Slith, it was being off-loaded again.

Even larger containers were trucked out from ware houses, were hoisted high, and were then slid into place between the ship's spidery frame members. Had Slith watched, he would have seen a unit the size of a small house loaded in, and might have been able to make out the label on it: BATH/KITCHEN MODULE 4C and a list of specifications:

Decor:	Desert Beige/Chrome
Envir:	Low Humid. Std. Atmosphere
Facil:	Fard Hdwe. w/Std. Litterbox
Adaptors:	Universal

It was a kitchen and a bathroom, complete with a self-cleaning fard-style oubliette, all enclosed within a box shaped like a wedge of lichen pie, with an outer wall that fit perfectly the curve of *Long Haul III*'s hull, that in fact *became* part of that hull, once installed.

Then there was Salon Module 3t with its own list of

specifications, complete with furniture suitable for a fard of high station, a module that melded perfectly with the doors, with the control and power wiring, the water-supply tubes and the air-supply ducts of Bath/Kitchen Module 4c and Bedroom Module 17k, whose closets came stocked with high-quality fard attire of the latest fashion, all in Slith's sizes.

When Slith was finally invited to board ship, he was impressed with the spacious luxury of his suite, with the fine materials, the well-stocked pantry, the study with state-of-the-art electronics and shelves lined with books and entertainments. "Everything but a nice little laboratory to play in," he mused. He was impressed, but not half as impressed as he would have been had he known that everything he saw had been assembled just for him.

"I know nobody can build starships without the star-drive John Minder the First invented, Dad," asked Sarabet, "but why can't people build plug-in modules that have bunks for forty men, instead of luxury suites?"

"They can," John Minder XXIII replied. "I—and my predecessors—haven't figured out how to stop them from trying. Right then, I'm sure they were building them, somewhere—and special modules with laser cannons and particle-beam weapons, too."

"And you couldn't stop them? Even if you had known where they were?"

"Think about that. What would they have been most likely to have done?"

Sarabet thought. Then she shook her head. "They would have gone right ahead, wouldn't they? Since they were already in trouble with you, they'd have *had* to keep on until you sent in your ships, and . . ."

". . . And I had no ships. Yes. If I had ordered them to stop, and did not back up my order with material authority . . ."

"So what did you do, Dad?" Rob interrupted. "What could you do?"

"The starships all require a special hull metal with a specific microcrystalline structure that the stardrive elements 'recognize.' If shipmasters try to go FTL with a module whose hull signature isn't right . . . No one's ever found one of those ships. Even I don't know where they've gone. All I know is that they never come back."

"So if they gut existing modules and use the original hull parts and decks, and . . ."

"Then nine times out of ten they have changed certain other patterns, too, and the ships disappear forever. And as they experiment, and lose ships and passenger modules, less people can travel from the ports they got them from, and people begin to complain. When that happens, my investigators look into it. Then, sometimes, there are yardworker strikes, and materials shortages. I try to stall them, or make them give up."

"But sooner or later . . ." said Rob, leaving the thought incomplete.

"Yes," his father replied. "Sooner or later, somewhere, one of them would have succeeded, and word would spread." He said no more. Parissa was there, oddly quiet, but listening. She was too young to be exposed to the fearful idea of interstellar war.

Slith did not know when the ship lifted off. There was no sense of motion, for one thing, and he was already deeply engrossed in the salon's library—old books, real books with plastic pages and composite covers, not mere recordings viewed on a screen. Even their content enthralled him, as if they had been selected precisely with him, Slith Wrasselty, in mind. Of course they had— because Slith's entire dossier had been examined with care by the shipping authorities, and his preferences taken very seriously. Slith noticed that some ethnology texts on the shelves were stamped with the University's sigil, and that the tiny readout windows inside their covers, where the required return dates were ordinarily displayed, said only INDEFINITE LOAN. He did not pay much attention to that, though he would have been amazed at how much difficulty getting those books had caused one unfortunate port authority clerk. The library held on to its resources with amazing tenacity, and Slith had not been able to order those particular sources before, because all copies had been on reserved status.

He did not notice many other things, either. He could have demanded more services and luxuries than he could have imagined—as most genuine "tourists" would have known to do—but as there was no menu at mealtime, only an attentive old-human crewman to take his order, he asked mostly for ordinary foods. Had he had the temerity to demand Achebian truffloids in fire sauce, they would have been forthcoming with no more delay than the kroon eggs, basted lightly and spines removed, that he ordered, thinking those the height of decadent luxury.

Had he wanted sexual entertainment, that too would have been provided, and had his tastes run to the unusual, there were holotapes, but Slith did not consider asking for such things. Instead, feeling secure in the Arbiter's ship, as he thought of it, he concentrated on collecting the ethnographic data previously denied him, and on trying to remember and write down all his formulae. Unfortunately, he could not be sure his memories were accurate, and there was no laboratory module in his quarters, and he could not test his memories' accuracy.

Still, time passed quickly for him, and one morning at breakfast his manservant informed him that arrival at Newhome was imminent. Slith had few preparations to make, and little to pack except his notes and the data modules he had filled. When he was led down a corridor to an elevator, and thence to the ship's debarkation hatch, he carried only a small valise with him.

"I am going to Thember," Bleth stated. "I cannot wait here in the desert while Slith Wrasselty piddles and muddles and furthers his own plans without concern for *me*."

"You cannot!" protested Thplet. "Here we are at least safe."

"Safe? You call this *safe*? We are at the mercy of wind, poisonous worms under every rock, and starvation. This is not safe."

"You cannot go alone. You need to nurse."

"I will not starve in three days—and if worse comes to worse, I will whine and cry at the orphanage door, and they will feed me chalk dust and water that will suffice."

"But that stuff will make you ill. How many fardlings die in spite of it?"

"I am *almost* mature. I will order krood livers boiled in salt water and will keep the broth down long enough to get a bit of nourishment from it. My *nurse* need not accompany me." She spat dryly, a gesture, not an actual waste of moisture.

The inflection Bleth placed on the word "nurse" had multiple meanings. First was anger—because the new nurse she had acquired was only a substitute for Slith, whom she had come to care for, if never to trust. Second was an affected scorn, because once having painfully broken the emotional bond with one male, she was not about to become any more involved with another than exigencies required.

"Very well then," muttered Thplet, who really had no control over her actions. "But say nothing about me, or this place. I do not know what Thradz has found out, or what his exact intentions are, but . . ."

"Do not concern yourself with that," Bleth said dismissively, making for the door of their uncomfortable cave.

Newhome! The brightness of the sun Prime filled his eyes, a gentler glare than Phyre's, but a welcome one even though his suite's artificial lighting had been tuned to his home star's spectrum. The first thing that impressed him was that there were green growing things everywhere, even in the inevitable cracks in the landing apron's surface. What profligacy, he thought. Only the highlands of Phyre, and only in brief seasons, permitted such growth. He sniffed the air, and caught scents of chlorophyll, of a hundred distinct pollens, of spores . . . Spores! He had carefully sprayed his fur with fungicides as suggested by his ship servant, who had informed him that unacculturated fards often succumbed to infections in atmospheres moister than they were accustomed to. Would that be enough? The air's moisture was almost palpable.

Slith was given little time to stand and ponder Newhome's ambience. By the time he had descended the boarding stairway, a fat-wheeled limousine had pulled up, and its door swung open. "Sar Wrasselty?" asked the driver, needlessly. Slith had not seen any other passengers, and in fact there had been none. He nodded, and took a seat in the luxurious car.

"Where are we going?" he asked.

"First to your hotel, the New Home," the driver responded. "And then, as soon as you are properly refreshed, to the Cariosh Table, a fine restaurant that specializes in fardish dishes from across the Xarafeille Stream."

"I am adequately refreshed," said Slith. "And I will not be hungry for a time. When will I see the Arbiter?"

"That is not up to me. I have only my instructions."

Slith nodded. Perhaps at the hotel, someone would be able to tell him what he wanted to know.

Now that he was on Newhome, Slith felt a sudden sense of urgency. He was so close to his immediate goal that he begrudged himself even a luxurious dust bath and the time to vacuum himself clean. He begrudged the time it took to arrive at the restaurant, and the waiting for a meal of exotic leatherbellies in cream sauce to arrive. The hotel folk had been able to tell him nothing. His arrival had been obviously well-orchestrated. Surely someone knew what was to happen next. . . .

"Sar Wrasselty?" that someone inquired. Slith looked up from the sole remaining leatherbelly still wriggling and swimming in the cream in his bowl. "May I join you?"

Slith nodded. He was enough inured to the sight of old-humans now that it would not spoil his meal. He pushed his bowl aside. "May I?" said the old-human, a youngish male, or so Slith thought him. Slith pushed the bowl to him, and he delicately lifted the leatherbelly, as fat with rich cream as Slith himself felt, to his mouth. "Not bad," said Slith's tablemate. "Sometimes they lose flavor once they get too full of the cream."

"I too have noticed that," said Slith wisely—though in fact he had never been able to afford that particular delicacy before, and had no idea how they should, or ordinarily did, taste.

"May we talk business?" the old-human asked. He proffered a flashy gold business card that bore his name in ornate ultramarine characters Slith could not read by the dim restaurant lighting, and the Arbiter's sigil, the famous balance-beam scale.

"You are the Arbiter's representative? Are you here to set up an appointment for me?" Slith thought the other man's arrival at his dinner table was most irregular.

"If needs be," the old-human said. "Consider this as an informal screening appointment. If all is in order, we will proceed. If not, I will expedite your further requirements. Now, tell me exactly what is the nature of your complaint."

Slith did so. He explained how Thradz had reregistered the Valbissag patents secretly, giving the former chief patent officer a false pretext to have him arrested for fraud. He told of his time in prison, of his research and writing, and of the irregularities surrounding the granting of his degree. He mentioned in passing the swift sale of his house, and his difficulties with Slem Banto and the basement vault. He bitterly recounted the award of his one single patent, the miraculous self-replicating crystal, to Gefke Jandissl, the tarbek lord of Low Diverness.

When pressed, he recalled further odd irregularities: the missing hololog of his meeting with the chief patent officer, and the trashing of the University contract that he had never signed by an untraceable, unexplainable current surge. "I think," said the old-human, "that something can be done. It is mostly a matter of correcting certain errors of record."

"What about my jail time?" Slith interrupted him. "What about my house, and reparations for my suffering?"

"There is that, too, of course," said the other. "I can see there are several things we will need. First, from the Patent Office on Phyre, we must obtain the entire contents of the data modules containing the Valbissag patents, and the one with your own patent now leased to the tarbek Jandissl."

"I tried to get those records before!" Slith protested. "They would not give them to me because of my false criminal record."

"This time you must use a different approach. And as the working copies of the records have been vulnerable to 'accidental' corruption, we must have the original datablocks, not copies or printouts."

"Impossible!" Slith expostulated. "No one is allowed near them. They are stored in secured locations, and guarded. Even a man with no shadow upon his record would not be allowed near them. Only a propertied nobleman or an official or . . ."

"Then, being a convicted felon, you must consider felonious means of obtaining them."

"I am not a felon! I am not a criminal or an expert in things felonious!"

"There is always a way around such things," soothed the old-human. "It may well be only a matter of careful research into the vulnerabilities of the Patent Office's security, and you are a researcher of proven merit, are you not?"

Caught between admitting himself a coward or an academic fraud, Slith did neither. "As you say," he muttered. "I will study it."

His tablemate nodded, satisfied with that—after all, it was not *his* risk any more than were the patents or house his! "Then there is the matter of access to your . . . or Slem Banto's . . . vault. . . ."

"Mine! It is my vault, whatever the ownership of the shop. The vault, the formulae, the . . ."

"Yes, of course! Yours indeed," the Arbiter's representative interjected quickly, forestalling Slith's indignant diatribe. "Yours—if we can only prove it. And as for that, I will need another data module, from the Registry, this time."

"Ah, and haven't I had enough trouble there, too? And for only a few record printouts? The irony of it all! The Arbiter's consul requires me to obtain mere printouts of records—which are denied me—and he sends me to Newhome for further help. Here I am, on Newhome, and what do you demand? That to accomplish the task of getting a few records, I endeavor the much more formidable and dangerous one of *stealing* the original data modules themselves! Where is the sense of it?"

The old-human sighed. "Nevertheless, there you have it."

"I protest! I must speak with the Arbiter himself. I am done with the flunkies and bureaucrats. Make an appointment for me."

"Very well," the other man said, again sighing as if overburdened by one too many vituperative fards. Again he proffered his business card, which Slith examined uncomprehendingly.

"What is this? I see no appointment time written here."

"Look more carefully, Slith Wrasselty. Look at the name on the card."

"I see it. What of it. A common name. I haven seen it somewhere before. John Minder. What of it? John . . ." Slith's nictitating membranes flashed down over his eyes, then back up again, as if to clear his sight, to verify what he had just comprehended. "The Arbiter's name is also John Minder, and you are . . ."

Slith shrank in his chair. He slumped not in awe of the Arbiter of the Xarafeille Stream, but in deepest chagrin, overwhelmed with the knowledge that his cause was lost, that there was no way he could avoid putting himself at further risk, and that the Arbiter had not helped him at all.

"There is an alternative," said John Minder XXIII. Slith looked up. "If there were only one crystal to be obtained, and if it were in the Fardish Archives, the History Division . . . would that simplify your task?"

Slith pondered. What were historic records to him, to his cause? Yet even felons were not barred from studying their history. Fard felons were still fards, and could not be denied their past, their very race—though few demonstrated much interest in their antecedents. The History Division was thus less heavily guarded and secured than the Patent Office, because of that very disinterest. "That might indeed be easier," Slith admitted. "What is it you want from there?"

"There is a datacrystal I need for . . . for my own researches. I would be quite grateful if someone obtained it for me. And being grateful, I might be inclined to sweep aside all the obstacles that surround the records you need, and to order a team of auditors to descend upon Thember, to freeze all the records, transactions, and documents, and to get to the bottom of your difficulties. If that proves unpolitic, I might instead reward you from certain discretionary funds."

"A datablock? A *single* datacrystal? One is surely easier than three. What module is it? How will I find it?"

The arbiter scrawled a number on a corner of a napkin and handed it to Slith. "This is its serial number. It should be easy to remember. There are exactly twenty zeroes."

Slith stared. 000,000,000,000,000,000,001. How did one say such a number? Had the numeral "one" been at the other end of the zeroes, he might have guessed "one hundred pentillion," but it was not. "That is number . . . that is . . ."

"Number one," the Arbiter confirmed. "It is the crystal first entered into the Fardic Archives on a far, forgotten world. It is so old that no one could read it on modern equipment even if they knew the passwords and codes, unless they had studied the ancient language it was written in. It is useless to anyone but me, and since no one can access the data in it anyway, none will notice a simple substitution with . . ." He paused, and reached beneath the table, then handed Slith a wooden box with a hook latch and tiny bronze hinges. ". . . with this."

Slith opened it, then shut it quickly. The crystal within the box glowed iridescent pink, as if with a light of its own. He was not confident. Surely the first fardish datacrystal ever was worth an incalculable sum, even as an unreadable antiquity. Surely it would be heavily guarded, in a special display case with alarms and sensors.

"There is no other way?" he squeaked. "No third alternative?" Even to fard ears, adapted to octaves higher than other humans could generate, it was still a pathetic squeak.

The Arbiter shook his head. "Deliver it to my consul in Thember," he commanded as he rose to his feet. Slith was so stunned, so overwhelmed with his own hopeless situation, that he did not realize he should have risen also. He did not realize it until long after the Arbiter had departed.

As Slith rose to depart, he saw something odd. On the smooth leather of the chair where the Arbiter had sat were two small flakes of something reddish-brown. Slith moistened a finger, touched one to pick it up, and held his finger to his nose. He sniffed it. "Swarrow root," he murmured. "I wonder where it came from?"

"Did I handle that one right?" John Minder asked himself. Fards were the most problematic of the human types. He knew that appeal to patriotism, human decency, or any higher code would have fallen on deaf ears. A formal audience would have been counterproductive also—being forced to stand at the foot of a raised throne, or before a vast, polished desk, would not intimidate a fard, only annoy him.

Giving a fard only one option was not practical, either. If it was not a suitable one—by whatever individual fard standard applied—he would pursue some parallel or circuitous alternative course that might meet his own needs, but not Minder's. Thus it was necessary to suggest several. The module or modules that held the patent records were of no use to the Arbiter, except that possession of them might be used to exhort Slith Wrasselty to further efforts later.

The Registry datablock was also of limited utility. It was of the same series as the one he, Minder, needed, but his agents' research led him to believe that the first of that series was a copy, and that the one in the Archive was the original. Possession of a later module might give his cryptographers a better sense of what he was seeking, but nothing concrete—the codes that would, in conjunction with the other six modules, release his inert fleet—would not be on it.

The Archive crystal—so old as to be unreadable by its owners—was the one he required. Had he been right to present it in such an offhand manner, as a possible simpler way for Slith to get what he wanted with less personal risk than he faced at the Registry or the Patent

Office? Would Slith take the bait and bring him what he really needed?

How much simpler it would have been if he could simply have *demanded* the seven data modules. But that was not possible. At best, he would expect at least one canny archivist to hold him up for a price he could not afford to pay, once his desire for the modules was known; his autocratic demand would raise suspicions that he had found some way around the ancient checks and balances his original namesake and the representatives of the races had created—checks both on Arbitorial power, mostly incorporated in his family's modified genes, and on those other races' ability to manipulate or command him and his office. In the worst case, knowledge of his present impotence would leak out, and the constant trickle of attempts to build interstellar warships would turn into a flood; then thousands of years of uneasy peace, all the effort of generations of Arbiters, would be wasted in vast conflagrations from which the worlds of the Xarafeille Stream would never recover. There would be a dark age, unlike any that preceded it, and no assurance that it would ever end.

Not for the first time, John Minder XXIII contemplated the frail vessels of human destiny—vessels like Slith Wrasselty on Phyre, like that big ikut and his bors friend on Glaice, and . . . What they all had in common was so pathetic—not ideals, but merely personal motive; not nobility, but merely opportunity: they were in the right place to get what they required, and they—he hoped—had the resources to get it.

CHAPTER 15

Pack no illusions in your traveling kit. On the Dry Worlds—as everywhere in the Xarafeille Stream—you will meet folk who seem entirely different from you. Rude fards who dwell in stone villages may compare unfavorably with the sylphlike presences who inhabit your own moist, green gardens. Rough, brash tarbeks who hawk tanned lizard skins from their market stalls may seem quite unlike the shy woodcarvers who leave carven flutes on your doorstep, hoping one may please you, and that you will leave him a coin or two.

Indeed, such differences are great—but beware! They conceal a dangerous similarity between you and those others; even though fard behavior and tarbek ambitions are not like yours, the intelligence that drives them is in no way inferior to your own. Understand that however different others are, however incomprehensible their goals, their capabilities are equal to your own, and their rages as deadly.

Know that, and your adventures among them may become the red spice of your old age's reminiscences, not a fatal dose of a darker blend.

> *The Wend's Guide to the Xarafeille Stream,*
> Volume 32, "In the Dry World Marketplaces,"
> Amos Parkoon,[2]
> Bermat Press, Newhome, 11994 R.L.

---

[2] Writing as the entirely fictional Minirelafen Pentranipet, "The Most Far-Traveled Wend."

Bleth returned to the bleak cave thinner than when she had left it. The soup of kroon liver she had ingested several days before had mostly passed through her undigested. The chalky milk substitute the orphanage had given her before that had sustained her, but not well. As a steady diet, it left her brain befuddled and slow, her motions sluggish.

In her weak and stupid state, only the encompassing vision of her nurse's full breasts had kept her feet on the proper path among the high desert's wind-worn boulders. Only her fierce determination to survive, to enjoy the fruits of her suffering, had kept her dulled eyes focused on the distant smoke column of Mount Afkak, as she trudged northward and upward from the highway into the wastes of High Diverness.

On the trip home to Phyre, Slith made little use of the library in his suite. The meals he ordered were even simpler than his earlier fare, because he had no taste at all for food. He sat at the table in his finely appointed dining room from the time he rose until the time he retired to his wide, comfortable bed, only stirring for infrequent trips to the automated sandbox to relieve himself. He sat, and he pondered his impossible situation. The Arbiter had promised nothing. He *might* reward Slith via those "discretionary funds." How much? The cost of his house, his business, and all of that he had lost? Hardly likely. And even if he considered it "politic" to send his auditors to Thember, what would they find? What good would his cleared name be, if he could not restore all that he had lost?

When the ship landed he disembarked sullenly and, as it was still early in the day, made his way to the University compound, to the one major edifice he had not yet visited—the Archive. Entering, he was not stopped by the single guard who dozed there, but he did notice the two small grilles, one on either side of the door, behind which sniffsnakes surely resided, alert for the scent of datacrystals or other contraband.

A brief examination of the records catalogue yielded no useful information. The oldest data modules still online or listed as available had seven-digit numbers, and were only centuries old. He sighed, and called up a floor plan and index of the museum portion of the building. The crystal he sought was an antiquity first and foremost. Perhaps in the Hall of Early Times he might find a clue to its whereabouts.

The Hall was on the fourth floor. He climbed from the first floor upward. It was as if the building had been designed to give indifferent fards an inescapable exposure to their history; the head of the stairs from the first floor was at one end and the foot of the ones to the third was at the other. Thus Slith had no choice but to follow a convoluted route among displays of no interest whatsoever in order to ascend another flight of stairs.

He breezed past showcases of traditional wendish musical instruments, blocking his ears against the recorded squalls and shrieks that demonstrated their capabilities. He ignored miniatures of great borish stamping-presses and other models of industrial prowess in his rush to get to the third-floor stairway.

Floor three held genealogical records. On impulse he stopped at a computer terminal booth labeled FIND YOUR ANCESTORS! In smaller print, it promised to trace the lineage of any tarbek back to his tribe's landfall on Phyre. Belatedly, he realized he had seen other booths specifically for fards and bors a few paces back, that differed from the tarbek one only in the height of the screen and the placement of the keyboard.

GEFKE JANDISSL, he typed. With all the dialects and accents on Phyre, a voice terminal would have been useless.

GEFKE JANDISSL: 12 RECORDS, the screen said. CHOOSE ONE. Slith touched the only one on the screen that had a birth date without a corresponding death entry. The screen refreshed, then displayed a series of options:

1) Ancestor Tree
2) Descendant Tree
3) Compressed Listing

Slith chose number one. The chart that then appeared told him nothing he wanted to know. He backed up to the menu and selected number two, "Descendant Tree." The chart was short, but so wide Slith had to scroll sideways several times to view it all. Jandissl had many offspring, but he was young enough that he had only a few grandchildren as yet, and there were no great-grandchildren listed. Slith ordered a copy of that chart for later perusal, and waited while it was printed out. He folded it carefully, and put it in a pocket of his smock.

Arriving at last at the fourth floor and the Hall of Early Times, he saw imaginative displays, mostly holographic, that illustrated the progress of fard colonization of the Xarafeille Stream. There were holos of old-fashioned starships that looked, to his unpracticed eye, no different on the outside from the one he had traveled on. Of course they had been different internally. In place of grand, luxurious staterooms the holos showed cramped and crowded barracks where pioneering fards had lain packed like podded seeds in a suspended semblance of life while generations of pilots and crew had sought suitable worlds on which to scatter them. Even with the first Arbiter's miraculous faster-than-light starship drive, such worlds were not easily found.

By the time the noonday sun shone in through the small windows set high in the hall's walls, Slith knew more of old fardish history than most fards learned in a lifetime—much more than any normal fard wished to know. But he did not know where to find one particular crystal that glowed peach and vermilion and pink, that looked just like the Arbiter's duplicate one now waiting in a storage locker outside the port area.

Slith did not dare inquire about the crystal—not, at least, until he had developed a cover story to explain his interest in it, and perhaps a false identity as well; he did not want the name Slith Wrasselty associated with a felonious doing even before the deed was done. The Arbiter's consul might be able to help him with that—the Arbiter had promised him all reasonable help, and an identity chip was surely reasonable, given the circumstances.

Slith left the History Division much wiser and better informed than before, but with the exception of his new grasp of the vast scope of fardish history, it was negative knowledge—he knew where the fluorescent pink and orange opalescent crystal was *not*.

He had money, or a means of getting it. The Arbiter had given him a card and numbered account at the Prospector's Bank and Savings Cooperative. He had few desires, though—few, at least that could be readily purchased. He wanted his name cleared of the felony conviction. He wanted revenge upon the treacherous and devious Thradz, whose trickery seemed the more despicable because Slith had not considered him capable of cleverness. He had feared violence from Thradz, heavy-handed and plain, but he had not suspected his brother capable of the kind of subtlety that he had shown by reregistering the Wrasselty patents quietly and not bragging about it.

Cataloguing his desires as he walked almost aimlessly to the storage locker where all his worldly goods resided, he added Lord Gefke Jandissl to the list of those he wished revenge upon: Jandissl, who was surely growing rich with the use of Slith's wondrous self-replicating molecule; Jandissl, who had—with such gall—actually sued him over Additive 3A, a false suit based on Jandissl's own stupid misunderstanding of the additive's utility. Or was it truly based only in unmitigated avariciousness?

Thought of his invention led to curiosity: How was the formula working? Did it live up to his great expectations for it? Had Jandissl's kin begun to spread outward into the marginal Vermous Hills? Since Slith had no clear plan how to satisfy any of his desires, and since he had a seemingly unlimited source of funds, he decided he could do no better than to go out there and see for himself. Perhaps a breath of fresh air—such as it was—and a few nights spent in the open would jog his creativity and give him some notion of how to proceed.

Perhaps too—if he were feeling generous—he might visit Thplet and Bleth in their distant exile. Surely the fardling had by now refixed herself on some other male nurse, or had learned to eat food, or had starved to death. He considered the latter overlong, surprising himself with a slight, guilty twinge and a vague sense of regret for paths not taken. If he did visit them, and found them alive, he might magnanimously release them from their bleak sanctuary by the simple act of informing Thplet that the "threat" from Thradz was now past.

Slith's immediate objective thus became an outfitter's shop where he could purchase what he needed for desert travel. Pedermat and Kneft was his choice, both because their outlet was nearby and because he had purchased things there before. They specialized in outfitting prospectors. He might, as long as he was there, purchase new and lightweight geological gear as well as camping equipment. It would not feel right, being out in the desert without the tools of his erstwhile trade.

At P&K he was unrecognized by the bors clerk, though the same man had waited on him many times before and had always been as fawning and servile as a bors could manage (though it was not one of their race's ordinary skills). Have hardship and disillusionment changed me so much? Slith wondered. Or was it only that he had arrived on foot, without panache or display, and that bors were not good at recognizing individual fard faces without such external cues as carriages with green and gold crests?

Nevertheless, the sight of the equally green-and-gold PBSC card guaranteed Slith polite and deferential treatment, and when he left the store an hour later he was both burdened and lightened. The lightness was his renewed faith in the goodness of humankind and the efficacy of green-and-gold debit cards. The burden, not great, was that of the most compact and technologically sophisticated gear that the Xarafeille Stream boasted. Why, his collapsible spectrograph fit in a case no larger than his forearm, and weighed only . . .

But Slith did not long contemplate his acquisitions. He marched—jauntily now—to the rail terminal, where he purchased a ticket on the high-speed train.

Ah, how good it felt to be away from cities, ports, spaceships, people, prisons, and all the other accoutrements of "civilization." The dry blowing sand whispered about his ankles. The faint sign of a krood burrow, which he skirted wisely, added spice to the air and a willful exuberant surge to his blood. *This* was life! This was the environment for which fards had been bred. All the rest was false and artificial.

That first day out, Slith walked lightly and tirelessly, and by nightfall he had left the railway far behind. He camped on the top of a solitary boulder with a view over miles of flat, gravelly terrain where nothing moved but the brushy tops of tasselgrab trees, the pale sandy wraiths of occasional dust-devils, and the slowly proceeding stars high overhead. Slith slept well that night, secure upon his lightweight yet soft and impervious sleeping mat, within the confines of his new repellant cord, which was saturated with an artificial oil superior to natural krood-tail fat for repelling vermin and bugs, an oil that never evaporated. He was far from any settlement that might produce inopportune fardlings but, nevertheless, he carefully arranged a sonic warning fence around his campsite. He did not wish to repeat his experience with Bleth, not yet.

When he awakened, finding himself still alive and alone and his mammaries unswollen, his new, optimistic attitude took firm hold. His dreams had not been of the past and his sufferings, but of a bright future of new discoveries, new patents, and new wealth of his own making.

PART THREE

LITHIFICATION

Sandstone, Limestone, and Shale

(HAPTER 16

Of all seven human races, tarbeks by and large
exhibit the very simplest manifestations of material
civilization, trading when necessary for the
amenities they are not equipped to produce. They
are, for the most part, simple hunters and gatherers
who do not stray from their seeps and wells, who
have no need for sophisticated vehicles, libraries,
or highly patterned behaviors.

The cautious tourist, however, will not equate
simple needs and simple methods with simple-
mindedness. A tarbek, in pursuit of his
streamlined goals, uses the same intellectual
tools as a sophisticated urbanite. Do not condescend.
Do not judge, lest you become incautious.

The Cautious Tourist,
Parkoon Publications,
Newhome, 12120 R.L.

Lord Gefke's lesser kin were indeed occupying the marginal valleys of the Vermous Hills. Driven forth by the
sheer concentrated essence of "Jandissl" that suffused
Low Diverness as unprecedented numbers of the lord's
females gave birth to his offspring, most males of cognate
lines or the subsequent generation took their females and
fled to the very limits of habitability. Slith assumed that
they paid well for the privilege of occupying the newly
opened lands, and that the payee was Lord Jandissl, having secured rights to the land while it was still worthless.

The migrating phenomenon, Slith remembered from his
studies, was called the Danl Boone effect, after an obscure early fardish explorer. As fards experienced it less

than tarbeks, perhaps Danl Boone had merely observed it in the other race, and described it. Slith concurred with various other academics in attributing it to an as yet unisolated pheromone. The effect was most clearly discerned in the species of spacegoing symbionts called "rats" that lived nowhere but within the walls and interstices of spaceship hulls.

Rats, when populations reached certain limits, were inspired to migrate. When this happened in shipyards, orbital spaceports, or graving docks, they merely occupied new or underpopulated ships. In fact, the covers on ducts and passageways of maiden vessels were deliberately left ajar to entice migrating rats abroad. Not that rats contributed much to the vessels they occupied, except feces and more rats, but they occupied a certain volume of space, and a unique econiche, and while they did so, it could not be occupied by other, perhaps less pleasant species that smelled bad, or stung, or carried nastier fleas or more virulent plagues. Rats had adapted. They were there to stay.

But sometimes, when no fresh rat-free environment was available, and when the local population rose above an undefined threshold, the entire rat population of a ship exhibited very specific changes in behavioral roles. Infants no longer squealed and nursed. Their new role was vastly simpler: they became meals for their mothers. Infanticide, at first, engendered fat and complacent former mothers—as long as the supply lasted.

Homosexual behaviors flourished to the point that little semen was deposited in receptacles appropriate for further rat propagation.

Inter-rat violence, hitherto limited to occasional tiffs, became rougher and more than common, to the point where "encounter" became synonymous with "slaughter." This irrational programmed violence in turn precipitated a fourth behavioral variation otherwise unknown: cannibalism. It might be argued that cannibalism was a subset or superset of maternal behavior, depending on one's scientific perspective, and given the common result of infanticide, but many students of rat behavior concurred that infants were not really rats until their eyes opened, or until they uttered their first semantically meaningful squeaks, or attained puberty, or . . . Nonetheless, the main objective was served: such rat populations were quickly and effectively reduced, usually well below the carrying capacity of their environments.

But the general phenomenon, known as "dahmerism" after some ancient and obscure rat or scholar, was of little interest to Slith Wrasselty. Perhaps, given the effects of Additive 3A without the release afforded by his miraculous self-replicating molecule as a well-water treatment, such words as "infant," "lover," "stranger," and "anybody" might have become, in some new tarbek lexicon, synonymous with "meal," but that had not happened. There had been new lebensraum for Jandissl cognates to occupy, thus leaving Low Diverness entirely to Lord Gefke, his females, and his very rapidly maturing offspring—who soon became too tough to eat, anyway.

Slith observed. Tarbeks sipped with relish from the springs and seeps of the Vermous Hills, waters which had once been poisonously pure. Tarbek semen swam, fought, and sought appropriate fulfillment within the confines of their newly hospitable waters. Tarbek females reluctantly, inevitably, necessarily visited those wet places.

Slith observed. A female tarbek approached small Defkapple Seep warily, hesitantly. Her thin, dull fur was dry and her skin had the unhealthy pallor of water-deprivation. At the edge of the muddy pool she squatted—all bones and knees, and coarse, callused elbows—and dipped a finger in the muddy ooze. She drew her wet digit across the back of her other hand, and she sighed. One small streak of skin softened and brightened to a healthy orange hue. One carroty digit stood out among its colorless companions.

Slowly, cautiously, the female dipped her whole hand in the seep, and dribbled opaque water on her opposite arm. Hand and arm immediately took on color. She sighed with—or so Slith interpreted it—relief. Driven perhaps by the uncomfortable contrast between *dry* and *wet*, or perhaps *pallid* and *orange*—or even between *feels awful* and *feels good*—she proceeded to spread liquid muck on her legs, her shoulders, and up and down her ribs. She was, Slith observed, very careful not to allow the slightest trickle to make its way anywhere within the vicinity of her vaginal opening.

After repeating the dampening process several times, the female arose. She sighed pitifully. Even from where he hid, the sulfurous offensiveness of that sigh, unfiltered by veils, almost overpowered Slith. He fought the impulse to retch, which would have revealed his presence. The female took three steps from Defkapple Seep. There she paused, locked—or so Slith surmised—in a prolonged battle of competing necessities.

Her skin glowed healthy vermilion, and her slicked-down fur, though sparse, had taken on a healthy luster. Yet she was not content. Invisible to Slith, one small portion of her anatomy remained unsotted, and its nerve endings transmitted demanding discomfort that was made all the more poignant by contrast with the pacific state of all the rest of her subcutaneous nerves.

She grunted wordlessly. Tarbeks were not known to mince words, or otherwise employ them, when an inarticulate noise would suffice. She returned to the seep. With infinite care, she dipped a finger in the water, let most of the droplets fall from it until it was merely moist, and reached between her legs. A beatific expression spread across her craggy features. Had she been wend, bors, or fard, Slith might have interpreted it as a sign of supreme solitary sexual gratification. As she was a tarbek, he quite correctly considered it as fleeting and temporary relief. Again she reached into the seep, and again let her fingers drip almost dry before replacing it in her most personal shadows. Again, her eyes widened and her jaw drooped. She grunted. Slith did not try to interpret it. Her hand trembled. Her fingers splayed wide, and her hand and arm seemed to move of their own volition. The wide-eyed tarbek watched, her horny-skinned face expressing horrified, defeated anger as the hand moved inexorably and independently toward the water.

"Aargh!" she said. *"Aaraghak, Aanardle!"* and plunged her hand into Defkapple Seep's addictive substance. There she squatted, madly splashing water up at her crotch, groaning, gobbling, grunting with supreme agony

and relief. *"Vadgh! Mfkat ragh!"* she said. Slith translated: "Oh, shit! I did it!" Again a beatific look crossed
her countenance. She muttered quiet words, and then
shrugged. "Oh, hell. Why not?" she had said. *"Megript
arhp aartenk"*—"The damage is done." Somewhere, in
some splashed droplet, had swum a single tarbek sperm,
an energetic, dedicated, motivated sperm. In fractions of
a second, responding to the subtlest cues of femininity, of
proximity to its natural goal, it had expended eighty percent of that motivation, dedication, and energy in a mad,
thrashing, tail-whipping dash. In mere seconds thereafter
it expended the remaining twenty percent in a slightly
easier swim across vast, uncountable, inches into the wel-
coming darkness and, at the end of its resources, had
there found fulfillment. Respite. Completion.

The new being created in the merger was no longer
sperm or egg, but already a complete cell—no, two cells
. . . no, four—triggering hormonal messages that burbled
into the newly pregnant tarbek female's blood and neuro-
transmitter messages that pulsed along her nerves. Within
moments of the unwanted joining, she knew of it.

"Oh, hell. Why not?" she had said, plunging headfirst
in the murk of Defkapple Seep. When her head emerged,
Slith felt no need to translate her satisfied sighs and de-
spairing grunts into words. He departed quietly, having
seen enough. His crystals worked in every way intended.
When she did speak in actual words, he was already too
far away to hear them. He hurried away because he
doubted his ability to withhold his triumphant laughter—
and an angry, depressed, and pregnant tarbek was not to
be taken lightly. Shorn of curses, blasphemies, and vitu-
perations meaningful only to a tarbek female, her words
amounted only to this: "Oh, damn. Oh, hell. Pregnant
again."

Everywhere it was the same. Tarbeks infested the once
quiet valleys that had formerly known only kroons,
kroods and wherts, insects and scorpions. They ate
(though Slith did not wish to contemplate just *what* they
ate). They mated (in distant tarbek fashion, though, as
Slith had recently observed, that was no less intense at

one remove), and they did other tarbek things of no significance or possible interest to a fard.

Slith contemplated the value of the real estate the Jandissl clan had gained at his expense. He calculated the past value of the entire Vermous Range (which was zero, of course) and added to it what he might have charged the tarbeks for it, had he only acquired it before he, or Jandissl, had doped its water sources.

He became freshly enraged. The profit should have been his, not Gefke Jandissl's! His discoveries, his formula, his Additive 3A, had set the stage for it, as had his years of work. And what did he have? Nothing. Or rather, a criminal record and a meeting with an Arbiter who made ridiculous, impossible, and risky demands.

That, then, was his situation. He vacillated between thoughts of developing entirely new resources, patents, and thus sources of wealth, and of satisfying all (or the minimum necessary part) of the Arbiter's requirements. Both courses of action had appeal. Was there any reason he could nor pursue both at once? Was there no possibility that, by doing so, he might achieve other objectives also? Objectives like revenge? The idea had a certain elegance to it.

As with all things worth doing, preliminary study was required. And where better to begin than the highest ground, with all Fellenbrath spread out below him, a vast canvas upon which to practice his arts? He considered: the Vermous Hills were foothills, and above them— beyond the Valbissag plateau to the north and west of them—were the high range where clouds impaled themselves and gave up their water to the sere, rocky crags. Up there, among the clouds themselves, might he gain some perspective unavailable below? And after all, he had no better idea.

Happily for Slith, not all the high peaks were active volcanoes, belching filth and poison into the air he must breathe. He chose a course that avoided the worst threat of gas flows, a sinuous trail that wound upward through valleys carpeted with groust and thimblewort which could not survive in noxious air. Barring catastrophic geological events, he should be safe there. He passed through layers of wispy clouds as he rose higher, clouds that obscured his immediate back trail, but as they did not extend far from the crags that generated or collected them, they did not block his further view. There, far off, was Low Diverness, a gray flatness of opaque gases held firmly in place by thermal inversion effects. There, but not so far, were the protruding tops of the Vermous foothills, where the foul vapors flowed and ebbed with the time of day and the vagaries of volcanic pressures within the planet. Nearer still lay southern Valbissag, though the town and the spring—and Thradz—were far to the north. At the limit of even Slith's superb fard vision was a smudge drifting from industrial Krat, and the Thember road.

High Diverness was mostly hidden beyond the curve of Mount Curble, which Slith was ascending. There, far across Valbissag, Bleth and Thplet awaited his call. Far to the south and east, also invisible with distance, was Thember. But no, there was a haze on the horizon, a haze of water vapor that could only be an effusion from the city, where water was sprinkled upon the ground to moisten offworld plants, where it flowed from ventilators and humidifiers and bathroom fan ducts. So there. All was visible, all the elements he must consider, except one: he would have to wait for night to view the Xarafeille Stream in all its scintillant glory, and would have to guess where, in that tremulous veil of stars, lay Newhome, and the Arbiter himself.

One of Slith's acquisitions from Pedermat and Kneft was a botanical and zoological reference chip that fit in his new voice-keyed computer, which in turn fit in the smallest pouch on his tool belt. With that handy source of information, he was able to identify species hitherto unfamiliar to him; the high ridges were unfamiliar territory for him, and though there was a certain overlap with the lower lands, plants and insects at home in both locales, there were also unique varieties unknown in the lowlands.

To the shallow thinker, knowledge of such things might not seem vital to the realization of Slith's complex desires, but Slith himself was not shallow in that respect. All the universe was, in his eye, one vast, interrelated complex of phenomena. The shape of the universe determined the courses of stars, and exploding stars transmuted hydrogen and helium into the heavier elements that made planets and more stars. Planets, in turn were crusted with minerals, chemical compounds of amazing variety. There were quartzes (sands, glasses, and hexagonal crystals) and feldspars (plagioclases, anorthites, orthoclases in white, pink, gray, and red) and sulfates and sulfites, nitrites and nitrates, ferrous minerals and ferric ones. Somewhere, within some rock, every element that occurred in the natural world was represented.

Such minerals only rarely existed alone. Most were intimately associated with others, and the particular combinations of minerals were called rocks. Where thick magmas congealed slowly, allowing large crystals to grow, quartz, mica, and feldspar together became granite. Where the cooling occurred more rapidly, and only microscopic crystals formed, such rocks were rhyolites. Where orogenous movement of the crust occurred, heat and pressure squeezed granite, flattening and aligning and distorting its crystals, metamorphosing it into gneiss.

Gneiss, granite, and rhyolite (and many other rocks of varying compositions) were eroded by water, wind, frost, and the plodding footsteps of bors, the mincing lightness of fardish treads, the burrowing of kroods ... and the detritus of such rocks was called sand, or lime, or mineral-rich water. Feldspars weathered to clay, quartz to sand. Clay, as it washed into quiet pools, slowly compressed into shale, and sand into sandstone. Again squeezed and heated as they sank beneath the weight of further erosional deposition and were racked by crustal movements, shale became slate, and sandstone became quartzite. Limy water released its burden as ocean-bottom ooze, which hardened into limestone, which was metamorphosed into marble, which ...

For Slith, such things were only beginnings. As the veil of the Xarafeille Stream lay lightly across the black depth of the universe, so sparkling, moving life lay across the bones of the world. And life responded to rock, and to the soils that exposed rock eventually became. The offworld pine trees bors loved favored acid, sandy soil of weathered quartz, while native carrowroot preferred limy

playas and alkaline gypsum flats. Red toegrab vines grew
in blowsands weathered from specific quartzites that were
rich in needle-like microscopic rutile crystals, and nowhere else. Thus as Slith walked, and observed what
grew, or did not grow, beneath his feet, he often knew
what soil he trod, and even what rock lay beneath it.

When his feet disturbed a nest of hotspit spiders, he did
not see them, but knew from hearing the crackle of their
acid droplets alone that tenuous ragthistle roots spread
through the sand, because hotspit spiders ate only
ragthistle nuts, which grew from the roots. From the
ragthistle he knew that the sand was rich in iron, or it
could not have grown there. Because the valley he tra-
versed had no outlet, and because the thick stratum of
rock exposed ahead of him in the wall of the declivity
was red, and sloped downward toward him, he knew that
he was viewing (and walking over) a particular sedimen-
tary layer called the Gleventrap Formation that was
formed in an ancient seabed then uplifted to mountainous
height in some only slightly less ancient orogeny, and he
knew that the valley-floor sediments were derived from
it.

From that knowledge he could surmise, with some degree of confidence, that the dark brown layer above the
Gleventrap rock was the Selderbeck Shale, and was younger. The gray lavas over the Selderbeck (that, where exposed, weathered to a nutrient-rich loam supporting
tumbleweeds and primrose) were recent, products of
Mount Curble during its more agitated phases.

Further, and finally, insofar as Slith Wrasselty was concerned, some rocks were porous and allowed water to
flow through them, and others were not. Gravity (a function of planetary mass that allowed rain and hydrostatic
pressure, and thus aquifers, springs, and seeps) worked
equally upon all, but with various results. Is it any wonder that Slith, immersed in the knowledge of such com-
plexity, might sometimes fail to take into account the
topmost layer of all, the thin human veneer upon Phyre's
surface, which had additional complexities of its own—
sex and reproduction, wealth and starvation, comfort and
suffering, and whether to have curdlefruit pods for dinner,

sauteed in milk, or to dine on beef sirloin imported from
Bekmadder, Xarafeille 1032, far across the known galaxy?

But now, atop—or almost atop—Mount Curble, with
all those millions of acres spread before him, Slith attempted to create a grand synthesis of what he knew,
what he did not know, and above all, what he wanted to
accomplish. There, in thin air that would have addled a
wendish brain, he considered his goals and his resources.
There lay Low Diverness and the Vermous Hills, infested
with Jandissls, a complex of people, plants, animals, rock
strata, and assorted waters rich in diverse minerals. Here
were valleys where rains sometimes fell, where cloud
masses deposited dews that ran down and were absorbed
by soils, by plants, by bugs of all sorts. Here was where
he would begin. The trail from dewdrop to the inner mo-
tivations of Lord Gefke Jandissl was not an obvious one;
the further track from there to the official buildings of
Thember was less so. Yet they were connected, and they
led by an even less obvious way to the Arbiter, on
Newhome, and back once again to Phyre, and to Slith
Wrasselty. It only remained to tweak the system a bit
here, massage it there. It was, as Slith conceived it, like
pulling on the end of a very strong string: if there were
no tangles, the bell on the far end would sooner or later
ring.

CHAPTER 17

For the most part, the V chromosome's hox-type genes merely regulate the actions of existing structures common to all humans; few of them actually code for anything not present in the old-human repertoire. Their effects are a matter of *when*, *where*, and *how much*. That is a good thing, from my point of view, because as Arbiter I must myself draw on those human capabilities that "typify" the variant races. At times I must be a superb technician, and thus much like a bors; my work sometimes calls for the fine sensitivities and sensibilities of a wend, the bold strokes of a tarbek lord, the determined acquisitiveness of a mantee, or the grasp of fine physical distinctions of a migratory ikut *shahm*. Yet most of the time, faced with situations composed of variables so sensitive and so intricately entwined as to seem purely chaotic, I must be, above all, a clever fard.

James Minder IV,
Unpublished diary,
Erne Museo, Newhome, 4321 R.L.

Slith's first task was to create a landslide. Moving eighty million tons of black, dense lava was not an obviously easy task. With pick and shovel, bucket and wheelbarrow, it would have taken hundreds of years to accomplish. It was much easier to walk about the rather small valley where the top of the Selderbeck Shale outcropped, looking for tiny brown leaves. The mountain pissberry was not named for its flavor, but for the sound made when one squeezed its fruit in the dry season. The berries, on mornings when there had been a substantial dew to swell them, actually tasted more like cinnamon tea, which bors loved. As fards would have preferred piss to cinnamon tea, Slith did not taste them. But where the mountain pissberry grew, beneath was the hidden Selderbeck Shale.

What he did do was dig a very small trench along the valley floor. It was a high valley, and there were other, bigger ones, farther down. As he had a very good eye for elevations and slopes, he was sure that his little ditch ran evenly downhill from the head of the valley to a point halfway down. Beyond that, no ditch was needed. When he finished his excavation, adhering to his commitment to maximum effect and minimum effort, he packed up his gear and departed. He would not return there except perhaps in years to come, for sentimental reasons.

Slith's next self-appointed task was not so easy. He surveyed the High Pan, twenty miles west of Mount Curble, and established that no rootmat plants grew there. He was sure they did not, or had not in the recent past. If they had, his earlier life would have taken a different course than it had. Never mind how. He knew it, and that was enough. But that did not matter to him now. Life was as it was. The future was as he would make it.

Another twenty miles westward lay another valley, where rootmat did grow. Unfortunately, it did not put forth seed pods unless there was rain. There Slith waited, and watched clouds. He waited for three days. Finally, a cloud in the southwest hinted that there might be rain soon. It was not a rain cloud, but a mass of high-flung ash from a distant volcano, Mount Blag, that erupted (or had, in the past, erupted) on a regular schedule. The fine ash particles, blown against the high peaks of Mount Curble and its companions, had been known to provide the seeds of raindrops. Water vapor supercooled at great heights, and the minute ash particles disturbed the water molecules just enough that they condensed. The consequent larger particles that formed, composed of ash and water—or ice—attracted more vapor, and grew. They grew heavy and fell, and as they fell into warmer air, they

melted. The tiny ash particles were no longer of consequence. They had done their jobs; rain watered the land.

Rain fell on Slith Wrasselty, who hated the feel of it on
his fur and skin. It fell on the ground, and seeped through
to the rootmat's root mats below, and within hours, the
mats put forth fruiting bodies with all the hasty eagerness
desert plants usually demonstrate when rain comes. Slith
went to sleep wet, as did the rootmat plants, but morning
found both dry. The first rays of sunlight shined on Slith,
and on the vast field of already-dry rootmat pods that had
formed and grown during the night.

Slith gathered pods. He emptied his knapsack and filled
it with them, and he carried it to his campsite. Along the
way, the pods, jostled, popped open and spat seeds.
Slith's jittery fardish steps jostled seeds and pods, and
by the time he arrived at his campsite, he was able to rake
the pods out, leaving the seeds at the bottom of his sack.
Those, he transferred to geological sample bags. Then he
went back for more.

In two days, he had collected enough seeds for his purpose. His belt was hung with sample bags. So were his
knapsack straps. His tunic bulged with them. When he
walked, he swayed and rolled with the weight and bulk of
rootmat seeds he carried, and it took him twice as long to
return to the High Pan as it had to come from there.
When he arrived, he divested himself of his sample bags
one by one, scattering rootmat seeds over the entire valley. He was very careful doing all of that, and he wore a
filter-paper mask, because rootmat seeds were tiny, and
had been known to lodge in a person's lungs, and to grow
there. By the time the seeds found out that human lungs
affected young rootmats much as gibberellins affect carrots, making them grow fast and spindly, it was too late
for them to choose a new home. They became infected
with several toxic (to rootmats, though not to humans)
molds, and died. Unfortunately, it was invariably too late
for the seedbed, too. The person usually died before the
rootmats did.

When all his seeds were scattered evenly across the
High Pan, Slith departed. When he was well away, and
standing with the wind at his back, he beat his tunic until

he was sure that the breeze had carried away any clinging seeds. Then he beat his knapsack. Then he ruffled his fur. Finally, he removed the filter paper mask he had taped across his face, and threw it away—downwind of himself.

Slith celebrated another task completed with a tidy meal of krebbet eggs—raw—and several chewy orange roots he had collected higher up in the mountains. There would be no visible results of his task until two rains had fallen on the High Pan. That gave him plenty of time for his other work, which he would begin in the morning.

Much of Slith's work consisted of getting from one place to another, sometimes carrying things with him, sometimes not. Often, as has been seen, the jobs he performed when he got to a particular destination were not especially difficult.

In the course of a month, he seeded several other valleys with rootmat. After that he collected borax and gypsum flowers and ground them into a fine powder, and mixed them with spores of the esophagus fern that grew in a cave he knew of. The mixture he poured into a krood carapace—an empty one. (Kroods, when living, admitted only things they found tasty into their carapaces, and those in small chunks via their gaping mouths.) He affixed a hollow stem atop the krood's former neck hole, and plugged its nether hole and leg holes with clay, thus making a dust-blower that distributed his mixture as a fine cloud when he blew in the stem.

He dusted the entire volume of Karibekl Cave—seven miles north and west and upslope of Valbissag, opposite of which lay the Vermous Hills—with his powder. He had to do that in several stages, over eight days, because though the spores immediately killed the fat, ten-inch-diameter pillowworms that inhabited the cave, the borax and gypsum took longer to desiccate their carcasses, often a day or more, and as the worms packed the cave so tightly a slim breeze could not have gotten through it, he could not get to the deep parts of the cavern until he had cleared a path that was free of worms—though it was now littered with crunchy, dried worm skins. As pillowworms were about ninety-eight percent water, the skins took up little room and provided no obstacle. Finally, his vermicidal task finished, he again departed without further ado.

The next time it rained, and water ran into Karibekl Cave, new esophagus ferns would flourish. They would gobble the rocksprats that came to feed on the rain-swollen worms that were no longer there—they were not called esophagus ferns for nothing. The rain they did not need and could not absorb would run farther into the cave, and would turn the vast assortment of droppings from previous preworm inhabitants of the cave into a noisome mud. Some of those previous denizens had surely been eyeless cliffhangers, which liked all dark caves except the ones with pillowworms in them, and which only came out of them on moonless nights. Slith was counting on that. Stupid Gefke Jandissl probably didn't know the least thing about pillowworms, caves, esophagus ferns, cliffhangers, or aquifers. Stupid—though far too clever—Thradz, Slith was sure, knew less than nothing about rootmat plants, mountain pissberries, or aquifers. "Too damn bad," he muttered in his sleep, when all was ready for the next stage of things. "What you don't know can kill you." Not that he had killing in mind, of course. Slith was not vindictive. Not especially, for a fard. Though when he thought of it, what he had in mind for Thradz and Jandissl was probably worse than killing them. He would have to ask their opinions, when all was done.

Now the groundwork was laid. Slith's next task was oriented more to people than to the complexities of geological strata and the biota that flourished on them. He would visit Thplet and—if all was well for her—Bleth. It was a four-day walk. Lightly burdened, Slith arrived just past midday and did a bit of scouting. Blendernet Seep showed signs of a human presence: a series of hand-dug pits in the moist sand where visitors had collected water; scrabbled gravel behind a low-growing juniper where fards had defecated; a foil wrapper, still bright green and smelling of mint, that bore the crest of the Hotel Xarafeille. Yes, Thplet had done his bidding, so far. Of Bleth there was no clear spoor.

Slith next sought the cave he had shown Thplet on the map—the only natural shelter within a day's walk of water. They would be there. Arriving, he lingered outside. Other things might also be there. He had no wish to explore the cave. "Thplet!" he called from the entrance to the dark place. "Thplet! Are you there? It is I, Slith!"

"Slith!" said a voice—from behind him.

Slith turned, his fur on end. "Ah, Thplet."

"Have you come for us at last? I was about to despair. Where have you been? I sent a song scorpion with news of our bare survival here, but you did not respond."

"You wasted a scorpion on that?"

"Wasted, you say? *Wasted?*" Thplet was more than annoyed. "There are still a dozen. Be glad I did not eat them!"

"They are toxic. You would not eat them," said Slith.

"Oh? They might taste better than what I *have* eaten, in this wasteland. I might have died—and that would have improved the quality of my existence whole orders of magnitude."

Thplet's hyperbole made no logical sense, but Slith caught the meaning of it: Thplet did not like High Diverness. But no matter. Slith had not liked prison, at least at first. He had not liked Thradz, either, or having all his well-laid plans destroyed by avaricious meddlers like Lord Gefke Jandissl. What one liked or did not like often had little bearing on the realities of existence. "Still, you are alive, and retain the capacity for unhappiness," Slith said by way of consolation. "That is more than the dead can say."

Thplet snorted. That is, had he been a bors or an old-human he might have done so. Being a fard, he released a very small breath from his nose, and made a finger-sign for blowing sand, coupled with an expression of distaste. "What do you want?" He was sure Slith was not paying a social call.

"The song scorpions are well?" Slith asked. "The ones you did not send forth or eat?"

"I ate none. As you say, they are toxic and . . . They are well. They like it here, I think. Several of them have bred."

"Good," Slith said, relieved. "That is what I hoped to hear. I will take a clutch of younglings with me. When all is safe for you and . . . But we have not spoken of Bleth! Is she well? Did you find her a nurse?"

"She is well. She is in the cave, looking at you and listening to us, but she does not wish to speak. She does not like you anymore, I am convinced."

"After all I did for her?" Slith was indignant. "Where would she be without my milk, my care? Dried and dead in a blind canyon deep in the Vermous Hills! She owes her life to me!" He spoke loudly, with his head turned slightly toward the cave mouth.

"That is so," replied Thplet. "She also owes the quality of her life to you, in one sense or another, and I suspect that may weigh more heavily in the balance-pans of her small mind than the abstractions you cite."

"Abstractions?" Slith's indignance grew. Nevertheless, he stifled it. There was business to be attended to. "Bah! Fardlings are inconstant. Fetch the scorpions for me, then, if she will not bring them out." He waited, as did Thplet.

"I will fetch them," Thplet said when it was clear that Bleth was not cooperating. He entered the cave, and emerged shortly, with a box. "The dormant younglings are padded with moss. I trust they are all viable."

"They had better be," Slith responded coolly, "because I plan to send one to you when all is safe for your return. If all goes well, that will be soon." Thplet said nothing. He did not have to. His brother was quite capable of reading his expression. Thplet was very near the end of his figurative rope. "Which was the one you wasted?" Slith asked. "I hope it was not the one with a three painted on its carapace."

"Of course not!" Thplet replied with his own degree of indignation. "Am I a fool? Am I inconsistent? It was number one, naturally. Had you not come when you did, I was about to send number two, and then number . . ."

"Three, of course," said Slith, straining to keep his voice pitched reasonably. He could not resist a mild jab at his brother's lack of careful thought. "It was good that it was number one. The message you sent did not find me for several reasons. One was because that particular scorpion was hatched in our father's scorpion pen at Valbissag, and was intended for Thradz."

"For Thradz? Have you betrayed us? Why would you have a scorpion for Thradz? What would you have said to him?"

"What I would have said is of no matter. Perhaps I would have said 'I have cut off my balls and am sending them to you under separate cover,' or yet I might have said 'The treacherous Thplet can be found at this location,' or . . . It is immaterial. Now I can send Thradz no message at all via that particular bug. In future, send no scorpions, because none will seek me, or a place where I might be. Now reflect on what you have done. What, exactly, did you tell Thradz in your message?"

"I told Thradz nothing! I told *you* to come for us, before we perished."

"Yet Thradz heard it, not me. He heard at least that you are alive, which is more than he knew before. Alive, and what else? Did you tell him your location? Did you mention your plot against him, or anything at all about me? Reflect carefully. Both our lives could be somewhat dependent on just what Thradz thinks he knows of us."

"I said only 'Slith, we suffer! Come for us, or soon we will be no more.' "

"Ah, fine! You merely told him that I too am alive, so he will not cease to consider me."

"I did not. I merely said . . ."

"Bah!" Slith spat. "Just bear in mind that the other scorpions of the first generation were hatched in separate clutches, in different places. You do not know what destination number two would seek, were he freed. Perhaps your plea would be heard by the Arbiter, or a clerk in the Patent Office, or . . ."

"The Arbiter is on Newhome. The scorpion has no ticket, and cannot fly between the stars!"

"You distort my meaning. Remember only that the scorpions will go where I wish them to go—though I did not wish number one to go anywhere, with your trivial message in its tiny brain." Slith saw that Thplet was about to contest his choice of the word "trivial," so he did not pause for that. "I will tell you what messages to send and when. Perhaps you may discover whom they are intended for, or perhaps not, if I choose to be obscure. Do not use them for your own purposes, or you may destroy your only chance of ever leaving this place."

Thplet threw back his head and opened his mouth, a gesture that among fards meant helpless surrender. Perhaps it derived from the position a nurseling took when its nurse was too busy to stop what it was doing to feed it, yet did not wish to hear the nurseling's hungry whimpers. That had a certain programmed effect on Slith, who felt indulgent. "Ah, Thplet," he said. "The Arbiter is not so far away. Console yourself with this: while you have languished here . . ." He told of his visit to Newhome and of the task the Arbiter had set him, and of the possible rewards. Or, he told part of the tale. Of data modules he mentioned only the one purportedly held in the History Division—the one he had decided he did not need. If he had the other records, the consul could straighten out his affairs for him. The Arbiter could send someone else to fetch the data module he desired.

At first Thplet considered him delusional, his tale a figment brought on by too long a time in the desert sun, but Slith's command of details and his consistency eventually convinced his brother he was telling the truth, however amazing it was—and Slith's recounting had the desired effect of impressing Thplet with the importance of remaining there in High Diverness and not meddling in great events beyond his comprehension.

Slith again eyed the cave entrance. When he spoke, it was very softly. "Now tell me of Bleth," he said. "Is she well—and do not expostulate about High Diverness or the quality of your own existence. Have you found her a nurse, or has she learned to eat food?"

"She has a nurse," Thplet answered obediently.

"Ah. Then he is with her in the cave? Call him forth. I wish to advise him of her preferences, the little things that please her." Slith's visage was not capable of the subtle expressions an old-human could employ, but Thplet was sure his brother was becoming quite sentimental.

"He is not in the cave," Thplet replied. "He is elsewhere at the moment. He will not return to the cave immediately. Likely not until you have long since departed."

"Where could he have gone?"

"I did not ask him," stated Thplet. "I seldom do. Suffice it that he is as healthy as circumstances warrant, and that he has great affection for Bleth. If she has preferences or desires that can be fulfilled with what poor resources exist, he knows of them." Thplet drew himself up to his full—though still slight—height. "Now then," he said, all businesslike. "If we have said all that needs saying, I will beg leave of you. There is much to do before sunset. Water to be fetched, fresh thorn branches to cut to cover the cave mouth . . ."

Slith had no more to say. Thplet's petulance had cured him of any immediate desire to free him from his unnecessary exile. "Goodbye, then," he said. "Remember what I have told you. Await the return of these scorpions for further instructions." He held up the box.

Thplet only nodded. At a loss for further comfortable formality or closure, Slith turned, and walked away.

Shortly later, Bleth's nurse returned to the cave, and for long minutes the sounds of his ecstatic reunion with her could be heard in and immediately outside the cave, but none was there to hear them.

None was able to hear the conflicting voices within Bleth's small head either; even as she drew sustenance from her nurse, she railed at the combination of circumstances that had split her needs, cravings, and capabilities into two such disparate and unreconciliable parts.

On the one hand, she was out of touch with the resources of the civilized world, helpless to further her own future goals, dependent upon the breast of a male who did not, she was sure, even care that she had thoughts, feelings, and frustrations; on the other, she was neither hungry nor dead of starvation.

On one hand she wept for the fate of scores, hundreds, thousands of fardlings much like herself who starved and died routinely, whose deaths only served the evolutionary fitness of the fard race by the unreproduced demise of their unfit genes; on the other, she willed their deaths, for their was no room in the grand scheme of things for the incompetent. She knew—though she did not enjoy thinking about it—that she herself was poised upon a very sharp edge between future life and death as just such an incompetent fardling, and that no final decision in her case had been reached. Only if she survived long enough for her own plans to reach fruition would she bring those contrasting and contradictory elements together. Only then would her genes be proven worthy of being passed on. As for her hypothetical offspring . . . they, males or females, each with their own problems and solutions, would live or die, reproduce or not, according to their own fitness and their own individual luck.

CHAPTER 18

Tarbek intelligence, we previously observed, is not inferior to other races', only directed to different ends. It would be incautious indeed to assume otherwise. Yet tarbek behavior has been shaped by cultural and evolutionary circumstances unlike those which other races have experienced, for they have never been urban folk.

As culturally inculcated behaviors can be learned and unlearned, tarbeks can adapt their customs to urban milieus. The self-abnegation we call politeness can be imitated, if not understood. Genetically determined predispositions, however, are less amenable to rapid change. Studies suggest that empathy arises as a survival trait only after generations of violent death in the cramped confines of narrow streets and tenements has culled the most aggressive and unempathetic migrants. Urban tarbeks wear filter masks because they will otherwise be beaten, jailed, or slain, not because they can place themselves in the shoes of others, who would choke on their effusions. The tarbek does not *care* what others may suffer. He has not been bred to care.

The Cautious Tourist,
Parkoon Publications,
Newhome, 12120 R.L.

"A fard? Here? What brings you?" the tarbek chiefling asked. Slith reflected that he was at present a minor member of the Jandissl clan and thus of little stature. That was why his intonation and expression were rude; too few others were beneath him, and those above were quite powerful, thus he made the best of his limited opportunity to be rude and abrupt with impunity. "Perhaps you have come to stay the night?" the tarbek asked in mocking tones. As Slith would die in bed, poisoned by gases that would fill the whole valley soon after first light, to judge by the winds and the ominous yellow cloud in the west, he did not intend to linger there.

"I am from the Office of Fair Practices," said Slith. "I am here merely to establish that no fraud has taken place. I see that all is well, and I will now depart." He made as if to leave.

"Wait! What is this of fraud?" He glanced around at his domain of rock, sand, and sickly plants encrusted with the yellow dust of the last sulfurous cloud to pass by. "Is there a problem with my lease? I knew that Lord Gefke could not be trusted. . . ."

"I know nothing of leases," Slith stated. "I investigate more nefarious charges. Since your happy presence here refutes them, I will be on my way." That time, he actually took a step back the way he had come—only to be brought up short, and up, indeed, off his feet. The tarbek had lifted him by his scruff. "Let go!" he cried. "My fur will be ruined!"

"It is your baggy skin I hold," said the tarbek. "I will release you when I am convinced I am fully informed, and not before."

"My mission is confidential!" Slith protested. "I cannot speak of it to just anyone."

"Then speak of it only to Chief Megidly Aptop—that is me—and you may depart." He jiggled Slith up and down a bit. "What loose and flaccid skin you fards have. It does not seem to stretch much, though. Perhaps if I shake a bit harder . . ."

"No! No more shaking! The fraud concerns Lord Jandissl, it is true, but as victim, not perpetrator. His only guilt is foolish complacency, and not knowing much chemistry. Now put me down!"

"Will your volubility diminish if I do so? In that case, my arm is not yet tired."

"I will tell you everything you wish to know."

"I doubt that," Chief Aptop responded, shaking his head. "I *wish* to know only pleasant things of advantage to myself. Yet I will put you down if you promise to tell me what I need to know—which is everything about your mission."

"Done! A bargain! Now do so!" The tarbek let go. Slith's knees buckled momentarily, but he kept his feet and did not roll in the dust. "It is Thradz of Valbissag. It was suspected that he adulterated the substances he supplies to Lord Gefke for the befouling of your seeps and wells here. As you are hale, and as I have seen your wives drinking your water, and one even now bathes there, I know that the informer was a base liar with a grudge. He is Thradz's brother Slith, after all, and has reason for that. I will report that the precipitates from Valbissag and Thradz's other wells are pure and of full strength, and will add slander to the growing list of Slith Wrasselty's unpunished crimes."

"I have heard of Slith Wrasselty," Megidly Aptop mused. "Was he not the originator of the compound that sweetens our wells?"

"He was. It is of no matter. He is a liar and a slanderer, to so impugn his own brother's honest practices."

"And what did you say about Lord Jandissl? I remember hearing an insult. . . ."

"It was no insult. I merely repeated what is well known, that Lord Jandissl is not by profession a chemist! Thus if Thradz were supplying him with inferior substances, no one could rightly blame him for not knowing it until it was too late, until your wells became poisonously pure and your females became pregnant with funny-smelling fetuses."

"What? Is that what Thradz is doing? Say it is not so!"

"I did that. I said it several times. It is not so. I am sure the odors of your infants and infants-to-be are like strong perfumes to you! Do not lift me up again!"

The tarbek did not. "You are sure?" he asked.

"I am as sure as I can be. I am a renowned chemist who can tell with a sniff the exact state of your water. The evidence surrounds me. Now may I go?" The tarbek nodded. He seemed to Slith to be lost in thought.

When Slith was out of sight on a nearby hill, he peered from behind a boulder at the tarbek encampment. There, squatting beside the poor seep Slith himself would not have dignified with the names "well" or "pool," was Chief Aptop. Even Slith's farsighted eyes could not discern his expression at that distance, or determine if the hand he held to his face was indeed wet, but his posture suggested his attitude was pensive and perhaps a trifle insecure.

The next day a similar drama unfolded at the camp of Jerbik Traglot, another tarbek chief. It differed only in detail from the last one—the chief picked up the false inspector by his ears, not his neck skin.

Two days later, at a greater distance, but still within the area of new tarbek settlement, the script was played out one last time. It was the last time, Slith decided. All the necessary seeds were sown—and he intended to quit while he still had ears and a bit of fur on his neck. He wished to keep both.

Now all was ready. Slith could only wait for winds to blow, for rains to fall, for Thradz, Jandissl, Megidly Aptop, and a host of others to act and react. Still, Slith was not one to await events, but to create them. *Strike!* an internal voice urged him. *Strike now!* Yet he bided. One could not rush the rotation of a planet, the slow rise of mountains, or any other thing of real and enduring significance.

Slith, at loose ends, visited Valbissag. That is to say, he skirted the edges of the town anonymously guised as an impoverished prospector, keeping his fine implements well hidden. He once caught a glimpse of Thradz as his brother strode proudly and arrogantly past on some important errand. Thradz wore fine robes of Giovan thistledown and upland linen, and was surrounded by an entourage of females and fawning officials. "Your time will come," Slith muttered, raising his eyes to the clear sky, then scanning the far western horizon.

It came. Yet at the time Thradz did not know it. At first, even Slith was not sure. It came as a chill morning in the month of Rath. Rath always brought cool air to the high places, and even some relief to the desert itself. With coolness came dew: in a certain high valley the mountain pissberries swelled, and the air acquired a faint, distinct aroma of cinnamon. Yet Slith was uninterested in dew or pissberries. They merely indicated that the rock itself was cooling, and it was that change Slith awaited. The temperature of the peaks high above the valley dropped by a few degrees, and no rising heat drove passing clouds up and away from them. Blown low and strongly against the peaks, the clouds delivered their moisture to the western slopes as rain, and the rain ran down them.

A few trickles, by fluke of topography, even ran down the eastern side of the divide. One small gully filled with cold water moving fast, and the water lifted sand and silt. The water reached the valley floor, and found a new, easy path to follow in its rush to oblivion in the dry playa far below. It was a straight path, not a meandering one, and it led the waters close to the edge of the valley, which was composed of sediments weathered from the Gleventrap Formation; it was the ditch Slith Wrasselty had so laboriously dug. Above the Gleventrap lay the Selderbeck Shale, resistant to sun, but not to water. The shale drew the moisture to itself, and became dark with it. Shale, of course, weathers to clay, and much of the exposure was half clay already. Clay, when wet, is as slippery as grease, and the Selderbeck clay was like any other. The runoff once destined for the desert floor detoured through the shale and down the strike of the strata to the northeast. As clay is slippery, the rocks above the Selderbeck Shale trembled, as if in anticipation.

The principle was simple. Had Fellenbrath been a wetter planet, one with seas, seaports, and shipyards, it would have been often observed. One built ships on land, as a rule, and only then moved them to water. With that move in mind, shipyards were located on high banks, and ships were built on cradles, which sat upon ways. Those ways were like massive timber on iron rails, and when a ship was ready to be launched, the ways were greased and the chocks that held the cradle were knocked out. Ponderously at first, then with increasing momentum, the ship slid down the greased ways, and met the sea for the first time with a great splash and all the fury of a brief summer squall.

The ways were greased. They were the Gleventrap rock, which sloped downward. The ship—such as it was—was the mass of lavas perched high above it. The grease was the deteriorated, water-soaked Selderbeck Shale. With a shudder, the top of the mountain moved. Fellenbrath itself groaned with wounded agony. Ragwort leaves trembled atop the ridge. Within the soft shale, burrowing snegs, kroods, and scorpions scrambled for their exits as their tunnels first deformed and then were obliterated. Crushed kroods, snegs, and scorpions gave up their own moisture to the process, and perhaps hastened it by some immeasurably small increment. The lava, the ship of the high desert, moved on its greased ways and slid downward. Soil and pebbles danced on its deck. A bow wave and wake of dust and superheated steam marked its course. Downward it slid, and then plunged, and with an impact that seemed slow and ponderous from afar yet was cataclysmic to the denizens of the lower valley, the crumbling, cracking mass struck.

Dust rose over the valley bowl, obscuring all. It slopped over the edges like an unruly child's bathwater (though of Phyre's population none but bors, wends, and old-humans would have known what bathwater was). The dust did not settle for hours—but then, there was no one nearby to see what was happening beneath its obscuring blanket.

On the western slopes of the range, rain continued to fall, and some small portion of it ran eastward, and down.

Elsewhere, rain also fell. It fell on the High Pan, dampening the dry dust of that depression, and dampening as well the rootmat plants whose seed Slith had scattered there. An earlier rain had quickened the seeds, which had put forth roots, tiny shoots, and leaves. The roots had, true to their name, formed thick mats that greedily captured the present rain, every drop. No moisture got through them to percolate downward through the porous sandstones beneath High Pan, and thus none passed through a certain thin seam of limy shale that was rich in soluble organic oils. Thus the waters that saturated the Belastipet Sandstone, an aquifer that supplied the well Valbissag, were subtly different in composition than before.

The rain that fell above Karibekl Cave was no different from any other rain that had fallen there, over many centuries. It fell, it collected into runnels, which joined into trickles, which merged into a sizable stream that flowed into the cave. But where once thirsty pillowworms would have captured the first flow, would have swollen with it, would have blocked the entire length of the cave with their fat, waterlogged bodies, the water ran through, unhindered by the esophagus ferns that had replaced the worms. It carried thrashing, dying rocksprats and uprooted esophagus ferns with it. It swept hundreds of thousands of eyeless cliffhangers from their perches and drowned them. Their deaths were of no account, a mere side effect of Slith Wrasselty's efforts.

The rushing stream splashed into the deep caverns below, roiling the centuries' and millennia's deposits of guanos, dissolving the nitrates and phosphates and other more complex compounds within them. The waters filled the caverns and then overflowed them. And the waters ran down.

Near Blendernet Seep, Thplet and Bleth endured heat, despair, bad-tasting water, a foul diet of small things that trilled, rattled, and attempted to scrabble to safety beneath flat rocks, and they cursed Slith Wrasselty's name. Yet they eagerly awaited a message from him.

While all those events were in process but not yet complete, Slith had one final task to perform. It was risky, and he would have been tempted to leave it for last if only for that reason.

He carefully packed his knapsack. First in was a metal water bottle, followed by several layers of sample bags as padding. He then put four of the young song scorpions from Thplet in the sack, and padded them carefully. Each one's carapace was painted with the number fifteen. Atop them he placed a small glass vial filled with a purplish powder. He hung his geologist's hammer and several other metal tools on his belt, and set out for Valbissag.

As before, he entered the town without incident. This time, he had taken the additional precaution of dying his face whiskers dull brown, and had painted a line of sticky sap on his forehead, across his eyelid, and down his cheek. When the sap dried, it shrank, and gave him the appearance of having once encountered the claws of an enraged kroon. His destination, this time, was not his brother's residence, but the scorpion-keeper's yard, which was just outside the wall. It was a soft stone enclosure not intended to keep humans out, only to keep scorpions in. Slith was able to chip an opening in the base of it with no great difficulty. He crawled in. He quickly verified that the keeper was not present.

Only the breeding scorpions were active, and even they became torpid when Slith dusted them with the cark-root powder from his vial. He then examined shelf after shelf of dormant scorpions within the keeper's hut, and selected several which had numbers painted on their carapaces. He knew his father's numbering system, and did not believe Thradz, or the older keeper, would have changed it. He replaced four of those bearing the number fifteen with his own scorpions, and dusted the rest of the fifteens with enough of the cark root to send them over a threshold of torpidity from which they could not recover. He blew off the excess powder so it would not be seen. That done, Slith departed as he had come, repairing the hole in the wall with mud made with the water in his bottle.

Chief Megidly Aptop, having for many days tested his seep religiously, having for just as many days sniffed his wives and offspring for the least trace of foul scents that would have indicated that they were not, indeed, his wives anymore, or his offspring, relaxed into the humdrum daily rounds of food seeking, basking, and solitary fornication that was his habit. Jerbik Traglot and other tarbek chiefs, elsewhere, did the same.

* * *

At about the time that the waters pooling in the deep caverns below Karibekl Cave overflowed their containment, the first waters from the Belastipet aquifer reached Valbissag spring, and the last of the dust settled in yet another valley, revealing what had until then been obscured. Where a trickle of water had once run was now a great dam of black basaltic lava, and behind it pooled glittering depths. Where once a black lava cliff had risen, now a bare face sloped evenly down to the new dam. It was the Gleventrap Formation, exposed, only thinly overlain with remnants of the weak, claylike Selderbeck Shale.

Gravity, time and the flow of waters were Slith's allies. The unique compositions of the rocks through which those waters flowed were his weapons, and his knowledge of them, unsurpassed by the likes of Gefke Jandissl and Thradz, "The Valbissag," was his strategy and his tactic alike. But it was not yet time for Slith to act. *Strike!* his every instinct urged him, but he did not. He waited. And he waited longer. He would be able to see when it was time to act.

CHAPTER 19

There are indeed "magic numbers"—digits that
occur in significant circumstances more frequently
than chance alone would suggest. In human
biochemistry the number seven (or a multiple
of seven) occurs often where matters of reproduction
and parturition are concerned. "The seventh son
of a seventh son" is the tail end of two
generations. He typifies the terminal
expectation—as the last child of the last child a
woman could expect to produce and still count on
living.

> *By the Numbers:*
> *Explorations into the Human Condition,*
> Peterifemen Eldariken,
> Agevant Press, Newhome, 12145 R.L.

The tarbek female ambled down the dusty path to the
muddy seep. She did not want to go there, because she
was not presently pregnant, having recently birthed her
seventh sprat, and women of her line had been known to
die birthing an eighth or ninth infant. She did not want to
die in childbirth. Neither did she want to die of dehydra-
tion and consequent madness. Thus she continued toward
the seep.

Yet within the murk and mud, all was not as before.
Where the water had once been alkaline, it was now
acidic. Where once it had swarmed with Chief Aptop's
zygotes, now it was lifeless. Where once it had been as a
soothing balm to the skins of tarbeks, now it was not.

The woman's eyes saw the thin iridescent sheen on the
water, but her brain did not immediately register it. Yet

within minutes of having immersed herself, she began to wriggle uncomfortably. Her skin itched, and it felt warmer than the sun-heated water could account for. Yet she lingered there. She had not been inseminated—she would have known. If the water was, as it seemed to be, safe—in other words, if there were no viable sperm in it—she really should hurry back, and tell the other women. A single dip in "safe" waters would give each one of them a week, even two weeks, of freedom from pregnancy, because they could avoid bathing again for just that long. Considering the way tarbek females' body clocks wound down a bit with each succeeding parturition, that was the direct equivalent of a week—or two weeks—of additional life. Yes, she really should go, she told herself, and eventually she did.

First as a trickle, then as a furtive stream that continued all throughout the afternoon and well into the evening, women visited the seep. Most were not currently pregnant; when they looked about them at the others, it became apparent that Chief Aptop's seed had been weakening for some time. Almost all the women in his tribe were there.

The first woman to have visited the seep did not notice, right away, how soft her ordinarily horny skin had become, or how sensitive it was to warmth and light; it had become, after all, nighttime. Only when the first warm rays of the rising sun struck her did she see that she was as pale as a newborn—but her discovery was masked by a more immediate one: the sun's rays felt like flaming torches pressed to her skin. She shrieked, but by then no one noticed her howls above all the other sounds of agony rising from the tarbek camp.

Throughout the Vermous Hills, wherever tarbeks had settled, similar sounds could be heard as the sun rose over each camp. In a few settlements where the women had not discovered their wells' sterility as soon, no cries were heard until a few of them arrived in the morning and attempted to bathe. By then those waters, even purer and less wholesome than before, were so obviously poisonous to tarbeks that even the most desiccated women refused to immerse themselves.

When Chief Megidly Aptop returned from a night's exploration of his farthest boundaries, his small settlement was as if deserted. Yet there were sounds. There were whines and moans from within ramshackle stone huts, from beneath rocky overhangs and the shadows of boulders, and from odd, dusty mounds that had not been there when he had left the camp. Aptop prodded one such mound, and was surprised to hear his eldest wife's harsh cry: "Do not expose me! It burns! It burns!"

"What burns?" asked the chief.

"My skin! The sun!"

That made little sense to him. The sun was the sun, no different now than on any other day, and whether it burned, or glowed, or merely shone was a matter of philosophy for men, not old women. And no flame or smoke arose from the mound, so the other half of her utterance was also nonsense. He said as much.

Between groans, his wife explained what had transpired—but only after exacting a promise from the chief that he would cease poking her covering of soil, and would cover her more deeply once she had told all.

Chief Aptop did not stay to listen to her woes, once she had told him of the seep. He rushed to it to see for himself. He did not have to stick a finger in it to know that the water was now dangerously pure, that his zygotes were dead, and that he, and all his tribe, were in very deep trouble.

"It is that treacherous fard Thradz!" he bellowed. "He has ruined us with his greed! It is Lord Gefke and his incompetence as well!"

Throughout the Vermous Hills similar scenes were enacted. By afternoon, those tribes that were least affected were on the march. By shortly after dusk, all the rest were also. Without exception, their destinations were all the same: Low Diverness, and the "palace" of Lord Gefke Jandissl.

The nature of the trails and terrain insured that most

tribes met up with others as they trudged throughout the
night, and their chiefs then compared experiences.
Megidly Aptop's tribe encountered no fewer than seven
others before dawn forced them to allow their women to
seek shelter.

Jerbik Traglot met five other tribes. Mrapelk Plig, the
third tarbek chief Slith Wrasselty had visited in his guise
as an official from the OFP, met four. Each of those
chiefs enlightened the others they met. By nightfall the
second night, when they could again travel, all nineteen
chiefs were equally well informed of Thradz's criminal
skimping and of Lord Jandissl's incompetence, and all
had worked themselves up to fine, towering rages.

Slith did not see any of the tribesmen until they ascended from the hills and converged on the well-kept
road that led into Low Diverness. The road ended at the
"palace" of Lord Jandissl, which was no palace by the
definition of anyone not a tarbek. "It is surely too full of
holes to store dung in," a wend might have said. "A heap
of rocks, oddly regular in form, but obviously not made
by a creature of any intelligence," a critical bors might
have speculated, wondering what odd combination of
frost, wind, and scrabbling creatures had made it. "What
palace? What dung-silo? What heap of rocks?" urban persons of any race but tarbek might have asked, seeing
nothing but the rubble of the desert floor.

Slith knew what it was, though, and he had stationed
himself not far away so he would be able to watch the arrival of the ever-growing throngs of refugees from the
now-hostile Vermous Hills. When the throngs diminished
to small scattered groups and the groups to lone strag-
glers, Slith departed, satisfied. He walked briskly over the
Vermous crest toward Valbissag, but stopped short when
he reached the place where he had hidden his remaining
song scorpions. At last the suffering Thplet and Bleth
would get their long-awaited message. Would it please
them? Slith did not think so.

Lord Gefke Jandissl, in a mood divided equally between
rage and despair, also spoke to a song scorpion, one that

had first seen light and breathed air within the scorpion-keeper's yard at Valbissag. There it would return, once it was freed, to repeat Gefke's angry accusations—which were quite similar to those the false inspector had so fiercely denied to Gefke's three chiefs.

"Thplet!" the song scorpion shrilled. "Thplet! Hear me! This is what you must do."

"What I *must* do?" Thplet expostulated. "*Must?* My brother oversteps himself. I *must* do nothing! I will do just as I please. He should plead with me, not order . . ."

"Shut up, Thplet! Now we have missed part of the message." That was Bleth. Yet it was not the Bleth whom Slith had known and nursed. She was taller by far—almost as tall as Thplet (who was of no great stature, but was taller than most female fards). She was dry and spare, yet she moved with smooth grace, womanly grace. Bleth was almost mature.

"Be precise!" the scorpion was admonishing Thplet. "A single error in execution of my plan could cause it to fail. For you, that would be a permanent sentence of exile. Be warned."

"See?" complained Bleth. "We missed the most important parts!"

"It will repeat. Give it a dribble of that water." Bleth dribbled water on the bug's shell.

"Thplet! Thplet! Hear me! This is what . . ." the scorpion began again. As it rattled off Slith's message a second and then a third time, Bleth scratched notes on a wind-smoothed slate. She did not intend to spend her life in the wilds of High Diverness. She wished to live in a fine house like the one in Varamin Park, to ride in carriages drawn by four matched thribbets and to enjoy the civil greetings of Thember's most important citizens. She would make sure that Thplet followed Slith's instructions exactly—as long as there was hope of success and no clearly better opportunity.

She stationed herself beneath the shade of a rock that faced the unmarked trail to Low Diverness and to Valbissag, beyond. When it was time to act, she would be ready.

* * *

Slith, elsewhere, would be ready also. In furtherance of that end he unpacked a sack of clothing that he had ordered shipped from Thember, and hung various articles out so they would be neat and unwrinkled when he put them on. Then again he waited, suppressing the small, insistent voice that said, *Strike now! Destroy your enemies! Strike.* That would happen, he hoped, but in its own time. Yet it was not easy to loaf around his small, hidden camp, to drink bottled water and prepare meals from dehydrated food packs, to review again and again his tactics past and future.

Were his plans overly complex, liable to fail at some critical juncture? Should he have been more straightforward—perhaps have hired offworld bors mercenaries to storm the Patent Office in search of the datablocks? When he considered what he had done, and what he planned to do, the connection between the distant eruption of Mount Blag—which he had not even seen—and the rootmat bloom in High Pan seemed tenuous enough. That its eventual result had been the march of unhappy tarbeks upon Lord Jandissl's stoneheap palace seemed almost coincidental, though he knew it was not so. To conclude that the eventual repercussions of that eruption would be felt in Thember, and even on Newhome, seemed ingenuous in the extreme, beyond the bounds even of coincidence.

Slith shrugged. The plans were laid. All the universe was interconnected. There was no genuine chaos, only the proliferation of possibilities from millions and billions of very specific events.

Jawal ad Heim, Xarafeille 95

The crimson-clad old-human motioned the robed and veiled figure to join him at the base of the airship's ramp. Steeling himself, the Arbiter pulled the hem of his disguising robe above his ankles, and descended.

"Can you guess what killed them?" the consul asked, gesturing around him. Everywhere, pathetic crumpled heaps of cloth and flesh were strewn across the dry ground.

"I see no wounds," said the robed man, his words slightly muffled. "Poison comes first to mind. Did fards do this?" All the bodies were tarbeks, none with any discernible sign of what had killed them. "No," the Arbiter said, retracting his first speculation, "it was not any poison I know of. Even the most toxic gases do not act quickly upon tarbeks, and these all fell before they had time to react at all." He pointed at a woman who had slumped over her cooking pot, her hand still in contact with her stirring stick. The dry air had stolen the moisture from the crusted porridge, and from the tarbek as well.

Nearby, in the doorway of a stone hut, another female sprawled, reaching for her infant, who lay just beyond her reach. The youngling's arms, legs, and neck were all stretched out from its body, an unnatural posture for the living or the dead—and the baby was quite dead. "Electroshock," Minder speculated.

"We thought so at first," the consul replied. "But there were no burns at all. A shock rod always leaves burns. We examined over fifty bodies and no burns."

"How many died?" Minder asked.

"In this camp, over a hundred—and there are many camps. It will take us weeks even to inspect all of them. So far, not a single band we have located has escaped death."

"I have seen enough," the Arbiter said, shaking his head slowly, sadly. "Let us walk outside the camp. If I find what I expect, then we will know at least the *proximate* cause of these deaths."

On the slight rise of the dunes that encircled the tarbeks' pitiful seep, the past week's winds had obliterated most of the evidence that might have confirmed Minder's developing hypothesis. There were, however, several shallow depressions, symmetrically spaced around the camp, that might once have been of a size to hold a man. Sifting the flourlike, alkaline sand through his fingers, Minder lifted a roughly disklike concretion. "It is as I feared," he said, even more sadly than before.

"What is that?" asked the consul.

"Someone urinated here," Minder replied, crumbling the artifact. "It bonded the sand grains slightly. It was a copious urination, far too much liquid for a tarbek or a fard."

"Then wends did this! There are not enough of any other kinds of men on the planet to encircle a tarbek camp. But why?"

"The proximate cause of the deaths was sound—the overtones and harmonics of wendish flutes," Minder said. "The wends surrounded the camp, and all at one moment began to play notes that ruptured the membranes in the tarbeks' oversized sinuses, and their brains themselves milliseconds later." He brushed the remaining chalky dust from his hands. "To confirm the *ultimate* cause of the deaths, I must use the terminal in your office." He strode purposefully toward the waiting airship. Even though he was more lightly clad, the consul had a hard time keeping up.

"There you have it," Minder said later, handing the consul a printout of names, dates, and ships' cargoes. "The ultimate cause of death was . . . a rumor. A rumor, and the fear it engendered."

The consul did not understand at all, until Minder explained: Whilernemin Filess, a wend cloth-merchant, had booked passage on a starship, and at his destination had bought several tens of tons of a rare carnelian dye dissolved from the silk-lined breeding nests of a kind of worm. The extraction process was known only to the fards who had perfected it. The source of the nests was known only to the tarbeks who collected and sold them.

On the same ship as Filess had traveled Kradlaot Badrille, elected overchief of Jawal ad Heim's largest concentration of tarbek tribes. The Arbiter was not sure why Badrille had spent what must have represented all the Jawallian tarbeks' meager earnings on a single interstellar trip. The cargo lists revealed nothing. Nonetheless, he told the consul, he was sure that somewhere en route or at their mutual destination the two men had met, and had spoken. Minder did not know their words, of course, but he understood the import of them. Upon his return to

Jawal ad Heim, Filess had spread word among the wends that the tarbek folk intended to poison all of them.

"If you have any way to identify the corpse of Kradlaot Badrille, among all these or among others, then publish the fact of his death among the wends. If they are satisfied that Badrille *and anyone on Jawal ad Heim whom he may have communicated with* are all dead, perhaps the killings will cease. If you cannot find his corpse, I fear that the wends will not stop killing tarbeks until they are absolutely sure that they are safe from tarbek poisoners."

When the Arbiter had boarded his starship to return to Newhome, his consul pondered the vast, dry reaches of Jawal ad Heim, Xarafeille 95. Tarbeks had settled there first, over eleven thousand years in the past, and had spread out across most of the desiccated planet. The wendish population had later occupied the few moist, fertile valleys near the poles—valleys the tarbeks could not use; they could not breed in such pure waters. Both groups had maintained peace and their territorial boundaries for millennia; both populations were stable, or they had been so until recently. Had the tarbeks really began to breed uncontrollably? Had they in fact planned to poison the fertile valley? The consul, aghast, considered submitting his resignation.

Wends were not prolific breeders, and even a hint of what they considered to be overcrowding caused females to become infertile. Tarbeks maintained relatively constant populations by other means: poor food—and little of it—kept death rates for infants and females uniformly high. Where pressures rose anyway, males fought with each other, slayed infants and females, or attempted fruitlessly to mate with members of the same sex and with immature tarbeks—both of which often caused death for at least one participant. Mothers consumed the infants they might otherwise have fed. It was all quite cruel—inhuman, some might even say—but it worked.

The consul sat down at his terminal. Where, he wondered, scrolling through a database of all the worlds of the Xarafeille Stream, was Phyre, and what discovery had been made there that had such tragic effects on the world he was responsible for?

Slith Wrasselty, though the consul had never heard of him, could have explained it. All the universe was interconnected. "There is," Slith might have said, "no genuine chaos, only the proliferation of possibilities from millions and billions of specific events."

CHAPTER 20

The tarbek condition typifies the human female's
lot, though it is the extreme case, because wends,
old-humans, bors, and ikuts do not consistently
die after precisely seven births. Bors seldom
experience so many parturitions at all, but have two
infants each time; among bors clesiopause, the male
counterpart of menopause, is of far more impact.
Mantees, of course, are a special case entirely.

Among fard females the tarbek situation is reversed.
The menopausal fard female who has *not* birthed
her allotted seven infants dies. Two, five, or six
do not ease the death agonies or prolong life one
day. Only seven will allow the female to enjoy a
long child-free lifetime after age forty-nine (which
is the number seven times itself).

By the Numbers:
Explorations into the Human Condition,
Peterifemen Eldariken,
Agevant Press, Newhome, 12145 R.L.

"It is here!" thought Bleth. The song scorpion scrabbled
down the last obstruction between it and the place where
it had hatched. Already, sensing its nearness, it had begun
to twitter, and to utter scraps of what she suspected would
evolve into words. Whose words? Slith had not been specific. He had not explained enough of his plans to
her—or rather, to Thplet—for her to guess the scorpion's
message, or what might result from Slith's instructions
concerning it. From his point of view that was probably
smart, she mused. The less she knew, surely, the less
tempted she would be to attempt to manipulate events to

her own ends. She was not one to stir up a brew just to smell the bubbles, not knowing what poisonous sweetness they might contain. She followed the scorpion to the cave, noticing the number fifteen painted on its carapace.

"My Lord Jandissl," the song scorpion began, in what Thplet recognized as Thradz's voice, though diminished and reedy in reproduction. "I am amazed and aghast! I cringe at your feet, shaken by your anger, crushed by your distrust.

"Who has lodged this false charge against me? Who will profit from the breach thus created? Consider those questions.

"My sons, nephews, and cousins work into the night to determine what has caused this disaster. It may be that a distant earthquake has modified the constituents of my springs. I will find out, and I will rectify everything! Be patient! The profits, the success, the very existence of both our houses hinges upon it. Give me the time I need.

"I am Thradz, the Valbissag, and I am your servant."

"Ah!" said Thplet. "I smell my brother Slith's fingers in this brew. Whatever has transpired, he is behind it. Has he pissed in Thradz's wells?" Thplet grew pensive. "I am afraid," he stated. "The simple anger of Thradz was enough to fear. Now another, more dangerous element is revealed."

"Would Slith use us cruelly?" Bleth was uncertain. Thplet had not told her of his conversation with his brother, there in the Hotel Xarafeille. He had allowed her to keep certain illusions about her former nurse, though he himself had none at all, where Slith was concerned. Still, he could not, from what little he knew, discern where his own suffering would be to Slith's advantage, except that Slith had needed someone right at this spot, to intercept this very song scorpion. He said as much.

"Then we do not dare do other than what Slith demanded of us, do we?" Bleth said. "We must trust that he has not abandoned us, that his machinations will free us of this exile, in time." Grudgingly, Thplet agreed—but only because he feared that Slith had indeed thought far enough ahead to insure that he, Thplet, would not profit from thwarting him. Thplet lifted his foot, then brought it down suddenly. The song scorpion's carapace made a muffled, sickening sound as it broke—like bones snapping.

Then Thplet lifted a live scorpion from its basket—one of the original ones Slith had given him, one with the number fifteen painted on its back, in numerals identical to those still visible on the back of the shattered, leaking carapace on the floor of the cave. He sprinkled a cup of precious water on the cave's gritty floor, and placed the live scorpion in it. Not much later, the revived creature emerged and preened itself, scraping clinging grains from its shell.

Thplet cleared his throat harshly. Hearing that, the song scorpion focused its antennae in Thplet's direction. It was ready. "Gefke Jandissl!" he began, lowering his voice to resemble Thradz's. "I am offended! My formulations are perfect! If your poor seed withers and your wells fail, blame yourself. Have you peed on the baskets of minerals I sent you? Have you failed to execute my precise instructions for the compound's formulation?

"Have you send payment for the most recent batch I sent you? If not, do so now, if you wish the next shipment to arrive on time. I will send an apprentice with the shipment, to retrain you and your bumbling laboratory workers, to make sure they do not fumble again. I am Thradz, The Valbissag."

Thplet slumped. Had he sounded like Thradz? He doubted the tarbek lord would be able to tell, as song scorpions distorted low octaves quite badly. Yet that did not console him much. He was more concerned with what he—in Thradz's voice—had said. Jandissl would be offended, not pacified as Thradz had intended. There was no telling how he would react. Or rather, there was no way he, Thplet, could tell. Thplet was uncomfortably sure that his brother Slith had made his own prediction, indeed that he counted on it. But why? What possible motive could he have for setting Jandissl and Thradz at each other's throats?

* * *

"Bumblers? Bumblers! The fard goes too far!" Jandissl kicked the scorpion, and his tarbek roar echoed among the loose stones of his palace. His female cousins, his aunts, his sisters, and their infants—the latter of whom were all his children—trembled at the sound. The refugees who clustered in separate groups as close to the still life-giving wells and seeps of Low Diverness as they could, grinned fiercely when word of Lord Gefke's anger reached them. He would show the cheating fard a thing or two! He would revenge their misery! Yet some among them, the more sensible ones like Megidly Aptop, wondered if their overlord's reaction did not bode ill for them: if Lord Jandissl's feud with Thradz were to prevent the further flow of vital formula to the wells of the Vermous Hills, what would happen to them? Better that Jandissl kowtow to the fard, pay whatever was demanded of him for fresh, efficacious minerals, than that all of them should remain crowded here in Low Diverness.

Already the signs of disaster appeared. Not within living memory had there been such a concentration of tarbeks in one small principality, but the tales were still told, the warning signs repeated from old chief to new, through the generations. And already, the signs of impending dahmerism appeared. Even this morning, walking among his wives and offspring, he had seen too few little ones about. Where were they, the latest crop, the most recent infants sprung from his loins, his waters? He resolved, when next he circled the constricted borders of his tribe's miserable camp, to dig up one of the small, fresh mounds he had seen there. What would he find? He was afraid he already knew: bones, tiny bones, gnawed clean.

It must not happen! The only sensible course was to restore the wells, not fight with Thradz. "Meglat!" he called out to his nearest wife. "Pack me a lunch of vechity grubs and a sip of water. I must visit the other chiefs, before it is too late." His wife obeyed, with tired, sluggish alacrity, the best she could muster. Her skin, healing slowly, was still blistered and weeping, and she still feared to expose it to the full light of the sun.

* * *

It took all day and part of the next for Chief Aptop to visit the chiefs of all thirty-six tribes. They were not all camped at the same wells; it was not the total increase in the population of Low Diverness that threatened disaster, it was the relative concentration in individual places. Thus he had to travel far, and talk much. By the time he had visited the last chief, all were agreed. They would call upon Lord Jandissl tomorrow and beg him to reconsider whatever angry plans he had made.

The next morning, just as the chiefs were arriving at their meeting place, a lone visitor arrived in front of Lord Gefke Jandissl's stone residence. He was not the usual desert wanderer whom someone like Lord Jandissl might expect to see. First, he did not arrive dusty and footsore, but left the dust behind him in the wake of his vehicle's sixteen tires. Even the finish of the late-model Pletz and Barnegal sandcrawler was unspotted with dust: a static-suppressor kept its light blue paint shiny and unflawed. It had no insignia on its flank, but was otherwise identical to the 'crawlers that various government agencies used.

The driver was likewise clad in light blue and wore no insignia, but before he turned off the dust-screen prior to disembarking, he remedied that: from a cloth pouch he took a blue and yellow badge, and affixed it to his chest. The fine lettering around its perimeter, gold characters surrounded with thick dark blue enamel, said CLERK FIRST CLASS, PATENT OFFICE OF PHYRE, not INSPECTOR, OFFICE OF FAIR PRACTICES, but they were small letters, and Slith Wrasselty counted on tarbek farsightedness to render them a blur to Lord Gefke Jandissl—and he counted on the lord's pride to prevent him from nosing close to Slith's chest to read it.

Slith had planned to announce his mission when he stepped from the sandcrawler, but he was preempted. "It is he, the agent from the Office of Fair Practices!" Chief Megidly Aptop called out. "Let *him* adjudicate!"

"Yes," cried another voice—Jerbik Traglot. "He is just the one to decide," concurred Mrapelk Plig, the third chief Slith had visited, thus firmly confirming Slith's identity as he pushed forward through the curious crowd.

"It is I," Slith agreed, pleased that he did not have to work to establish his bona fides. "I am disposed to listen to you, but bear in mind that I strongly prefer to remain on my two feet. My disposition often suffers from being lifted by the skin of my neck or by my ears. Is that understood? Else I can return whence I came, without . . ."

"No one will so elevate you!" Aptop assured him loudly. "We will defend your dignity as if it were our own!" As Slith did not consider them to be at all dignified, that was small comfort to him, but the other chiefs—all thirty-six of them were there—agreed that Slith would not be molested even in the justified heat of argument, not even by the august Gefke Jandissl himself. As Lord Jandissl was not there outside the palace to speak for himself, that warranty quite clearly confirmed that the chiefs were not kindly disposed to him, at that moment.

When those terms were established, Aptop urged him forward. "Come! Jandissl even now prepares to visit the adulterer Thradz with hostile intent. You must dissuade him. A war with Valbissag serves none of us whose wells have been fouled. We prefer to convince Thradz to resume shipment of his substances, and to oversee the crystal-making process ourselves, as it is too important to leave it to Jandissl's road-camp cooks."

As Slith had expressed a similar sentiment about Jandissl and his chemists at one time, he readily agreed. He went forward toward the Grand Portal of the palace. Had he not researched it, he would have done so less confidently, for the Grand Portal resembled nothing more than a large hole, a dark shadow across the heap of irregular stones. The three chiefs flanked him as an honor guard, and the others trailed immediately behind.

"Jandissl!" Aptop called out. "We come with an adjudicator. Harbor no hostile thoughts about us!" Whatever hostile thoughts the lord might have entertained, he did not follow through on them. He sat upon a boulder in the middle of the palace's Great Hall, which became close and crowded once all thirty-six chiefs and Slith were inside. "This fard is the inspector of whom I spoke, here to assure the government in Thember that we are dealt fairly with," said Aptop. Lord Gefke Jandissl demanded no further identification than those words and the shiny blue and yellow badge Slith wore. Perhaps he assumed his chiefs had authenticated the fard's credentials.

Though the chiefs were less irate than they had been earlier, their united presence, and Slith's own, seemed to daunt the tarbek lord. He listened to their complaint without protest. "Your proposal to give Thradz another chance," he said to Chief Aptop, "has merit. I suggested as much to him in my recent missal—though I was perhaps harsh in my expression of it, having just learned of your problems at that time."

"They are your problems too!" cried one chief.

"Indeed," agreed Lord Gefke. "They are that." With a pensive, desultory air, he scratched the flaking skin of his vermilion wattles.

Slith was distinctly uncomfortable with the air of reasonable accommodation that prevailed. His plan depended upon decisions that would be made only in the quite unreasonable heat of anger that he had hoped he would find. His eyes kept slipping toward the doorway, bright with sunlight. He had been wise to arrange for further stimulus—but would it arrive in time?

It seemed like hours had passed, though Slith's chronometer indicated it had been less than one hour since he had arrived. Though he might have preferred otherwise, he found himself in the position of arguing for peace and reasonableness. Would his diversion never happen? The chiefs and the lord had already agreed upon a course of action: they would send carts with Thradz's payment, and would insist that the OFP inspector verify the quality of the shipment before the payment—mostly rare pebbles gathered on the windblown flats of Low Diverness, with a few bales of iridescent lizard skins thrown in—was offloaded. That was all well for the tarbeks—though Slith knew that even the purest form of his crystalline molecule would have no beneficial effect on the wells. The contaminants introduced by his manipulations of the upland aquifers (and the vital compounds no longer present in their waters) made his crystal ineffective. The problem was that Slith, unrecognized by the tarbeks, would not be so by Thradz. His plan did not include presenting himself before his brother at any time soon. Yet the one key event he counted on had failed to occur!

"Gefke Jandissl!" It was Thradz's voice, yet it was oddly high and tinny. Slith rejoiced—though he remained outwardly impassive. "Gefke Jandissl!" repeated the song scorpion. "I am offended . . ." The message continued through to its end. With each offensive phrase Lord Jandissl became progressively more agitated. His bushy eyebrows twitched and the brushy hairs in his oversized nostrils took on a life of their own. His wattles inflated with russet blood. "I am Thradz, The Valbissag," the scorpion concluded. There was no sound, no murmur, in the Great Hall of Low Diverness.

Slith waited. He eyed first Lord Jandissl, then the chiefs. All seemed dumbfounded. None had expected Thradz's insults. Jandissl was first to recover. "This changes our plan," he said, stating what was immediately obvious to him—though not to the chiefs. "This cannot be borne. My workers do not fumble and bumble! He casts aspersions upon my . . . my . . ." He choked, unable even to think of tarbek seed, his chiefs' seed, though not his own, now only thin, iridescent scum on the waters of the Vermous Hills. The chiefs were ultimately of his blood. Their seed was in that sense his.

"The insult is to you alone," insisted Chief Traglot, less inclined to abstraction. "The deficiencies in the crystals affect us all. You must make peace with him!"

"Never! It has gone too far. He refuses reasonable accommodation." The arguments went back and forth, the chiefs concerned only with their wells and seeps, and Lord Jandissl with his impugned honor. Slith let them have it out. He waited until the chiefs and Jandissl began to repeat themselves.

"There is a third alternative," he murmured quietly to Megidly Aptop.

"What?" the chief whispered back. "Tell me, or this meeting will soon degenerate into a brawl."

"It is subtle and devious, quite unworthy of a noble tarbek," Slith said. "I dare not propose it."

"Tell me alone, and let me decide," Aptop responded.

"It is Lord Jandissl who must agree to it," Slith reflected, "and if others know of it too, he will surely refuse. I see no way to implement it." He sighed. "Ah, well, perhaps you can go to the Arbiter's consul in Thember for redress of your grievances. I hear that he sends worthy cases to Newhome, to be heard by the Arbiter himself. In six months or a year, all this could be behind you."

"We do not have six months! Already my wives . . ." Chiefs as well as lords have certain hardwired inhibitions; Aptop could not bring himself to speak of the many small bundles of infant bones he had uncovered, bones sucked clean of marrow and polished by their own mothers' tongues.

"That is too bad," said Slith. "Then perhaps Lord Jandissl's war against Valbissag is inevitable."

"No!" Aptop protested. "There is a way. *You* speak with the lord. You tell him what must be done, and we will follow his commands, ignorant of whatever shame he perforce brings upon himself. Where there is ignorance, there can be no true shame."

Slith thought that argument sententious. Shame was shame. Or was it? Since Slith himself, a true fard, had no concept of *guilt,* which was internal and not dependent on public review, he had nothing against which to contrast the tarbek's conclusion. Perhaps it was so. "Perhaps that is so," he said aloud. "But will the chiefs trust me, a fard? Will they let me act in their interest without knowing just what I might do or say?"

"You are more than a fard," said Aptop. "You are the voice of the government—of the Arbiter himself, here in the desert. We will follow Jandissl where you lead him."

Slith considered. Chief Aptop's words were more astute than he could know. Though Slith was not truly affiliated with the Patent Office or the Office of Fair Practices, he was in a very real sense affiliated with the Arbiter and served his ends, however indirectly he seemed to do so. "That is true," he agreed. "But I cannot speak for all unless all agree to it."

"I will handle it. Wait!" Aptop moved off among the crowd, and Slith observed him whispering to first one of his peers and then another. With increasing loudness and diminishing sense, the arguments of the other chiefs and Lord Jandissl went on around them.

Gradually, as Megidily Aptop spoke to chief after chief, their protests faded. In a short while, Jandissl noticed this, yet he wisely forbore from confronting Chief Aptop until the latter had spoken with the last chief and absolute silence prevailed except for the harsh breathing of thirty-seven tarbeks and the swift pants of one small fard. Not for the first time did Slith congratulate himself for having pushed bors-made nose filters high up in his nostrils before exiting his sandcrawler. He was not even remotely curious what effect the respirations of three dozen tarbeks would have had upon his unprotected mucus membranes or the insides of his lungs.

"Lord Jandissl," said Aptop softly—there was no need for volume. "The inspector from the Office of Fair Practices is trusted by all of us. Perhaps the two of you, in quiet conference, can find a solution that is not obvious to this large convocation."

His quiet words mollified the lord: by calling the gathering a convocation, which suggested that it had been Lord Gefke's initiative—though it had obviously not been—Aptop demonstrated a degree of respect, and restored Jandissl's much-battered pride. Jandissl nodded, and looked about the room. All understood the order implicit in that gaze, and the chiefs began to file out in quiet order. Soon Lord Gefke Jandissl was alone with the fard, who had not yet been required to give so much as a false name, yet who held the fate of many in his hands.

Jandissl did not speak first. He merely raised a bushy yellow eyebrow. Slith began: "I would not shame you with mention of devious thoughts worthy only of a fard, Lord," he said. "I fear I might insult you by asking your consideration of them."

"We are alone," replied Jandissl. "Whatever fardish lies you might tell of this meeting at a later time will have no basis. I would simply deny them; thus there is no dishonor in listening to your plots." He shrugged. " 'Use a fard to foil a fard,' as the saying goes," he said. Was that how the saying went? Slith had not heard it before, though in the circumstances he agreed wholeheartedly. Perhaps the very avatars of tarbek culture were allied on his side, if the saying was indeed common among them.

"This is what I propose . . ." he began.

Much later, Lord Jandissl recalled the chiefs. "The fard has a plan," he stated. "I am satisfied with it, and with him, though without knowing the fardish intricacies of his plot. Obey him as if he were me." Those words satisfied his tarbek "honor": he did not know those things that might otherwise be used to impugn him. The "fardish intricacies" could later be "misunderstood," if they crossed some fine cultural line. Being the fard's plan, all could be disavowed and blamed on innately dishonorable fardish nature. That, Slith reflected, was not far from the truth.

The chiefs accepted Lord Jandissl's brief approval on the basis of their confidence in the "official" from the Office of Fair Practices. Jandissl himself knew otherwise, for Slith had told him the truth—not *all* the truth, of course, but Jandissl knew he was Slith Wrasselty, the crystal's inventor, who alone might find a solution to his problem, for Jandissl knew it was not a flaw in the molecules formulated in his laboratory. He had done the work himself, or had overseen it; the crystals had been made properly. Either Thradz had adulterated the raw materials, whether purposely or accidentally, or the contamination had occurred at the source—the aquifers that supplied the wells.

Alone with Jandissl, Slith had revealed his true identity. The tarbek lord knew there was no better man to solve his problem than the one who had first studied the wells and the sources, who had invented the formula. Yet Slith had revealed his own helplessness—the false charge of felony that kept him from the records he needed not only to prove his own innocence and to show Thradz's guilt, but those that concerned well logs and assays as well, records that could be obtained, Slith explained, only with the help of someone of unsullied reputation, someone of sufficient rank who would not be barred from the storage rooms of the Patent Office.

"Go back to your camps," Lord Jandissl told his chiefs. "There is much planning to be done. Endure but a while longer, and all will be resolved." Uneasily—but what choice did they have?—the chiefs obeyed.

"Now," said Jandissl, "explain how you will make good my promise to them."

"We do not know if the materials Thradz has supplied you were contaminated by him or were adulterated by some natural cause before he precipitated or distilled them from the well waters," Slith said. "I suspect the former, of course, but without the Registry's listings of all the wells of the Valbissag domain . . ."

"I will demand them," Jandissl said. "They will not refuse me."

"It is not so simple," Slith replied. "Perhaps Thradz has submitted false assays to the Registry. The data on file may themselves be false."

"Then we are lost," Jandissl said glumly.

"Perhaps not. Consider that the records are entered chronologically. Thradz's submissions would be recorded on a recent datacrystal, one still on-line in the Registry. No attempt would have been made to check them against earlier records, those submitted by my grandfather's grandfather, for example. It is those records I must have, and they are surely archived, not on-line in the crystal readers. I must have those original crystals."

"I will demand that they be put on line, and printouts made."

"Printouts can be falsified. It must be the originals."

"Impossible! The Registry would not allow them out."

Slith shrugged eloquently. "Then explain to your chiefs that the Vermous Hills are forever lost to them," he said unsympathetically.

"How can I get the crystals?" the tarbek asked skeptically, surrendering. "There are guards, and sniffsnakes at the portals."

"I have examined both the Patent Office and the Registry," Slith claimed, with a degree of truth—though his memories of being dragged through the halls of the Patent Office hardly constituted a careful examination of the facility, nor did his research visits to the outer offices and reading rooms. "I do remember seeing windows in the Registry from which a tall tarbek might be able to toss an object, thus circumventing both the guards and the sniffsnakes."

"And are there windows throughout the Patent Office as well?" Lord Jandissl asked.

"I saw none," Slith admitted, "except in the suite of the chief patent officer. And those had no latches or hinges."

"Then what do you propose?"

"If you throw the crystal with the original well assays from a Registry window, I will be outside to recover them."

"What will warrant that you will not then abscond with it, leaving me with nothing?"

"For my own purposes, I need *three* crystals—one from the Registry, and two from the Patent Office. You may keep the ones from the Patent Office until you are satisfied that your own difficulties have been resolved."

"But there are no windows in the Patent Office."

"You must go there with a servant—or one of your chiefs, like Megidily Aptop, in the guise of servant—and recover the datablocks. I will supply you with their numbers and where they are stored. Hide the blocks under the voluminous filter robes all tarbeks are required to wear in the city. And I will give you this . . ." He drew a small leather pouch from his uniform tunic's pocket. "It is a comingling of pollens and dusts that will irritate the nostrils of the sniffsnakes and will confuse them. Dust your clothing and Chief Aptop's with it when you are both ready to leave the Patent Office. Have him precede you through the exit portal, and you will see that it is safe for you too to depart without the attention of the guards. Once away, keep the crystals in your possession until all is accomplished to your satisfaction."

He gave the tarbek the pouch. "There is enough there to test the mixture's efficacy on a sniffsnake or two," he said. "I saw a nest of wild ones only an hour's walk from here. I will furnish you with a greater quantity of the dust at a later time."

Lord Jandissl grudgingly acknowledged that the plan had merit. He would make preparations for the journey to Thember. Perhaps Slith could convey them hence in his fine sandcrawler?

"There must be no visible association between us," Slith demurred. "Besides, I must make a side trip into the high desert before returning to Thember. There I will gather more pollens and mineral dusts. If you travel by ordinary means and I drive cross-country at great speed, we can meet in the tarbek caravanserai at the far end of the Western Highway, four mornings hence. I will there give you and Chief Aptop each a sack of the dust for the Patent Office's sniffsnakes."

Shortly thereafter, Slith reentered his sandcrawler and headed up the slope of the land toward High Diverness. He stopped briefly at his cache of song scorpions, and recorded a message for Thplet.

"Thplet! Hear me! Soon your exile will be at an end. Certain information has come my way that is of no use to me, but from the goodness of my heart and my loyalty to you, I supply it. It concerns Thradz, and a threat to his welfare. Give it to him and beg his gratitude, or bargain with him for amnesty, as you think best." What followed was an only slightly edited description of the plan that Slith and Lord Jandissl had agreed upon.

"I am Slith, your brother and your friend."

Slith watched the song scorpion scramble away. He did not start up his sandcrawler until it was well along; song scorpions were sometimes startled by large things that moved, and he wanted that one to arrive as soon as possible. He then set out for Thember, for the Hotel Xarafeille, where he would take a luxury room with a dust-bath and electrostatic shower. He would have a fine dinner of simmered rock cress and spicy blue spider mites from the slopes of Mount Blag, whose eruption had aided him in an earlier phase of his complex endeavor. The next day he would stroll by the shop Slem Banto occupied, the shop that contained his vault and his records—and would contemplate his revenge against the stubborn bors. He would soon be wealthy and important again, and the shop would once again be his. Perhaps, if he felt magnanimous, he might keep Slem Banto on in some capacity—he would need a janitor to sweep the floors and to polish the dials and handle on his vault door. On the second morning, he would take the outer belt highway to the outskirts of the city, and reenter it as if he had just arrived from the west, near the tarbek caravanserai.

At midday on the second day of his luxurious rest, Slith strolled along Booksellers' Way, contemplating his future. At that exact hour, an unmarked song scorpion was approaching the scorpion-keeper's yard in Valbissag Town, just outside Thradz's palatial dwelling. "Thradz! Thradz of Valbissag! It is I, your brother Thplet . . ." it chittered.

The scorpion-keeper netted it, placed it in a wicker cage, and immediately sought Thradz. There was a small passageway to the main house at the back of his own dwelling.

"Slith Wrasselty is nasty and selfish," Parissa said angrily. "I do not like him. I do not like this story. Bleth is much nicer than Slith."

John Minder smiled. Parissa had, exactly, though inadvertently, positioned herself where she would get the most out of this "lesson"—though she might not be pleased with its conclusion. "Sometimes such things fool us, dear," her father said. "Sometimes the nastiness we understand is nicer than the niceness we don't." Parissa—as her father had expected—looked mostly confused by that odd weaving of words. "If you know *why* someone is being nasty, you can protect yourself against his nastiness—so isn't it just as important to know *why* someone is being nice?"

Parissa, to her credit, did not respond immediately. When she did, her father was pleased with her response.

"When Robby is nice to me," she said thoughtfully, "he is planning a mean trick. When he is mean ..." She smiled. "It's better when he's mean, isn't it? Then I *know* what he's doing."

CHAPTER 21

I seldom arbitrate. Yet would the folk of the
Xarafeille Stream accept my rulings if my title was
"Manipulator," not "Arbiter"? By the time a
matter reaches actual arbitration, my real work
has often been done. I have then brought together
in one fine and somber courtroom all the disparate
self-interests that I have secretly prodded,
tweaked, nudged, encouraged, and shaped, the
predispositions I have encouraged or thwarted.
   If I have truly understood those things, then those
often-angry, oft-hostile participants I see on
either side of the courtroom aisle will of their
own accord perform the final steps in my
choreographed sequence and will give me credit
for the resolution of their conflict.

James Minder IV,
Unpublished diary,
Erne Museo, Newhome, 4321 R.L.

All was ready! It was a fine fall morning, the tenth of
Krad. Late-blooming syllipherns scented the air of
Thember and the first clouds of the season mounted the
western horizon, looking as if the far peaks themselves
drew near. Slith was light-footed and cheery. He had
given the Hotel Xarafeille's concierge a fine tip to be distributed among the staff. He had breakfasted on fat
blunderneffs in a nest of slivered perslips. He had ordered
his sandcrawler cleaned and polished inside and out and
brought to the front door.
   No longer did he slink, head down, and dart furtively
from the service entrance! Slith Wrasselty strode proudly

through the hotel's stately lobby and out through doors held wide by uniformed bors. His vehicle awaited him there.

"It is time!" he stated ebulliently to the tarbek lord and the chief. "Today is the first day of a new life! Here are the sacks of dust I promised you." He handed a red sack to Lord Jandissl, and a blue one to Chief Aptop. "This one is the stronger mixture," he said to the lord. "The sniffsnakes' noses may become inured to the first dust they inhale. They will not withstand this other, to which I have added capsicum extracted from an offworld spice that wends fancy."

He wished the tarbeks luck. "I will proceed to the Registry. Have you surveyed the grounds where I will be waiting? Do you know where to throw the datablock?"

"We will throw it from the fourth window from the right, on the south side of the edifice," said Lord Jandissl. "There is a garden bed below that will cushion the impact if you cannot catch the crystal, and the periwhistle vines will hide it if you are delayed or otherwise not there."

"Then all contingencies are prepared for. It is a good day, indeed," Slith effused. He reiterated their plans to meet, when all was done, in the tarbek wing of the Hotel Xarafeille, where he promised that a fine meal would await them. Tarbeks were not allowed to dine in the regular restaurant, because they could not bring food to mouth without lifting their veils, but the tarbek restaurant was immediately adjacent to the other, separated only by a glass partition wall. It was identically appointed to make it seem part of the larger layout, and its three solid walls were mirrored to give it depth and to reduce any sense of isolation the tarbek guests might otherwise feel. The glass partition was mirrored on the far side only, so the wends and bors who dined there would not suffer imaginary twinges brought on by the mere sight of unveiled tarbeks at their repasts. The tarbeks' scents would not bother Slith; he had become quite used to the feel of his nose filters, and now carried fresh ones in his pocket as a matter of course.

* * *

Once Slith had departed, Lord Jandissl eyed the red bag skeptically. "Perhaps we should exchange sacks," he said. "I will leave the Patent Office first."

"Indeed, lord," Megidly Aptop answered him. "If so, perhaps I should hold both datablocks. I am sure that with my greater stature I could conceal two on my person."

Jandissl's skeptical expression intensified. He lowered one bushy eyebrow until it almost concealed his yellow-tinged eye. "And why is that?" he asked.

Aptop turned his head aside, and exposed his neck wattles, a gesture of nonthreatening submission. "I only assumed you expressed doubt of Slith Wrasselty's intentions—that if the sacks hold only ground meal and sand, you would not wish to be caught with a stolen datablock in your possession."

"It is so—I trust the fard only to serve his own ends. He is too facile, too forgiving. I had thought he would be angrier with me, that I came into possession of his treasured formula as a result of his adversity." He pondered the blue sack Chief Aptop held. "Or perhaps I should go first, but with the contents of your sack clinging to my clothing."

"Perhaps so, lord. Then you take both crystals with you. If the blue sack's contents are indeed stronger stuff, then I would not dare depart with both a crystal and an inferior deterrent for the sniffsnakes. I would be caught, and if you were still in the vicinity, you also might be apprehended." He picked up two wind-worn rocks, approximately the size of the datacrystals they planned to steal. "Try to conceal these on your person, lord. If they do not bulge in unseemly places, or knock painfully against you . . ."

Jandissl eyed the rocks. "I cannot carry two," he admitted. "One, slung from my belt and between my legs, I can manage without unmanning myself, but not two. There must be another alternative." Tarbek genitals, like their noses, ears, and wattles, were adapted for intense lowland heat, radiators of large surface area, and were thus overlarge.

"Can we mix the contents of the two sacks?" Aptop wondered. "Then if I precede you with one crystal . . ."

"Or I you . . ." Jandissl suggested. Both men looked at each other, realizing the futility of that alternative. If the sniffsnakes indeed became inured to the effects of the first sack, the second would be no better than none at all.

"It seems that we must trust the fard, in this matter," Aptop concluded. "No alternative occurs to me." That was not entirely true. He suspected that if both men were to walk out of the Patent Office side by side, equally covered with both sacks' contents, both would win free at once. That would not occur to Jandissl, who was lord; the habit of precedence was ingrained in him. Perhaps that accounted also for his reluctance to allow Aptop to go first—though in that case, it would be as if they were unaffiliated, and precedence did not apply.

Yet Aptop was oddly reluctant to propose that they go out together—for reasons entirely his own. "If the fard plans treachery," he mused, "I am less likely a target of it than are you. If he indeed intends that one of us be revealed by the sniffsnakes and caught by the guards, then perhaps only one of the two crystals he has required is of true worth to him. Can we determine which one?"

"It must be the first one," said Jandissl. "The one you would win free with, if you went first."

"Then if we switch crystals . . . He did not actually demand that we carry them out in a particular order. He only laid out the shortest route from crystal to crystal to the exit, and only conversationally suggested that I pick up the first one."

"Indeed, let us switch them, then!" Jandissl exclaimed, relieved that a solution had been found.

"And shall I go first, or you?" Aptop asked.

"Why . . ." Again, Lord Jandissl realized that the dilemma remained unresolved.

Chief Megidly Aptop brightened. "I have it!" he blurted. "There are four exits from the Patent Office. Or three—I forget which. You, carrying one crystal, can exit from the northernmost portal and I, at the same time, will depart through the southernmost one."

Lord Jandissl immediately discovered the flaw in that plan. "And which sack of dust will each of us use?" he asked.

For a moment Aptop was stymied—but only for a moment. "We will mix the contents of each," he said. "When we tested the stuff Slith gave us earlier, a tiny pinch was enough to confuse the wild sniffsnakes. We can be sure that one sack of the new stuff must be efficacious, even if the other is not. Otherwise neither of us would fare free with a crystal. Thus both of us will be adequately dusted to confound different sniffsnakes at different exits at one time."

Jandissl could find no flaw in the plan. There were still imponderables, but they were remote possibilities: if Slith planned only revenge on Lord Jandissl, and in truth needed neither crystal for his own ends, then both sacks might contain useless cosmetic powder or a patent nostrum. If he in truth needed both, then both would function as promised.

"Then it is agreed," the tarbek lord stated. "Only one final change in plan must be made: we will meet at Jerbandly Seep, the first way station on the Western Highway, instead of in the restaurant of a decadent hotel. When the fard wishes to use the crystals they will be still in our possession, and we will be safely back in Low Diverness, where he will be able to use them only with our supervision and approval."

Aptop agreed to the change, and complimented Lord Jandissl on his perspicacity. All was now set. They set out for their first destination, which was the Registry. Neither of them thought any difficulties would arise there. After all, they had only to find a crystal and throw it out a window.

"There he is!" growled the thickset fard. Of course "growl" and "thickset" were both relative; to anyone not another fard, his phrase would have seemed a trill, not a growl, and to a bors or even a wend he would have seemed not thickset, but downright skinny. Yet he was an imposing figure to the lesser fards who accompanied him—and he was, of course, Thradz, The Valbissag, and was the master of their lives. "That is the vile Jandissl, carrying the staff of his rank. Mark him well. Things are just as Thplet claimed!"

"Thradz! Thradz of Valbissag!" Thplet's message had began. "It is I, your brother Thplet, who beseech you. I live to serve you, and I have discovered a plot by the foul Jandissl. I ask only my life, and that of a nurseling who accompanies me. I ask only to serve. Grant me audience, mighty brother. The tarbek lord, at the instigation of your brother Slith, plans your downfall.

"I am Thplet, a humble no-man. I exist at your whim."

Thradz had then gone to the seep Blendernet and had there found Thplet and the fardling Bleth. Thradz had questioned both of them. Now Thplet was with him, watching as Lord Jandissl entered the Registry. Bleth remained at Valbissag, luxuriating in the steams of the spring Valbissag, nibbling on latherwort leaves and sweet morsels, for which she was rapidly acquiring a taste. Soon, thought Thradz's wives (who were also his cousins, his aunts, and his sisters), she would lose her affection for her nurse's breast and discover the utility of a different male organ. Bleth was growing up.

Thplet had told Thradz more than Slith had suggested. He had wished to protect himself thoroughly; thus he admitted that it was Slith who had informed him of Jandissl's plot—and thus that Slith might have his own plans, though he had no knowledge of those. All he could really say was what Slith had told him to say: that Gefke Jandissl, desperate, deeply angered by the failure of the Vermous wells and Thradz's purported responsibility for it, planned to steal the original modules with the data from Valbissag's well cores, the original deed to Valbissag, and what other information he would need to prepare a lawsuit claiming that Valbissag had never belonged to the fards but had been leased to Thradz's family, and that the lease was now expired. Thplet suggested, though without concrete knowledge of it, that Slith, perhaps knowing what had caused the problem with the minerals refined from the Valbissag wells, and thus knowing how to remedy it, might then take over Valbissag himself, under a new "lease" from Jandissl.

It was necessary to stop Jandissl. Whatever Slith's plan, and the tarbek's, as long as the records were safe in the Registry, or even safe in Thradz's hands, the plot could not go forward. "He enters the Registry! Thtenk! You and Pranth go to the far door to the place, and watch it. If he attempts to leave, one of you follow him, and the other come for us. We will then overpower him and take what he has purloined." Two fards broke away from the group. Others, with similar instructions, left to cover the remaining exits from the Registry.

Thradz and Thplet remained where they were, hiding behind a well-pruned sweetthorn hedge near the Registry's south portal. "Watch for anything unusual," Thradz instructed his brother. "Slith is involved, and where that is so, nothing is truly predictable. If you see anything out of the ordinary . . ."

They waited, and saw nothing remarkable. Men went in and out of the Registry. Men walked by it without entering. Lizards and skinbirds scrabbled and pecked in the gravel of the path beyond the hedge. A vendor hawked bits of dry, black meat from beside his one-wheeled cart. The day became hotter as the sun rose toward zenith. High up within the Registry, someone opened a window.

Thplet was first to notice that the fard in the black tutor's cloak and hood was the same one who had passed by a few minutes before. He had picked the tutor out from the others walking the path next to the Registry wall only because he seemed to linger overlong as he passed the patch of periwhistle, listening to the faint tunes the flowers generated as the sun heated them and forced expanded air from their bladders. He only faintly heard the melody they played today; it sounded almost like a quaint tune his mother had sung to him when he was a fardling. *It is Slith!* he realized; the concurrence of the periwhistles' tune and something about the gait of the black-robed fard triggered that conclusion. The hooded man was Slith Wrasselty! Ever cautious, Thplet refrained from revealing his discovery to Thradz, whose eyes were fixed on the portal, awaiting Lord Jandissl's return.

Nevertheless, fard eyes and brains were uniquely adapted to sense motion where none had been before. Thradz's eyes flashed to the window on the fourth floor, and to the shadowed form within. He thus saw the sparkling object that flew from the window and landed among the periwhistles, and he heard the faint, shrill cacophony the flowers made as the falling datacrystal crushed several of them. He saw, too, the black-robed fard who dashed forward and snatched the crystal from its whistling nest. "Was it Jandissl in the window?" he asked Thplet urgently. "I must know! If it was Jandissl, then the fard tutor is allied with him, and we have just seen the theft we came to prevent."

"I did not see the thrower clearly," Thplet replied, quite honestly. "Should one of us follow the fard?"

Thradz was torn. He had to decide! "I will follow him! You watch for Jandissl. This may be only a distraction." He dashed off. The fard was already out of sight, around a corner of an academic building.

"Good day, miss," said Slith to the receptionist, who looked up from her acrostic. "Tutor Chelemerin left his robe in the refectory some time ago. It was discovered only when painters came to redecorate the anteroom. I will hang it in its proper place." He proceeded to do so.

"What was Tutor Chelemerin doing in the Patent Office refectory?" she asked, eyeing Slith's uniform and his clerk's badge.

"I do not know. Perhaps when he returns, you can ask him. Now I must go. I am very much behind already."

"Thank you!" said the receptionist, too late. Slith was already hurrying down the path.

He did not slow down as he passed Thradz, who was no longer running, but was looking wildly about himself, having lost his quarry. Slith's change of clothes—and his false facial scar—had done the trick. When he rounded the corner of a building, he chanced a peek back. There was Thradz, now trudging slowly back the way he had come. And there, still behind the sweetthorn hedge, was Thplet. "Good day, Thplet," Slith whispered as he passed by. "You have done well. When I have completed my successes, I will remember your service this day." Thplet said nothing. Thradz was on his way back. He did not look happy. And Slith's data module was gone. His snug uniform could not have concealed it. Slith had thrust it into the sleeve of Tutor Cheleremin's robe. He would recover it later, when the tutor returned from his three-day holiday at Forest Dome—at Slith's expense.

Slith walked away from the Registry, in the general direction of the Patent Office. He was in no hurry. Either the tarbeks did well or they did not. Matters were outside his control, and there was no use worrying about them. He thus did not see Thradz's minion return, out of breath, to cower before his master. "Gefke Jandissl has left the Registry by the entrance I was to watch. He was ahead of me, and I dared not accost him. There were constables present. I have sent Bradth to follow him."

"We know where he will go," said Thradz, who had recovered his composure now. "He will enter the Patent Office where the other data modules are, probably by the east portal."

Thradz deployed his men where the few high windows and all the entries of the Patent Office could be watched. He himself stood outside the southernmost entrance, reasoning that the tarbek would likely be inclined to leave by a different one than he had entered through. If, unlikely as it was, his men could not recover the datablock Jandissl threw out before his robed fard accomplice did— the thought crossed his mind that the fard might be Slith, but as Thplet had not mentioned it, he only speculated— then they would have to pursue the tarbek.

Time passed, and Thradz's men grew impatient and bored. No windows were opened. Thradz knew this because he had assigned one man as a runner to check on the rest and to report to him each time he circled the Patent Office building. Thplet remained perforce with Thradz, who did not entirely trust him in spite of his revelations and seeming loyalty. "He has been in there a long time," said Thplet. "What can he be doing?"

"Perhaps he is having a hard time getting what he went in for," replied Thradz. "Perhaps the Registry staff were more impressed with his credentials than are the Patent Officers, who are a hard-nosed breed." Thplet agreed it might be so.

Elsewhere, not far away, within view of both his brothers and also within sight of not one but two of the Patent

Office's entrances, Slith, too, wondered what was happening in the Patent Office. He had twice as much to wonder about, because unlike Thradz and Thplet, he knew that two tarbeks from Jandissl's domains had entered the building, not one. He, unlike some of the other watchers, was not the least bit bored. He awaited events yet to come with both zest and anticipation.

There! He observed Chief Megidly Aptop's tall figure and flowing filter robes as the tarbek emerged from the leftmost portal. The chief's ordinarily sweeping stride had a certain almost fardlike, mincing quality to it. "He preserves not the usual two, but three precious things beneath that robe," Slith concluded happily. He watched as Aptop passed the watching fards without incident, until he disappeared around a corner on his way to the Western Highway out of Thember. He had no further time to become bored, either. He scurried from his hiding place, a ragleaf clump beside the Textbook Repository, which was closed until the next University term began.

"Quick!" he exclaimed, approaching one of Thradz's men watching the east portal. "The thief Jandissl will be coming out with a datacrystal slung between his legs! He has a powder to fool the sniffsnakes' noses. You must tell Thradz!"

The man, whose name Slith had once known but had forgotten, grunted for his partner to continue watching both windows and door; he had not forgotten who Slith was, and he was not at all sure his advice was on the up-and-up—no one had told him anything about Slith's recent status, yet he had heard what had been said before about his boss's recalcitrant and disloyal brother.

"Oh no!" he said as Slith attempted to sidle off. "You remain here. We will wait and see. If this is some trick, you can explain your part in it to The Valbissag." He was large, and his grip on Slith's arm was firm.

"No matter," Slith said, shrugging, and gazed tranquilly toward Thradz's position.

They did not have long to wait. Thradz left Thplet and the message-carrying fard, and he entered the Patent Office by the nearest door. He would accost Jandissl inside and catch him with the evidence! Thplet would inform

the constables, who would catch the tarbek at the door.
Thradz would stay close to Jandissl to prevent his dispos-
ing of the evidence before he was truly and surely caught.
Slith only wished he could have been close by to see and
to listen when the two of them met inside.

When Thradz and Jandissl emerged into the bright
Thember sunlight, they were arm in arm—a ridiculous
circumstance, because the tarbek was much taller than the
fard who clung to him. Yet Slith knew such things were
deceptive. The assorted human races were, he knew from
his extensive readings, quite evenly matched. What fards
lacked in height they made up in speed and dexterity.
Combat even between a heavy bors and a fard had no
foregone conclusion.

Yet there was no indication that the two were other
than best of friends. They strode, heads leaning slightly
toward each other as if in intense conversation. Only the
first shouts of the constables affected their seeming concentration.

"It is them! Arrest them." Hearing that—and hearing
the plural pronoun employed—Thradz hesitated, drew
back, and attempted to distance himself from his companion. "I am Thradz The Valbissag," he essayed. "I have
brought out the thief. He carries the data module in a sack
between his legs. I am on your side. It was my minion
Thplet who called you!"

The bors constables had none of that. "You are clearly
Thradz, the thief's accomplice, caught in the act," said
the bors corporal. Other constables quickly recovered the
evidence of the crime from beneath Jandissl's robes—
though not without much grunting and complaining; there
had not been time for them to fetch nose filters or gog-
gles, and by the time they produced the crystal, their eyes
were streaming with the effects of tarbek bodily effusions.

Thradz loudly protested his continuing detention, but to
no avail. "Accomplice or arresting citizen, it is for the
courts to decide," said the corporal. "Now remain still.
The police wagon is on its way."

"Thplet!" howled Thradz. "Explain to these bors what

has transpired!" Thplet, standing at some distance, merely shrugged apologetically.

"Do not address the witness!" the corporal commanded Thradz. "There will be a time for that in the courtroom."

Jandissl was less vociferous, confining his protests to inarticulate growls, though his eyes sought out Slith among the bystanders.

The wagon arrived, and the offenders were bundled into it less than gently. "Now we shall see," said Slith to his smaller brother.

"Indeed," replied Thplet. "I await the unraveling of events with a certain eagerness." Slith, who eagerly anticipated recovery of one crystal from the tutor and another from Chief Megidly Aptop, did not stop to wonder just what it was that his brother hoped to see transpire.

PART FOUR

METAMORPHOSIS
Quartzite, Marble, and Slate

CHAPTER 22

FROM: CONS. HANS VANOVERBEEK, VELA
     (X-1029)
TO: ARBITER
TEXT: Subsequent to analysis of (*proscribed
chemical 32a-42-var beta, details autocensored
at source*), bulk manufacture at (*offworld loc.
autocensored at source*) and final distribution on
Vela, the hostilities have ended. Clipping file and
suggested official media release appended.
PERSONAL: John, it took 3 whole years to analyze
the molecular structure, and seven more to reproduce
the stuff in commercial quantities, but it was
worth it! Who ever dreamed we'd have to decode
the DNA of a fossil microorganism to do it?

John Minder crossed his legs, and Parissa climbed up on
him. Rob settled into a corner chair, and Sarabet onto the
floor at her father's feet. "The unraveling, as Thplet
called it," Minder began, "was not a sudden thing." As it
turned out, he told the children, all of the people involved
in the events concerning Valbissag, Low Diverness, and
the Vermous Hills had a lengthy wait for the final disposition of their cases—for the last threads to become
straight. Slith Wrasselty, the Arbiter said, spent much
time with consul Van Dam, poring over data from the
crystals removed from the Registry and the Patent Office,
and even more preparing for the court appearances that
one by one cleared up the blemishes upon his future happiness.

The third crystal, the one Jandissl had been caught
with, was of no import, a red herring introduced by Slith

to fool the tarbek: Megidly Aptop made sure it was he himself who had carried forth the one Slith needed. Of the other crystal, the one the Arbiter had hoped he would acquire, little was said. "I do not need the Arbiter's favor now," Slith stated. "We have the evidence we need right here. Why should I risk my skin on yet another pilfering venture?"

Indeed, his attitude was sensible, George Van Dam agreed indifferently. The consul's attitude seemed slightly disloyal even to Slith.

For the sake of his youngest child, who was easily bored by tedious detail, Minder glossed lightly over undramatic events, compressing into a few sentences the reversal of Slith's felony conviction, the return of his patented formula, and the recovery of his notes and formulae from the vault under Slem Banto's shop. But as luck—or nature—would have it, Parissa was unsatisfied with that.

"Did Slith get even with that dirty old bors?" she demanded. "Did he get his shop back and make Slem Banto sweep it for him?"

"Come on, Priss! It wasn't Banto's fault," Rob interjected, rumpling her hair affectionately. "If my books were under your bed, would you want me to come in and crawl under it without your permission?"

"You keep your books in your own room, Robby! You stay out of mine!"

"Rob is just trying to say that Banto was only an innocent bystander and within his rights," their father said, heading off further hypothetical distraction. "My consul merely had to ask him politely to allow Slith to recover his records, and the bors complied. Slith was able to patent all his formulae without further difficulty."

"Did he get rich again? Did he get his house back?"

"He opened a new shop only a few doors from the old one, and yes, he made a lot more money. But as his old house in Varamin Park had been sold, and as recovering it for him would have caused an innocent buyer much hardship, he instead bought another house—in an even finer neighborhood—with the proceeds from his lawsuit against the city of Thember."

"Did Bleth get her very own room in it?" Parissa asked.

"Ah ... Bleth did not live there with him," Minder said. "Bleth had her own life to live.

"Rob," he said then, abruptly changing the subject, "did you bring your staff? What have you done with it recently?"

"It's in the corner. Just wait till you see! I finished carving Chief Aptop picking Slith up by his scruff, and now I'm working on the knob on top. I think I'll make it a globe of the fard homeworld like the columns in Valbissag, and ..."

"Are there holos in Valbissag that show such detail?" Minder had not seen any himself.

Rob smiled slyly. "There may not be, and perhaps the fards themselves do not remember it accurately," he said, "but the *Arbiter* never forgets ... or his library does not."

"You found the original corporate surveys, didn't you? Very good." That surely meant Rob was mastering the reference software, and more. He would need that, if he were himself to become Arbiter someday. Minder did not want his own children to be as unprepared as he had been when his father had died.

"Bleth," said Consul George Van Dam, "how good to see you again. You look well. Please, sit down." Bleth sat. Indeed, she did look well; her fur was shiny, her eyes bright, her smock of the finest semberdown with a hem of gold threads—and her belly was quite swollen under it. "I carry the first son of The Valbissag," she said proudly, seeing his interest in her condition.

"Oh? Is Thradz now free?"

"Thradz? Why speak of Thradz? Thplet is The Valbissag now. Thradz languishes in his cell, or he has already starved—I do not know or care. Thplet is The Valbissag, and I am his first wife—and his only one."

The consul's expression was unreadable. "Are you happy?"

"I am content—for now. When I have produced my share of contenders for the Valbissag inheritance, then who knows? I may visit you again, with a request."

"And what might that be?" Van Dam asked. He was impressed. What had become of the shy fardling he remembered? From whence had sprung this poised and assured young fard?

"I would prefer not to say. I hope first to incur your gratitude—which brings me to the purpose of this visit." She lifted the small shoulder bag she carried. "I wish to leave something with you. Do with it as you wish, when I have gone." She stood.

Van Dam sensed he would get no more from Bleth. He saw her to the door of his office, now eager to see what she had left in the unopened bag on the chair. But there was one question he was unable to resist asking. "Thplet? I thought Thplet was a . . ."

"An unman?" Bleth laughed humorlessly. "So did Thradz, to his detriment, yet a pair of balls can be purchased cheaply in the dry middens, often from their original owner himself. I once suggested as much to Thplet. All along, Thplet plotted to become The Valbissag in Thradz's place. Thradz was unsubtle. Thplet is a true and worthy heir." She departed.

"Amazing," Van Dam muttered. He could not quite understand how it had all come about. Thplet, retaining his manhood, was now The Valbissag! Bleth, in a manner quite unlike the oppressed, enslaved, and uneducated women Slith had described as Valbissag's finest, was poised, sleek, and articulate. But how had that happened? And she had said she was Thplet's *only* wife. What did that mean? Were not all the women of Valbissag now Thplet's wives, in a sense? Was Bleth's spousehood a legal fiction, or would her male offspring indeed be the only contenders for inheritance of spring, town, and territory?

He shrugged. There was one question he *could* find an answer to—and it was in the bag Bleth had left behind. When he opened it, his eyes widened and he drew in a short, sharp breath. Then, settling the bag gently in the chair without removing its contents, he went to his terminal and began to compose the first of many messages he would send out that night.

Van Dam did not know it, but it was to be several years before he had answers to all his questions.

John Minder's children were perhaps wiser than Consul Van Dam. By the end of the evening, all three were quite sure they were still some way from having all their questions answered. Of all his children he was proudest, at that moment, of Parissa, who was for once uncharacteristically silent, but upon whose face lurked a wise, smug, knowing smile. "Yes," Minder murmured beneath his breath, "there, I think, is the next Arbiter of the Xarafeille Stream."

In the Arbiter's mind, right then—allowing for the difference in physiognomy between smooth-faced old-human child and whiskered fardling—the expression on Bleth's face might have been quite like Parissa's, exuding the confidence only a child could feel when it had taken a big bite out of the universe, chewed it, tasted it, and understood it. Parissa's bite was, of course, more abstract than Bleth's, because her essential survival did not depend on it. For Parissa, success would bring perhaps relief from her brother's teasing, and a sense of control over her existence. For Bleth things were different. If the gratitude of Thplet, Slith, even Consul Van Dam counted, she would win some of what she strived for. If the results were based in purest pragmatism, she would win all.

Slith was too busy reestablishing his commercial empire to bother with distant Valbissag, with Thplet, Bleth, or with anyone's unanswered questions. His "nose" for both chemistry and commerce had not dulled, and his past reputation as a chemist of note now stood him in good stead. His shop soon became an obligatory stop on all the offworlders' tours. He recovered most if not all of his old customers, and gained many new ones. He sold licenses to produce many of his patented concoctions, and the royalties from those alone amazed his accountants.

The irregular nature of Slith's doctorate was regularized when the University, at Consul Van Dam's suggestion, granted him an honorary degree with all the rights and privileges of one gained by more usual means. Dr.

Slith Wrasselty, PhD, was content with that. It looked the same on the "Contents" pages of many academic journals where his work was published.

By carefully choosing his managers, supervisors, and agents, Slith left himself plenty of time to spend long days and weeks in the deserts and mountains, pursuing the real love of his life, his geological research. Whether by accident or intent, his ever-widening areas of interest seldom took him near Valbissag, Low Diverness, or the Vermous Hills, so it was only by accident that he discovered what was happening there.

"Enclosed is my last check for production rights to your fine formula," wrote Lord Megidly Aptop Jandissl's scribe, in a fine wendish hand. The words were, Slith knew, a "translation" of Aptop's own, which were hardly so fair or coherent. "Our association has been profitable for both of us, and I will treasure my memories of it, for without your cleverness, I would not be sitting here now, in this fine palace."

Indeed, Slith thought, nodding his agreement. If it had not been for his quick comprehension of the meaning of the Jandissl genealogical chart he had copied in the History Division, he might have approached some lesser tarbek than the former Lord Gefke's firstborn son. If it had not been for his open mind, his easy realization that the document showed that tarbeks practiced primogeniture instead of the more practical and eugenic fard custom of parricide, he might not have conceived of that phase of his plan at all. But he had understood, and though he had used Aptop—now Lord Jandissl—he had not used him ill.

But what was the tarbek lord telling him? His *last* payment? Did he no longer need the crystal to pollute the Vermous colonies' seeps? Slith read on. "With the kind help of your friend Consul Van Dam, the former colonists have all been relocated in distant places where they will thrive without additives for their wells. Of course with the Vermous valleys empty, I will be lord over many fewer tarbeks than was my late father—who died in his cell almost a year ago—but I will be more secure in my

holding than was he. The fard chemists your little friend
Bleth sent to me maintain a constant watch on the state of
my wells and seeps, and we both know how honest and
clever she is!

"I remain your loyal friend Megidly Aptop, Lord
Jandissl."

Colonists relocated? Consul Van Dam? Bleth clever?
Slith had no idea what was going on. "Preletemifen!" he
bawled at his secretary. "Order my sandcar readied! I am
for Low Diverness!" The clerkish wend scurried to do his
bidding.

Even the finest vehicle could not make smooth the
rough roads, nor straighten out the curves and hills. The
route seemed to stretch out forever ahead of Slith, and
the edifices of Thember shrank behind him only slowly.
He could not wile away the long hours in sleep, with his
sandcar on automatic, because he was too anxious about
what he would find. He was doubly frustrated because the
road through the Damplag Trench was closed by new
landslides, and he had to take the longer route, through
Krat and past Valbissag.

The first hints that his fears were justified came miles
before he reached the turnoff from the main road. Passing
west of Bladnost Gap the road became churned and rutted
by the tracks of heavy vehicles. He backtracked, and
found where the tracks joined the main road. A minor
trace, a road only by definition, ran off to the east, into
the hills sloping not toward Low Diverness, but toward
Valbissag. He rounded a jutting crag, and there before
him was a great trench, ten, even twenty times as deep as
the length of his sandcar, and a hundred times that wide.
Huge machines deep within the gutted earth looked as
small as firespit bugs, from his high perspective. A sheet-
iron tower, an ore mill, rose at the far side, and on it was
painted the logotype of a notable mining firm. CONSOLI-
DATED INTERSTELLAR MINERALS, the sign beneath it read.

"CIM! Here? There is nothing worth shipping offworld
in those rocks!" Slith headed toward the tower. As he approached, he saw that there was indeed a mine shack with
barracks, as he had suspected. Yet it was like no mine

shack he had ever seen. It was a fine three-story building, prefabricated of glass and shiny metal. The barracks attached to it resembled a five-star hotel, and through the expanse of tinted windows he could even see the glitter of that ultimate offworld decadence . . . a swimming pool.

"What is this?" he demanded of the first hard-hatted bors he saw in the mine office. "What are you doing here?"

"We are mining vanadium," said the bors. "What are *you* doing, tracking dirt onto our clean carpet?"

Slith ignored his dusty feet. "Vanadium? Vanadium! That is the Peldiment Formation, and there are only useless traces of vanadium in it. Fill in your hole and be gone! You will destroy the flow of groundwaters to a thousand wells in the valleys beyond!"

"We have received no complaints," the bors said. "And again I ask, who are you to come in here and order me to depart? We are properly licensed. We hold mineral rights to this land. We hold as well a direct commission from the Arbiter himself."

Just then the conversation—such as it was—was interrupted by a deep, palpable thrumming sound that seemed to come from everywhere at once. "I must go," the bors said. "The ship is arriving."

Ship? "Is this an ocean?" Slith asked himself, having seen photographs of one in a book. He soon realized what kind of ship it was when a shadow crossed over the broad span of sun-filtering glass overhead. A spaceship. A spaceship was about to land here, in the middle of the high desert!

Slith darted outside. The ship was just coming to rest beside the ore mill. The sound of lesser machines now replaced the deep note of its engines. Conveyor arms reached out from the mill tower and penetrated hatches up and down the shiny swordlike hull of the ship. The rattle of low-grade rock, that could hardly be defined as an ore at all, deafened him as the first chunks landed within empty holds.

"Why are you doing this?" asked Slith of two bors miners as the ship was being loaded. "There is no point to it. The ore is useless." The bors did not answer him.

They instead picked up their helmets. "Back to work," one said. "Next ship arrives at seven in the morning."

"Another ship?" Slith was astounded. "How can you keep up?"

"It isn't easy. If we had to trace seams or anything, we'd never make it. But 'take it all,' the foreman says. 'No need to pick and choose. Just take it all.' "

That made even less sense to Slith. Take the overburdened along with the so-called ore? He now realized that indeed he had not seen any tailings heaps. Everything excavated went into the ship—the ships.

Another visit to the office did not enlighten him any further. The engineers and executives were all polite, and seemed themselves wholly uninformed, and the geologist was "in the field" and unavailable for questioning. Shortly later, Slith climbed back into his sandcar.

Before he reached Jandissl's palace Slith saw three more major operations. One was another open pit "mine" from which useless rock was being excavated. A rail spur had been run to that pit, and a constant stream of hopper cars removed overburden and "ore" alike as fast as it was lifted from the hole. "Where are you taking it?" Slith asked the engineer in charge of the train that was currently being loaded.

"We are filling a canyon in Blanderstan," he was told. "It is a flood-control project, I believe."

"There are never any floods in Blanderstan," Slith said.

"And now there never will be, will there?" was the reply.

The next operation Slith saw was a subsurface mine. There, he saw tailings piles, mountainous heaps of rocky rubble drawn from deep in the planet. Yet he saw no processing facility, and no provision for ore to be removed from the site. "What are you mining?" he asked the first man he saw, another bors, of course. All the miners on Phyre were bors. All the miners everywhere were, he suspected. He was standing beside a chart table on which complex subterranean shafts and laterals were outlined.

"We are looking for the chromium layer in the Feldnap Basalt."

"You are mad! There is no chromium layer in the Feldnap or any other basalt."

"Then I will have an interesting paper to present at the next Geological Society meeting, if we indeed find chromium," said the bors. "Besides, I will be a rich man whether or not chromium is found. My crew is being paid by the hour for all this. We work three shifts, and still everyone gets a bit of overtime too."

Madness! thought Slith—though by now he was beginning to see a glimmering of collective method behind the insane activities, when they were all taken together.

Slith saw evidence of the third project long before he got near it. Huge trucks blocked most of the poor road, limiting Slith's pace to theirs, which was very slow. They were like tank trucks with the kind of bins that held dry powdery products. When he saw several of them pulled off the road, their drivers sharing a pot of kaf, he also stopped.

Over a tin cup of strong brew, Slith asked, "What are you carrying?"

"Cement for the new Ballanbuff Dam," he was told.

"The old Ballanbuff Dam is in fine shape," Slith said. "I drove over it only last month. Why must there be a new one?"

"The new one is a mile down the canyon. I hear it will be twice as tall."

"What good is that? Ballanbuff is a reservoir dam, not hydroelectric. The periodic floods only supply enough water to fill the old reservoir. A new one, with greater surface area, will only enhance evaporation. There will be less water to be piped to Thember, not more."

"Are you a geologist?" the driver inquired.

"As a matter of fact, I am," replied Slith.

"Well, I'm not. I am a truck driver, and it's time for me to get back to work."

The palace at Low Diverness looked no different than it had the last time Slith had visited it. Only its occupant had changed. "Arrgh. Slith Wrasselty!" said Lord Jandissl.

"Megidly!" Slith replied in kind, then got right to business. "What's this I hear? Are you abandoning the valleys?"

"We already have," replied the tarbek. "Now that Valbissag can no longer produce the ingredients to make your formula . . ."

"What? Is it true?"

"So says little Bleth, who runs things there. The wells that supplied the raw materials no longer do so. We had no choice. I am quite thankful to your friend the consul, for taking all the former settlers off my hands. Low Diverness was getting downright dangerous. People were going crazy, just like before, when the old man was running things." He shrugged. "But now I am rich, and do not care. I bought an interest in the firm that's construction the Ballanbuff Dam, and in a mining firm looking for chromium up in those hills, and . . ."

"Enough! I know! And in a firm mining vanadium, too!"

The chief looked puzzled. "No, I do not own shares in such a firm. Everyone knows there is no minable vanadium on Phyre. I bought shares in a shipping company—six fine interplanetary spaceships. I am supplying bulk rock to be used as shielding around the new solar monitoring station that will orbit Phyre—Phyre the sun, I mean. All I have to do is dump rock from a mine just off the Thember road into orbit, where the constructors can find it later. And my ships earn not only premium freight rates, but there is a hazard allowance and . . ."

Slith had heard enough. "I must visit Valbissag!" he said, standing abruptly. "I must see Thplet and find out more." Megidly Aptop Jandissl was disappointed that his friend Slith, who had made him lord of Low Diverness, was to leave without sampling his grateful hospitality. Slith, however, not only felt an urgency to get to the bottom of things, but had not brought extra nose filters with him, and already he experienced a sensation like worms crawling inside his snout.

"Thplet! Are you mad? You are throwing away your patrimony! Why have you allowed those excavations to proceed? The hydraulics of the whole region are being disrupted. Valbissag's wells will produce unpredictable products far into the next millennium."

"What do I care?" said Thplet, lounging in the steamy mist of Valbissag, the spring itself. He was well groomed and becoming chunky, Slith saw. Yet he did not seem even as happy as he had been when his kingdom was a cave in High Diverness, and his only subject one small fardling. Slith had long since realized that it was Thplet himself who had nursed Bleth then, and that there had been no third person living with them in the hills. "What do I care?" Thplet repeated. "If the wells and seeps and springs all change, why then, there will be new discoveries to be made, new processes and formulations to patent in the name of Valbissag. Then, perhaps, I will have wealth of my own."

"What do you mean? You are wealthy already—or you were, before you threw it all away by not contesting the mining firms, the dam construction company, and . . . The patents you inherited from Thradz were worth uncounted millions."

"How true. And how false. The patents were worth millions before the mining changed the groundwaters— but I inherited nothing from Thradz but the real estate and the title. Thradz himself owned no patents, and I express a certain vindictive satisfaction that their present owner will soon become a poor impoverished fard just like me. *Then* certain things will change around here, you can be sure."

"I do not understand," Slith protested. "The patents are yours. Who else would have inherited them?"

"No one did. Are you so slow? Haven't you figured it out yet? It was not Thradz who bought up the rights on father's patents when they expired. It was not Thradz who caused you to be thrown in prison when you falsely claimed them. It was Bleth who did that! Bleth, my wife—my only wife, as long as the royalties her patents earn continue to trickle in."

"Bleth? Bleth had me thrown in prison? But Bleth *saved* me when I was there!"

"And Bleth saved me from unmanning myself! I did

not know balls could be bought from indigents in the dry middens. Yet am I grateful to her for that? Indeed I am not! My life here is hell! I, The Valbissag, am forbidden from mating with my female subjects—among whom I do not count Bleth, who rules *me*. No sons but hers will compete for my estate, when I am killed. I am a miserable fard, Slith, and I have Bleth to thank for it—and now that she deems her four sons and three daughters to be enough, I am even denied the fleeting pleasure of congress with her. Four sons, can you imagine? I think she used offworld medicines for that."

Slith was startled, but when he considered that Bleth owned all the original Valbissag patents, and that there were many kinds of hormone-altering compounds among them ... Yet he did not speak of it to Thplet.

"But how did she do it?" Slith wondered aloud.

"I suppose she ordered them from one of the jobbers on Colony Boulevard," Thplet replied.

"No, no! How did she get the patents? I could not acquire them because I was as yet a minor. How could Bleth, a fardling with less legal standing than I had, have registered for those patents?"

"I do not know. Perhaps it has something to do with her trust fund and its trustee."

"Trust fund? *Trust* fund? Bleth? But where did she get the money for that? I do not understand. She did not yet have the patents and their revenue, so where did the money come from?"

"I suspect it was your money, Slith. How often did she beg funds for 'charity'?"

"Charity? You mean that silly orphanage? Keeping useless fardlings alive?"

"Bleth did not ignore your complaints about that," Thplet said. "She came around to your point of view— that keeping alive those who could not survive on their own resources diluted the health of the fard race. Yet, she did not tell you? I imagine the 'charity' she came to favor was the Bleth Wrasselty Trust, which was administered by the Arbiter's consul himself. . . .

"Ah, yes," Thplet continued, "I will be glad when she is again poor, her patents worth nothing because they depend upon Valbissag's waters for their utility. Then, at least, I will truly be The Valbissag, however poor I am."

Slith rose to his feet and snorted Valbissag's mists from his nose. "I must see Bleth," he said. "Where is she?"

"She is in Thember at this moment," Thplet told him. "She is overseeing her interests there."

Slith did not inquire what interests Bleth might have in Thember. He would find out from Bleth herself. He again climbed back in his sandcar, and headed for the rail terminus in Krat. He would leave the car to be fetched later, and would take a fast and comfortable train back to the city.

"Dad? Why didn't you find an easier way to do it?"

"To do what, son?"

"To destroy Valbissag, of course."

"I had no intention of destroying Valbissag. I merely wished to maintain the equilibrium of all the worlds of the Xarafeille Stream."

"I don't understand."

"Rob, can you imagine what would have happened if Slith Wrasselty's formula had been distributed among all the worlds where tarbeks dwell? Chaos! Whole economies would have been created and destroyed. The stable demography of vast regions, even worlds, would have been disrupted. There would have been wars. Even the rumor of the formula's existence caused thousands of deaths on Jawal ad Heim. There was no way to guarantee that the substance would not be used to pollute wells in territory already occupied by fards, wends . . ."

"You could have regulated its use! There was no need for such extreme measures. There had to be a less expensive way—how much did you spend hauling rocks into orbit, and . . ."

"Think larger, son. And think of my mandate, as Arbiter. *Money* was not a concern. Money never is. The interstellar shipping industry alone, for all the false expense of passenger travel, would pay for a thousand such operations every year, and no one would notice the drain. The one thing I do not concern myself with is money. Whatever money that is created in the system must be put back into it, in some way. I merely use it to further my ends while returning it to the Xarafeille Stream. Lives, now, are another matter. I do not spend them profligately, if at all."

"I understand, I suppose. And as for your mandate . . . As Arbiter, you do not regulate much, do you?"

"Only shipping, really. I control the flow of goods and people among the worlds, because only I know the secret of interstellar flight, but I do not meddle on the worlds unless I am called to do so, or unless the interstellar peace is threatened—or to protect my monopoly on shipping."

"So hiring those miners and dam builders wasn't exorbitant, only roundabout?" Rob looked as if he would have to think about that.

Bleth Wrasselty frequented the finest restaurants in Thember, places even Slith, wealthy as he was, seldom visited. "Miss Bleth," said the host, "your table, as always, is waiting. Please . . ."

"You have your own private table here?" Slith was amazed.

"Blame yourself for my profligacies," Bleth replied, smiling. "It was you who introduced me to fine hotels." A slight frown crossed her face. "It was you who introduced me to food, too, if you will recall."

"That may be so," he allowed. "But do not blame me for your difficulties. From Thplet I have learned that you betrayed me long before I even considered deserting you."

"Is that so?" Bleth's ears flattened against her head. "Were you kind to me in the Vermous Hills when we first met? Then who was it who threw stones at me? Who left me for dead amid the fumes and poisons? Was that another fard you do not know?"

"That is unfair! That was before I nursed you! I was within my rights."

"Perhaps so. You were within the range of allowable behavior, perhaps—but I do not have to like that. I do not have to like you." They were seated by attentive waiters. Conversation ceased while they decided upon drinks and appetizers. Slith chose a bitter wrass cocktail, which suited his mood. Bleth chose something mild and sweet, which suited her outward aspect.

"But now you are about to become poor, when the Valbissag patents are of no more use," said Slith. "Haven't you thought ahead?"

Bleth laughed. "I think further ahead than anyone," she said. "A fardling must think ahead, or die. It is the nature of things. It improves the race." Was she bitter? Slith could not tell from her bantering tone.

"Then what will you do? Will you stay with Thplet?"

"I will not stay with Thplet. I do not like Thplet, though I once thought I did. I would have preferred to stay with you, I think. I remember our times in Varamin Park with warm regret. I even have happy memories of the old shop where we made Additive-Three-A for the late Lord Jandissl."

"Me too," Slith admitted, sighing. "You were so small and cuddly then. . . ." He would have blushed, had he been an old-human. He had just thought of that first time he had awakened with Bleth beside him, and his now-shrunken breasts tingled with a kind of bodily nostalgia.

Abruptly he changed the subject. "Thplet said that you have . . . interests . . . here. May I ask about them?" Thplet had seemed confident that once the Valbissag patents were rendered useless, Bleth would have to fall back on him. Slith was less sure of that. She had dealt cleverly with both him and Thplet in the past, to her advantage. Why should Thplet believe she would not succeed a third time?

"I invest in my future. A bit of real estate, a few stocks, other things."

"I suppose one of them is a vanadium mine," Slith said.

"Why, no, not exactly. But I have stock in Consolidated Interstellar Minerals, which operates a mine not far from Low Diverness."

"And does 'Blanderstan' mean anything to you?"

"My railway has a lucrative contract hauling quarried stone there. A flood-control project, I believe."

"Bah! It never floods in Blanderstan!"

"And now it never will, isn't that so?" Bleth smiled brightly. Slith felt a sense of disorientation, as if he were in a feedback loop where the same things were repeated over and over.

"And you must own shares in the firm that supplies the cement for the Blanderstan dam."

"What odd ideas you have, Slith! I am not well versed in heavy industry. No, I merely lease trucks and drivers to them—through a subsidiary of my railway."

"Then Thplet is wrong," Slith concluded. "You will not, when all settles out, return to Valbissag?"

"Of course I will! My sons and daughters are there. But I will not stay. Thplet suffers from a deficiency of humor, of late. I have a fine home here in Thember."

An uncomfortable prescience of how Bleth might answer those questions most on his mind kept Slith from asking them. He doubted his ability to remain calm, and he had not yet eaten, and did not wish to be ejected from the restaurant unfed. Bleth observed how his ears flattened and that his flared, black nostrils had narrowed. She asked the source of his discomfort.

Slith did not respond directly. Instead, he merely speculated aloud on a tangential subject. "I am curious," he stated, "as to how you acquired the means to become wealthy."

"I knew the people whom you knew. Many of them had means, and saw my favor as your future mate—or so they anticipated—as an asset worth cultivating. It was not hard to put together a nest egg of my own. The rest was mere hard work. A pity, isn't it, that we did not breed? Think what bright, hard fards our union might have produced."

"Ah, Bleth," Slith sighed. "We are both of a kind. In a way, it is almost a shame we are not still together."

"Do not let simple nostalgia cloud your common sense, Slith," she replied sharply. "You were selfish, and did not wish to have sons. You feared death too much." She made an apologetic grimace. "As did I, I suppose. I feared not experiencing seven parturitions."

Bleth wriggled in her chair. "I must excuse myself," she said, and stood up suddenly. Slith did not know what to make of that. Fards' water-retentive desert adaptation precluded their using a sudden need to urinate as an excuse for a sudden departure, so Slith simply nodded, nonplussed.

He was alone at the table for several minutes. Then a waiter approached diffidently. "The Lady Bleth apologizes, Sar Wrasselty. She has been called away on a matter of urgency. She asks your forgiveness. Please enjoy your meal at her expense."

Slith ate with less than his usual enthusiasm. When he finished, he simply departed. "Bleth is paying," he muttered, "thus Bleth can supply the waiter's tip, if she wishes to."

CHAPTER 23

FROM: Arbiter
TO: Hans VanOtterbeek
TEXT: Congratulations! Citation appended. Report
to Newhome in person 3-22 CSY for retirement
ceremony and formal award of Legion of Merit
medal. Expect full media coverage. Draft press release
appended.

"I am not pleased with this story," Parissa stated, imitating Bleth's manner—the Bleth of the latest episodes, not the innocent child of the earlier ones. John Minder was thus reminded that his own daughter too would someday become a woman. *She might even become Arbiter*, he thought, vacillating again, *though she is yet too young for me to be sure her adult personality will be suited to that*. There had never been a woman Arbiter but, he thought, there was no rule against it. "I see no happily-ever-after in it," Parissa explained with Bleth-like inflection. "Why do Slith and Bleth not marry?"

"Bleth is married to Thplet, The Valbissag," Sarabet explained. "She cannot have two husbands. After all, would you want Mom to marry again, so you would have two daddies?"

"Would my new daddy tell me happily-ever-after stories?" asked Parissa, thus innocently avoiding the thrust of her sister's intention. Divorce was not mentioned; the older Minder children knew their sibling's literal turn of mind and her tendency to take the examples from stories to heart, and they did not want to have to reassure her that there was no possibility that *her* mother and father would divorce.

"Not all stories end happily, dear," John Minder said, "But you have not yet heard the end of this one. It takes place years later, but I will tell it to you now, because nothing of real note happened in between."

A muted bell chimed over the door of Professor Slith Wrasselty's fine book-lined study. He carefully set his cup of tea—Kemp and Bastian's Finest Old-Earth Green—on the long, finely polished granite table, carefully avoiding his spread-out notes for tomorrow morning's lecture. He often sipped warm tea to make himself drowsy an hour or so before bedtime. "Who is it, Fenethelem?" he asked his aging wend majordomo. "Who could be calling this late?"

"It is an agent of the Parkoon Messenger Service with a parcel for you," said Fenethelem. "He insists on delivering it into your hands alone."

"Very well," Slith said, rising from his antique leather chair, grumbling softly at the inflated officiousness of messengers with very minor responsibilities.

The package was wrapped in the azure and maroon of the Parkoon megacorp, and it thus blended with the identical colors of the thickset bors messenger's tunic. Slith took the parcel and was about to set it aside until morning, but the messenger, he saw, had not departed. "Go!" Slith commanded. "What are you waiting for?"

"I was instructed to remain, to verify to the sender that you have indeed opened the parcel and have viewed its contents."

"What? Your customer commands the door of my very house?" His annoyance had brought him to full wakefulness. "Begone!"

"Hah! I was also told to expect such obstreperousness," snorted the bors. "The sender instructed me to give you *this,* if you become obnoxious." He proffered a gold-colored business card.

Slith had to squint to read the ornate ultramarine blue script. It was a hauntingly familiar card. Where had he seen its like? As often happens, the memory of an odor and a flavor surfaced before that of an event or a face. It was the smell and the taste of live leatherbellies plucked from their pool of thick, fresh cream. "The Arbiter!" Slith gasped. "What has that greasy-headed old-human sent me?" He did not hear the bors's grunt at such *lèse majesté;* he was now quite curious, and the sound of wrapping paper tearing had masked the bors's muffled exclamation. "A newspaper?" Slith expostulated. "And it is not even today's! It is two weeks old!" Then he saw that a certain front-page article had been highlighted in a shade of fluorescent green specifically tailored to fard vision, drawing the eye much as certain reds and oranges do for other races of man.

Consular Program Vindicated Again!

Adding to the glorious successes of the Arbiter's consuls on worlds across the Xarafeille Stream is the resolution of pending conflict on Vela (X-1029). Consul Hans VanOtterbeek brought together the efforts of wendish paleontologists, bors geologists and technicians, and intrepid tarbeks who volunteered for experimental medical doses. Their mutual goal was the isolation and reproduction of a hitherto-unreproduceable chemical discovered by an obscure fard chemist, who wishes to remain anonymous. Consul VanOtterbeek was recently awarded the Arbiter's Legion of Merit for his part in the happy affair.

The substance (whose compete nature and formulation are known only to the Arbiter himself) renders the wells and seeps of certain deep deserts palatable to tarbeks. On Vela, use of the chemical has averted a devastating war between local tarbeks displaced by geological events and the wendish population currently in possession of lands the tarbeks coveted.

Have you heard it said "We have no choice but war?" Have your world's leaders, your newspaper editors (or you yourself) called upon the Arbiter to send his white warships and his ferocious poletzai to resolve an otherwise-unresolvable dispute? The Arbiter's consuls can help you too! The cost of their services is not measured in creds or human lives; it is mere pennies dropped into the fare boxes of bus, train, or taxi. There is a consular office in every major city, on every world of the Xarafeille Stream.

Maintain the peace of your neighborhood, your community, your world, and the Xarafeille Stream! Save yourself the burden of paying for the launching of white warships, the mobilization of marching men! In Thember, call 45-ARBITER or visit the consulate on Park Street at the corner of Booksellers' Way. The Arbiter's consul in Thember is no outsider, no offworlder; she is one of you, familiar with the streets of your towns, the sands and rocks of your deserts. Do not complain to your friends, or suffer silently. Take action! Call or visit your consulate this week, this very day!

Slith was stunned. He was, for several moments, too irate even to speak, and when he did, it was in Old High Fardic and consisted of expletives and obscenities inexpressible in any other tongue. It was wholly indecipherable to the bors messenger, who nonetheless understood the tone of it, and who then decided that his mission had been completed. He departed, unnoticed by Slith.

"My formula!" spat Slith. "He analyzed my molecule and mass-produced it from substances that came up through no well! He stole my treasure, my hope of immeasurable wealth!" Slith did not stop to consider, not then, that with the changes in Valbissag's groundwaters his formula was no longer of any use. He did not consider the years and the millions of creds that had gone into the new synthesis of the compound. He continued to expostulate in that vein until another offending phrase caught his eye. " 'An obscure fard'!" he squalled. ". . . Wishes to remain anonymous'! The old-human wretch has stolen not just the substance but the glory! Where is *my* Legion of Merit medal? I will protest! Fenethelem! Call my carriage! Call and announce to the Arbiter's consul that I will arrive shortly with my grievance!"

"It is nighttime, Dr. Wrasselty," murmured the wend. "The consul will not be there."

"Are you stupid? Are you slow? Call anyway! Leave a message. I will see him at dawn's first glimmer."

"Very well, Sar. But are you aware that there is a new consul, and that it is a she, not a he?"

"No matter! All old-humans are the same to me. Obey immediately!"

Fenethelem, not willing to risk further verbal abuse, departed to do as he was ordered. If his employer was unduly taken aback by what he discovered in the morning, it would be no fault but his own.

In the dark hours before dawn and his impending appointment, Slith did not sleep. At some time during his fourth or fourteenth rereading of the offensive article he discovered the sticky-note affixed near the bottom of the page, hitherto hidden by the paper's central fold. "Slith," he read, "I thought you should see this. Of course the still-sensitive nature of the situation and the danger of misuse of the chemical in the wrong hands precludes my public recognition of your seminal contribution, but if you will visit my new consul in Thember she will have something for you. It is only a small token of my gratitude and esteem, and no recompense for your true costs, but it is from my heart. Sincerely, John Minder."

"My 'true costs' indeed!" complained Slith. "What does he know? 'No recompense'? Fah! Of that I am sure."

Slith's words were angry, sullen, and bitter, but in his high fardish intonations could be heard a softer note, too. After all, Slith was again very wealthy. He could not spend half what his patents, licenses, and sales brought in. Of what use then would greater wealth have been? And he was a respected professor at the University as well. Graduate students, even eminences, nodded to him on the walkways between the great edifices of Thember. What need had he of further recognition or public praise? No, Slith was not half as bitter as he pretended to be, but he did not wish to stray much from his public character.

In the morning, he decided, he would indeed pick up his "token" from the new consul, and he would not create a scene or scatter dander about—well, not much of a scene, and not much dander, anyway; only enough to maintain the carefully cultivated irascible image his students and colleagues loved and feared.

* * *

Thember's dawn appeared with its usual diffuse brilliance, with the suddenness characteristic of clear, dry air and an almost equatorial location. The many effusions of vapor from the rich sources of water in the cosmopolitan, multiracial city took the sharpest edge from the light, but little of its fresh intensity. The smallest pebble in the pavement sparkled and glowed with its truest color, made glossy with rarefied dew.

Slith noticed none of that as he strode purposefully toward the consulate, though dawn's promise rapidly gave way to the beginning of a delightful day. Yet his step was lighter than a fard's usual nimble prance. What, he wondered, would the Arbiter's "token" be? He pushed through the fine new etched-glass doors of the consulate without seeing the name of the new consul engraved thereon. "I am Slith Wrasselty—Dr. Slith Wrasselty—and I am here to receive the Arbiter's gift," he announced.

"Come in please, Doctor," said the wend receptionist. "Please take a seat in there, in the consul's office." Slith did so. The office was appointed in the style of a Thember town house (and such town houses were of course appointed in the style of fine desert palaces like Valbissag). The walls were hand-pressed stucco, the sills and lintels were metamorphosed conglomerate polished to a high sheen—a conglomerate that Slith recognized as being from the Pfibest Formation, quarried near the edge of Valbissag, perhaps from within Valbissag territory itself.

The rearmost wall, behind the imposing marble desk, was adorned by a single great painting, one that Slith recognized immediately as Fratteth's "Epiphany in the Colors of Sunset," which was painted with colored sand and coarsely ground minerals in a matrix of spatterslug glue. Slith recognized it not because he was a connoisseur of the arts, but because it was the very same painting that had hung in the anteroom of his own house in Varamin Park!

His emotions, at that moment, were indecipherable even to himself. His state became, if anything, less clear, in the moments that followed.

"Hello, Slith," said the new consul as she stepped through the door into the room.

Slith did not say hello. At first, he merely stared, his jaw hanging, at the small fard in the crimson Arbitorial tunic, at the black piping on its sleeves, lapels, and hem. When he did speak, it was only a croak. "Bleth?" he croaked. "Bleth!"

It was an odd reunion. Both parties had much to say, but—at least at first—lacked the wherewithal or the courage to say it. Only gradually, as the morning wore on over bowls of rootsap soup, did they become enough used to each other and to the strained circumstances to begin to tell their individual tales.

Bleth explained the strange circumstances of Slith's PhD, of the abortive attempt to enlist the university dons to gain control of the patents. When she saw the fur on his neck rise as his anger grew, she hastened to say, "That was Thplet's idea, not mine! He had already approached Prethelerimen before I knew of it. He would have *shared* the patents with them, rather than lose them." Slith understood that her indignation was genuine—"sharing" was an unsavory concept for a fard. Either one owned a thing, or one did not.

"Thplet's failings are now manifest!" he spluttered. "I begin to suspect a wandering scatmonger was his true sire. If Mother still lived . . ." He suppressed his ire, realizing that he still did not know all. "What happened next?" he demanded.

"As the Wrasselty patents were already registered to the Bleth Wrasselty Trust . . ."

"My patents!" Slith began—and again forced himself to be silent.

". . . Only your self-replicating molecule was still unassigned new ownership. Unfortunately, in the furor that then arose, amid accusations tossed back and forth between Thplet and the dons, the rights to it were assigned to Lord Jandissl before my friend Consul Van Dam could intervene and suppress it. That was most regrettable, considering the eventual cost of revising groundwater patterns throughout all Valbissag and of reinventing your discovery and redesigning it without self-replicating properties. But once the rights were assigned . . ."

Slith's anger gradually diminished. After all, that was dust long blown away on the wind, wasn't it? A good fard does not dwell forever on past failures or past wrongs. Besides, Slith was at that moment experiencing odd sensations he could not explain. To distract himself from them, he asked, "How did you obtain the consulship? I thought all consuls were old-humans."

"George Van Dam owed me a favor," Bleth said, fingering her tunic's crimson sleeve. "Of course I still had to pass the tests by myself, and attend the interviews. . . ."

"What favor was that?" Slith asked, interrupting.

Bleth smiled—a mature, womanly smile that did funny things to Slith's composure. "At the cave in High Diverness, you spoke with Thplet, but I did not come out because at that time I was quite angry with you—but I did not stuff my ears with sand to mute your voice. Later, when you were enjoying your new successes, I remembered a loose ravel that you had not seen fit to tie off."

Slith pondered. What had he and Thplet spoken of? Bleth, enjoying her game, allowed him time to guess at what she hinted. It was good that Slith was quick and clever—good for his self-esteem, anyway; he did not have to ask Bleth to explain. "The Arbiter's crystal! The one I could not find, in the History Division. You stole it for him!"

"I did not steal it! Hush, or my secretary will hear, and think ill of me. I merely borrowed it, and replaced it later when the Arbiter was done with it."

"How did you do it?" Slith demanded. "I could not even find it."

"Professional curiosity?" she asked, grinning—a grin that drew Slith back across several years to a much smaller Bleth whom he had once played rough-and-tumble with. Her expression was no less appealing to him for the years that had passed. She shook her head. "That is a long story, for another day."

"And will there be another day?" he asked. "You are no longer angry with me?"

"Would it please you, if that were so?"

"It would please me. I am not too proud to admit it. I often think of the old days when . . ."

"When together we made Additive-Three-A in the crumbly old shop on Colony Boulevard, and nursed hopes of a richer, fuller life, and . . ."

"And when I nursed a small fardling whose eyes lit up when I brought her shiny trinkets and . . ." Slith stood, and reached across the desk toward her. She moved around the obstruction, and when she was quite near him, lifted her head and turned it sideways as if ready to nurse. What transpired between them thereafter was not nursing, nor was it a tale to be told. Merely suffice it to say that upon later reflection Slith decided that if it had not been as sweet and joyous and pleasurable as nursing Bleth had been, even his phenomenal memory was not good enough to allow him to compare.

"*Now* they are happily-ever-after," Parissa crowed.

"Oh, how do you know?" growled Rob. But even Parissa, however literal-minded she usually was, did not take offense. She was not able to articulate her feeling, but of late she had sensed a certain affection beneath her brother's gruffness.

"What happened next, Dad?" Rob asked. "I mean, after they . . . Did Slith get his token? What was it?"

"You mean you haven't guessed? I thought it was quite an appropriate gift for Slith Wrasselty."

Rob's eyes widened. There were no more wood chips caught in the pile of his bedroom carpet, but no long time had passed since he had finished that project he had worked on for so long.

"It's beautiful!" Slith exclaimed, fondling the glossy swarrow-root staff. "And what are these carvings?"

"That is supposed to be me, I think," Bleth said between giggles. "Was I really that skinny when I first met you?"

"And this? No, never mind," said Slith. "I see that it is Chief Aptop waddling out of the Patent Office with the datacrystal between his legs."

"I think it is Lord Gefke," Bleth countered. "See the staff in his hand?"

"Then where is Thradz? No, the carver simply did not

know that Aptop did not have a staff, then, but it is he."
He smiled. "No staff is as pretty as this one!" he exclaimed. Slith stood straight and tall, as if he, not Thplet,
were The Valbissag, appearing in state before his subjects.

No staff would ever be lovelier for Slith Wrasselty.
Perhaps part of his attachment to it was mere ego, because it was a gift of the Arbiter. More likely, knowing
Slith, Bleth suspected it was lovely to him because all the
events symbolized in the tiny carvings that adorned it
from tip to knob where events from his own life. For
whatever reasons, not least because Slith had already admitted to himself that he had more wealth than he could
spend, and more honors than he could gloat over, it was
indeed a far better gift than money or medals would have
been.

Now, looking over the shiny fist-sized knob atop his
new staff, he saw Bleth. "There is nothing else, is there?"
he asked. Then he shook his head. "There is no need for
anything else," he answered himself, taking her small
hand in his own. "I now have everything."

"Everything?" Bleth queried. "What about heirs to
your clever genes? What about . . . children?"

EPILOGUE

Being Arbiter, even for one bred to the task, is not easy. I work long hours and my family suffers for that. I would like to think that they and I are reimbursed by a greater diminishment of suffering throughout the Xarafeille Stream, but of that I am not sure.

Still, hidden out there, perhaps behind vast obscuring nebulae, in orbit around some dim and unappealing star, is my fleet, unused. Out there lie the worlds where my poletzai raise a generation of children that may never wear my service's uniforms. Had I access to either, I ask myself, would I have used them? I am not sure. As things have unraveled thus far, I have not needed them, not really. Of that, I am sure.

John Minder XXIII's diary,
Newhome, undated

Slith was happy, but happiness did not make him foolish. "No fool is more foolish than one who is happy in his foolishness," he would have said. Thus there were no children. Bleth did not require more offspring to insure her own survival, and she often visited the ones she had—even the females. She had quietly, in an unfardlike manner, arranged for each of them to bond with fine and clever young fards who would, if her daughters were as wise as she, go far in the world. Such nepotism, she reasoned, did not dull the sharp edge of evolutionary fitness, because it was still Bleth who was preserving her own clever genes.

Slith would have accepted children—and a shortened

life span—as a fair price for the joys he shared with Bleth, but it did not prove necessary. An arbiter's consul had access to many things, including offworld contraceptives, and had that not been so Slith, a fine chemist, would have formulated them himself.

Both of them had their work, usually apart from each other, and they had their times together. As time passed, they were more often seen in far, wild places—the deep deserts or the high, bleak mountains—than in the fine restaurants and glittery nightspots of Thember. Once a lone prospector reported having run across them in a small valley in the Vermous Hills, not far from an abortive surface mining effort. "Fools they were, prospecting there!" said the prospector. "Everyone knows there's nothing good in the Bright Limes. Never was, either, even before the strip mines changed everything."

He was wrong, of course. The waters that had once trickled through the ancient microfossil beds in the white limestone had—along with other waters elsewhere, also now changed—shifted the balance of events far and near. By their part in this tale, they had determined the future history of all the worlds in the Xarafeille Stream.

"Oh, yes!" the prospector remembered. "The big fard was carrying a staff, mind you! A big, fancy swarrow-root staff, like he was The Valbissag himself." He laughed, as did his companions, at the foolishness of city people on holiday.

"Did they have babies, Daddy? Did they?"

"I haven't looked in on them for a while, dear," said John Minder, "and Bleth has had little to report to me, of late. Besides, Slith did not want children—not when I last heard of him."

"*Will* they have babies later? I want them to! They *need* babies to be happily-ever-after."

Rob suppressed one—no, several—acerbic comments. Then he smiled. "I can tell you what happened later, Priss," he said—though Rob, his sister Sarabet, and John Minder himself were aware that "later" had not truly happened yet. But as far as Parissa was concerned, *all* stories were "once upon a time," and told of events that were at once quite immediate and yet a long, long time ago. "Many years went by," said Rob, "and Slith celebrated his birthday with a party at the governor's palace in Thember. . . ."

"The governor's wife said again how smart I was," Slith commented. He never tired of such observations. "I said, 'I'm seventy years old. Even a rock can learn a lot, in seventy years.' I guess I'm not as puffed up as I used to be years ago, am I?" Yes, it was the eleventh of Plet by the old fardish calendar, and was Slith's seventieth birthday. Bleth, of course, was only forty-eight or thereabouts—she did not know for sure, having been too young to count when her mother had weaned her. "She— Governor Blant's wife—asked why I didn't have any kids to pass all my smarts on to. You know how those bors talk, as if nothing is too private to speak of."

"Lady Blant had a good point, though," Bleth observed. "It is a shame that such good fard genes as yours will be wasted."

Slith did not reply immediately. He was thinking, performing a mathematical calculation. Though it was a simple one, he was not—and never had been—a fool, so he recalculated several times before reaching a firm conclusion. "I am seventy years old," he said at last.

"And it took all that figuring to figure that out?" Bleth giggled. "Happy birthday, again."

"And you are what? Forty-eight?"

"About that," she replied, now understanding where he was leading. "And no, I have not yet passed my time."

"How did you know I was going to ask . . ."

"I am no fool, Slith Wrasselty. Now . . . shall we begin?"

Slith thought that was a fine idea. First, and obviously, such activities were . . . fun . . . even at seventy. They could not compare with nursing a fardling, but they were quite pleasant in their own way. Second, less obviously, even unconsciously, though Slith was knowledgeable enough to understand that his own fine genes were already conserved, because Thplet was his full sibling, there was still an ingrained proclivity to guarantee that they carried on.

What they did then needed no description. It was much the same between individuals of all races, all ages, even most species. Suffice it to say that over the course of a few years of such activity, Slith and Bleth produced not one but two children, a boy and a girl, before Bleth experienced her change of life, and that both of them benefited from their parents' genes and example, and were proud tributes to the fardish race.

And were Slith's lifelong fears warranted? Of course they were, for he was a good fard, and I have already said that his genes and Bleth's held true. By Slith's ninety-fifty birthday he had become not just old but crotchety and befuddled most of the time, and he had been bedridden for the better part of a year. Poor Bleth knew how he hated that. They had not been into the desert for half a decade, and when Slith was coherent enough to recognize Bleth, he complained to her of that. "I hang around only because I do not know how to die," he said, "and because I do not want you to be lonely."

Bleth assured him that however many years she lived, she had her memories for company, not to mention her work as a consul and her visits with her children and grandchildren by Thplet. Slith nodded. "Our son Splart is not stupid, is he? What is he doing these days?" Splart, a fine young fard who was almost an adult, was not stupid, merely patient. On his next visit he elegantly exchanged his father's bladder-infection pills for a potent poison made from spitbug eggs, and Slith died shortly thereafter, in his sleep.

Did Bleth have regrets? Of course she did, being human. But what she regretted were circumstances, not her reaction to them. Above all, she never felt one shred of remorse for the way she had sometimes treated and cheated Slith, in those long-gone early years. A fardling, she reflected, imbibed more than nutrients from his nurse's milk, and whatever she had done to Slith, he had really done to himself.

Bleth lived many years after Slith's passing, and worked for most of them. She occasionally visited Slith's drawer in the fine family mausoleum, a drawer right above Fladth's, and between Gleph's and Thplet's. Bleth's second son by Thplet, Kratz Wrasselty, was The Valbissag then. As he was a wise son and sometimes listened to his mother, the town and countryside were much nicer now than when they had been ruled by Thradz, Thplet, or even old Fladth—though with the exception of Thradz they had been good fards all, and exemplars of the race.

If you liked *The Wells of Phyre*,
be sure to read the first book
in the Arbiter series
Stepwater
on sale from Roc now

Finding nothing else of note, he returned to the glass case, and lifted it aside. The blue crystal gleamed brighter still. It was cool to the touch, no heavier than a crystal of that amazing size should be, and when his ring clacked against it it made a sound much like any crystal might make, but still, Barc felt uneasy handling it. Perhaps it was the setting he had found it in—obviously, someone had once thought it important, and worthy of great respect. Though Barc could not explain his own feelings, he set the blue gem down gently, and replaced its cover. He was hungry and thirsty. The sodden feel of the surface underfoot reminded him that water ran from the room. Did it come from somewhere high enough to be clean, free of mahkrat feces and slither slime? He searched, holding his globe high and slightly behind. There! It was coming from behind one of the wall medallions, the "doors." Poking and prying, he pulled an edge of the heavy metal rectangle free. It *was* a door. It swung open without much effort, on a narrow passage.

The water on the floor was still suspicious, but the passage seemed to lead upward. Barc followed it. He followed it and continued to follow it, ever slightly upward. The trickle was undiminished. By now, he had forgotten his thirst, and was consumed with interest in the passageway. It seemed an entirely natural passageway, and it was unlike the wide, branching ways he was familiar with. Where did it lead?

A scent tickled his nostrils. It was nothing strange, but for a moment it surprised him. It smelled like rain, like the ground outside smelled after a shower, when soil bacteria freshened and bloomed. Barc pushed on. It *was* rain.

When he muffled his globe in his shirt, he saw a glow not from his own lamp or another glow light, but from outside.

Barc's thoughts raced. Outside? Had he found a secret exit from Margal Town? One without gate guards to stop him and humiliate him by calling his mother for permission to let him out? One unknown to his nosy cousin, Dird, and even to Uncle Grast? The possibilities the discovery promised were limitless. "Barc, where are you?" he imagined his mother asking. "Just exploring the old caves," he imagined his reply. "Ah well," he imagined her sighing, "at least it's safe." Safe. Even the oldest caverns were stable. There had not been a cave-in in a century. They were safe, stable, and to Barc's dismay, they had begun to become . . . boring. Today was different, of course, but in how many old rooms could he expect to find things like the blue crystal? The most exciting thing he had found before this was old bones, perhaps of an explorer less skilled or lucky than himself. The thought of death in the lower caves had spiced his wanderings for a while, but the more he looked at the bones, the more they resembled leftovers from some old-time barbecue.

The enticing, fresh glow inspired him to great effort. It was a very small glow, from a minute hole—the source of the water. He had to dig his way out. He had to claw past cobbles, push past roots, then scrabble over rubble and through dense brush but, finally, he got out.

He stood in cloudy daylight within a few paces of the river, just a few obels downstream of the South Margal bridge. He was outside. He was . . . free. Glancing behind him, he could see no trace of his exit. Next time, he would have to bring something down from the upper caves with him, something unsuspicious to mark the spot.

Becoming aware of the time, of the low sun-glow behind the clouds, he realized it was already late. Barc pushed back through the brush, then scrambled over the rubble, and ran most of the way down the long, narrow passage. It was clean and clear; he had encountered nothing on the way up it that might have caused him to stumble, and he was comfortable in the dark, even more than most of his kind.

Exiting the crystal's shrine, he could not replace the fallen door—but then, no one but he had discovered the place in ages, anyway. It did not matter. Barc hurried back through familiar caverns and passageways. About halfway home he realized that, with the river so near, he had forgotten to assuage his thirst as had been his initial intent.

GLAICE

an Arbiter tale
on sale late 1996

Tep Inutkak, of the ikut race of man on Glaice, stood over two meters tall and was covered with white fur. His fellow students at the Metok University, most of whom sprang from other kinds of parents, considered him a man mostly because he was half again the height of a lissome mantee male, weighed three times as much as a jittery fard, and was not afraid of a good rough-and-tumble with the bors males in his dormitory.

But tonight, he was working on his paper, which was a week late. He had filed his long, yellow claws to blunt nubs that did not slip off his terminal's keys or obliterate the letters on them. He had adjusted his chair just so, to accommodate his stub of a tail. Those things helped, but they didn't aid the flow of words and ideas from his brain to fingers to keys, from the keys to the multi-terabyte data-storage crystals somewhere deep within the clammy basements of the university.

It wouldn't be the end of the world if Tep didn't get the paper in by the end of the week, but he was afraid it might be the end of his academic career. He envisioned his ignominious return to the Inutkak ikut band, and his future thereafter. There was nothing wrong with the Inutkak life, Tep assured himself. Someday when he was much older, he'd be ready to challenge the old *shahm,* to take his place as chief. But now he was too young, and enjoyed city life far too much.

Tep struggled with the paper for another hour before he pushed his keyboard aside and waited for a printout.

"Maybe somebody down at the bar can help me with the last part," he muttered. Maybe a beer or two would loosen his head just enough so he could finish it himself. In all likelihood someone at the bar *would* be able to help, because the Last Atopak Tavern was a hangout for Metok U. grad students.

As luck would have it, Tep recognized a group of potentially useful fellow students the minute he entered the bar. Also as luck would have it, they were wholly engrossed in a discussion, and did not welcome his persistent efforts to change the subject to his paper's topic. "Tep Inutkak," said Velanda, a bors archaeology student, "don't you even care if the mantees kick you off your own planet?"

"Huh? Kick me off Glaice? I was born here."

"Don't you watch the news?" Velanda and the others seemed surprised, but not excessively so. Most of them were old enough to know what it was like to be a second-year grad student. There was seldom time for anything but study. Velanda took pity on Tep, and brought him up to date.

It seemed that an ikut band somewhere on the other side of the planet had purposefully disrupted their usual migration pattern so they could mate with another band that occupied the same territories, but in other seasons. Everyone knew how finely choreographed ikut migration cycles were, and how disastrous it was if a band got off schedule. If a band missed its regular voyage through the equatorial waters, they would also miss out on certain kinds of fish they needed to stay healthy.

The Ketonak band missed the southern half of their migration and ended up back in their northern camp at just the time the local mantee throng arrived to mate on the offshore rocks. Happily for the Ketonak, the mantees contained many of the trace nutrients they had missed by not completing their voyage south. Unhappily for them, the mantees did not willingly submit to being eaten.

"Cannibals?" exclaimed Tep. "They killed and ate other people? Are they still living in the stone age?" he asked, shaking his head. They were, his fellow students agreed.

"But that's only part of the story!" insisted Blent Dagro, another bors, a chemistry postdoc. "The Warm Stream mantee throngmother is taking them into Metok High Court. She's brought murder charges against their shahm."

Tep had just drained his second mug of beer and, realizing that he would get no help with his paper from anyone present, decided to go back to his room and try again. "Well, it *is* murder, isn't it? Mantees are people, too." He stood, and set down his empty mug.

"It's killing—but *murder?* The Ketonak only did it to live. In the old days before there was a High Court, all ikuts ate mantee, didn't they? You tell us, Tep. You're the expert on food chains."

"I wish I was," Tep said, sighing. "I never will be, unless I get this paper done, though, since all you guys want to talk about is mantee stew . . ." He turned to leave.

"Wait, Tep!" said Velanda. "I'll go with you. Maybe I can help with your paper, and then I'll tell you the rest of the story about the Ketonak and the mantees."

"Sure," he said. "You can tell me some on the way. Especially about how what the Ketonak did affects *me.* I didn't eat any mantees."

Velanda told him. "It would have stopped right there. The court would have awarded the Warm Stream throng damages, and probably would have ordered the Ketonaks disbanded and scattered among the other bands, which is traditional, isn't it?"

"That's what people did centuries ago," Tep agreed. "But I don't think there's been a similar case in generations. I suppose now that there's a formal court and all, things are different. But you still haven't said how—"

"As I said, it would've stopped right there except that Professor Rakulit, who's been putting together a book on radiocarbon dating of prehistoric sites on Glaice, and—"

"Rakulit? Isn't he a seel, too?"

"Tep! Don't call them that. Professor Rakulit is a mantee. Calling him a 'seel' even makes him *sound* like he's something to eat."

"It's the ikut word for 'mantee,' " Tep protested. "It doesn't mean anything bad."

"Hah! If there was an ikut encyclopedia, I wonder if 'seel' would be cross-referenced along with *bors* and *tarbeks* as 'other human subspecies' or with *ritvak* and *etolat* under 'traditional ikut meals?' "

"So did they eat your committee chairman, or what?" Tep asked facetiously.

"Tep! Professor Rakulit has proven that the mantees have been on Glaice longer than anyone else." She rushed to finish the tale. In short, Rakulit proved that the mantees inhabited Glaice in 650 R.L. and that the ikuts didn't arrive until around 800, and the bors a century and a half after that. That meant that the mantees were the original charterholding colonists of the planet, and the others were there only on their sufferance. The Warm Stream throngmother heard about Rakulit's work, and before long she had gotten all the mantee throngs on Glaice to join a class-action suit against all the ikut bands, to have them declared displaced persons who had to apply to the mantees for licences just to remain on the planet where they were born.

"They can't do that!" Tep exclaimed. Suddenly his own problem didn't loom so large. "I belong on Glaice just as much as they do! I was born here, too!"

"So was I," Velanda replied. "So far, the mantees haven't included us bors in the suit, but it's still scary. Where could we go? We'd have to appeal to the Arbiter himself, to find us a new homeworld."

"The Arbiter! Hah! I sometimes think the Arbiter is a myth, like the bogeyman who lives in holes in the ice, and—"

"Just for your information, Tep-with-your-head-in-the-snow, the Arbiter has opened a consulate right here in Metok. It's right down the street from the Last Atopak, as a matter of fact."

REDISCOVER THE STAR TREK UNIVERSE